Katharine Prescott Wormeley

# The United States Sanitary Commission

SALZWASSER
VERLAG

**Katharine Prescott Wormeley**

# The United States Sanitary Commission

Reprint of the original, first published in 1863.

1st Edition 2022 | ISBN: 978-3-37500-293-0

Verlag (Publisher): Salzwasser Verlag GmbH, Zeilweg 44, 60439 Frankfurt, Deutschland
Vertretungsberechtigt (Authorized to represent): E. Roepke, Zeilweg 44, 60439 Frankfurt, Deutschland
Druck (Print): Books on Demand GmbH, In de Tarpen 42, 22848 Norderstedt, Deutschland

# THE

# UNITED STATES

# SANITARY COMMISSION.

A SKETCH OF ITS PURPOSES AND ITS WORK.

COMPILED FROM DOCUMENTS AND PRIVATE PAPERS.

PUBLISHED BY PERMISSION.

BOSTON:

1863.

It may be necessary to inform the reader that this Book does not originate with the United States Sanitary Commission, nor with any of its Officers. But it is written by one who has served with the Commission from the first, and who may claim to comprehend its purposes and its work, and to relate its facts with accuracy.

# TABLE OF CONTENTS.

## PART I.

### ORGANIZATION.



### INSPECTION.

## BRANCHES. — SOURCES OF SUPPLY.



# PART II.

## GENERAL RELIEF.

## PART III.

### SPECIAL RELIEF.

## CONCLUSION.

THE

# UNITED STATES SANITARY COMMISSION.

## PART I.

### ORGANIZATION.

The Sanitary Commission is the great artery which bears the people's love to the people's army. The following pages will show, briefly, and in some sense superficially, how the people's confidence has been given to it; what were the motives of that confidence, and the reasons for it; and how it has been justified.

When, in April, 1861, the guns of South Carolina were pointed at the life of her country, and the first shots were fired at the breast of that august form of Liberty, lifted here in the West, and shining with an aspect of redemption to the world, men were aroused to vindicate the vital principle of nationality: and in that great uprising nothing was more marked than that the principle which actuated the men was shared alike by men and women. As the men sprang to arms, the women rose to find what they should do; nor had they far to seek. For one side of war is theirs, and that the dark reverse of it; theirs not only in the patient act of yielding their beloved, — to receive them back, it may be, in widowhood and bereavement, — but theirs in the actual succor which, God be thanked, it is their right and their place to render to the suffering. This, no doubt, was the first aspect of the work to the hearts of women. Time was to show them that, by a great united effort, the work was to broaden out into a material good to the whole army; that lives were to be saved, the vital force protected, and that women, guided by the wisdom of men, were to bear no small part in helping to maintain the efficiency of the army, and thus to share upon the field itself the work of husbands and brothers.

As the men mustered for the battle-field, so the women mustered in churches, school-houses, and drawing-rooms, — working before they well knew at what they ought to work, and calling everywhere for instruction. What were they to do? Where were they to send? The busy hands went on, but where was the work to go? Some fitted out regiments; some sent to various points on suggestions afterward shown to be unreliable; some sent anywhere, rather than nowhere. Little circles and associations were multiplying, like rings in the water, over the face of the whole country; they were all in need of direction, information, guidance, and they felt it.

At a meeting of fifty or sixty women, informally called, in New York, April 25th, 1861, the providential suggestion of attempting to organize the whole benevolence of the women of the country into a general and central association ripened into a plan, and took shape in an appeal addressed to the women of New York, and others "already engaged in preparing against the time of wounds and sickness in the army." This met with such an answer as showed the deep-felt need of it:—and thus commenced the "Woman's Central Association of Relief." But still the need of instruction, and the futility of trying to carry on the association without better knowledge of the work to be done, pressed anxiously on the minds of all. Then the Rev. Dr. Bellows — out of the many men, professional and other, who had come forward in the right relation of men to women, to teach and guide — was ready with the true advice: "You want inquiry from the only correct sources. You must find out first what the Government *will* do, and *can* do, and then help it by working *with it* and doing what it cannot. You must have advice derived from the Government." Accompanied by a few gentlemen, afterwards members of the Commission, he went to Washington, and discovered there, in that moment of national emergency and inadequacy, the need of a far larger machinery, and a more extensive system than that already contemplated; and so, through details which need not delay us here, he formed, he gained the basis of "The Sanitary Commission." The wisdom and devotion of one man gained, on that day, for suffering humanity, the greatest relief ever perhaps wrought out by any human organization.

The following extracts are passages from the letter to the Secretary of War which initiated that relief, and in which is found the first suggestion, on record, of "The Sanitary Commission": —

## AN ADDRESS TO THE SECRETARY OF WAR.

To the Secretary of War:

Sir: The undersigned, representing three associations of the highest respectability in the City of New York, — namely, the Woman's Central Association of Relief for the Sick and Wounded of the Army, the Advisory Committee of the Boards of Physicians and Surgeons of the Hospitals of New York, the New York Medical Association for furnishing Hospital Supplies in aid of the Army, — beg leave to address the Department of War in behalf of the objects committed to them as a mixed delegation with due credentials.

These three associations, being engaged at home in a common object, are acting together with great efficiency and harmony to contribute towards the comfort and security of our troops, by methodizing the spontaneous benevolence of the city and State of New York; obtaining information from the public authorities of the best methods of aiding your Department with such supplies as the regulations of the Army do not provide, or the sudden and pressing necessities of the time do not permit the Department to furnish; and, in general, striving to play into the hands of the regular authorities in ways as efficient and as little embarrassing as extra-official coöperation can be.

These associations would not trouble the War Department with any call on its notice, if they were not persuaded that some positive recognition of their existence and efforts was essential to the peace and comfort of the several bureaus of the War Department itself. The present is essentially a people's war. The hearts and minds, the bodies and souls, of the whole people and of both sexes throughout the loyal States are in it. The rush of volunteers to arms is equalled by the enthusiasm and zeal of the women of the nation, and the clerical and medical professions vie with each other in their ardor to contribute in some manner to the success of our noble and sacred cause. The War Department will hereafter, therefore, inevitably experience, in all its bureaus the incessant and irresistible motions of this zeal, in the offer of medical aid, the applications of nurses, and the contribution of supplies. Ought not this noble and generous enthusiasm to be encouraged and utilized? Would not the Department win a still higher place in the confidence and affections of the good people of the loyal States, and find itself generally strengthened in its efforts, by accepting in some positive manner the services of the associations we represent, which are laboring to bring into system and practical shape the general zeal and benevolent activity of the women of the land in behalf of the Army? And would not a great economy of time, money, and effort be secured by fixing and regulating the relations of the Volunteer Associations to the War Department, and especially to the Medical Bureau?

Convinced by inquiries made here of the practical difficulty of reconciling the aims of their own and numerous similar associations in other cities with the regular workings of the Commissariat and the Medical Bureau, and yet fully persuaded of the importance to the country and the success of the war, of bringing such an arrangement about, the undersigned respectfully ask that a mixed Commission of civilians distinguished for their philanthropic experience and acquaintance with sanitary matters, of medical men, and of military officers, be appointed by the Government, who shall be charged with the duty of investigating the best means of methodizing and reducing to practical service the already active but undirected benevolence of the people toward the Army; who shall consider the general subject of the prevention of sickness and suffering among the troops, and suggest the wisest methods which the people at large can use to manifest their good-will towards the comfort, security, and health of the Army.

It must be well known to the Department of War that several such commissions *followed* the Crimean and Indian wars. The civilization and humanity of the age and of the American people demand that such a Commission should *precede* our second War of Independence — more sacred than the first. We wish to prevent the evils that England and France could only investigate and deplore. The war ought to be waged in a spirit of the highest intelligence, humanity, and tenderness for the health, comfort, and safety of our brave troops. And every measure of the Government that shows its sense of this will be eminently popular, strengthen its hands, and redound to its glory at home and abroad.

The undersigned are charged with several specific petitions, additional to that of asking for a Commission for the purposes above described, although they all would fall under the duties of that Commission.

1. They ask that the Secretary of War will order some new rigor in the inspection of volunteer troops, as they are persuaded that, under the present State regulations throughout the country, a great number of under-aged and unsuitable

persons are mustered, who are likely to swell the bills of mortality in the army to a fearful percentage, to encumber the hospitals and embarrass the columns.

. . . . . . . .

3. The committee represent that the Woman's Central Association of Relief have selected, and are selecting, out of several hundred candidates one hundred women, suited in all respects to become nurses in the General Hospitals of the Army. These women the distinguished physicians and surgeons of the various hospitals in New York have undertaken to *educate and drill in a most thorough and laborious manner;* and the Committee ask that the War Department consent to receive, on wages, these nurses, in such numbers as the exigencies of the campaign may require.* It is not proposed that the nurses should advance to the seat of war, *until directly called for by the Medical Bureau here*, nor that the Government should be at any expense until they are actually in service.

. . . . . . . .

It is believed that a Commission would bring these and other matters of great interest and importance to the health of the troops into the shape of easy and practical adoption. But if no Commission is appointed, the Committee pray that the Secretary will order the several

* Adopted; and nearly every nurse thus selected is still in the service.

suggestions made to be carried into immediate effect, if consistent with the laws of the Department, or possible without the action of Congress.

Feeling themselves directly to represent large and important constituencies, and, indirectly, a wide-spread and commanding public sentiment, the Committee would most respectfully urge the immediate attention of the Secretary to the objects of their prayer.

Very respectfully,

HENRY W. BELLOWS, D. D.
W. H. VAN BUREN, M. D.
ELISHA HARRIS, M. D.
J. HARSEN, M. D.

WASHINGTON, *May* 18, 1861.

This was strengthened by a letter from the acting Surgeon-General to the Secretary of War, advising the institution of "A Commission of Inquiry and Advice in respect of the Sanitary Interests of the United States Forces."

LETTER FROM THE ACTING SURGEON-GENERAL TO THE SECRETARY OF WAR, ADVISING THE INSTITUTION OF "A COMMISSION OF INQUIRY AND ADVICE IN RESPECT OF THE SANITARY INTERESTS OF THE UNITED STATES FORCES."

SURGEON-GENERAL'S OFFICE,
*May* 22, 1861.

Hon. SIMON CAMERON, *Secretary of War:*

SIR: The sudden and large increase of the Army, more especially of the Volunteer force, has called the attention of this office to the necessity of some modifications and changes in the system of organization as connected with the hygiene and comforts of the soldiers; more particularly in relation to the class of men who, actuated by patriotism, have repaired with unexampled promptness to the defence of the institutions and laws of the country.

The pressure upon the Medical Bureau has been very great and urgent; and, though all the means at its disposal have been industriously used, much remains to be accomplished by directing the intelligent mind of the country to practical results connected with the comforts of the soldier, by preventive and sanitary means.

The Medical Bureau would, in my judgment, derive important and useful aid from the counsels and well-directed efforts of an intelligent and scientific Commission, to be styled, "A Commission of Inquiry and Advice in respect of the Sanitary Interests of the United States Forces," and acting in co-operation with the Bureau, in elaborating and applying such facts as might be elicited from the experience and more extended observation of those connected with armies, with reference to the diet and hygiene of troops, and the organization of Military Hospitals, etc.

This Commission is not intended to interfere with, but to strengthen, the present organization, introducing and elaborating such improvements as the advanced stage of Medical Science might suggest; more particularly as regards the class of men who, in this war of sections, may be called to abandon the comforts of home, and be subject to the privations and casualties of war.

The views of this office were expressed in a communication of May 18, 1861, in a crude and hasty manner, as to the examination of recruits, the proposed organization of cooks, nurses, etc., to which I beg leave to refer.

The selection of this Board is of the greatest importance.

In connection with those gentlemen who originated this investigation, with many others, I would suggest the following members, not to exceed five, to convene in Washington, who have power to fill vacancies and appoint a competent Secretary: —

Rev. Henry W. Bellows, D. D.
Prof. Alexander Dallas Bache, LL. D.
Prof. Wolcott Gibbs, M. D.
Jeffries Wyman, M. D.
W. H. Van Buren, M. D.

It would be proper, also, to associate with this Board an officer of the Medical Staff of the Army, to be selected by the Secretary of War, familiar with the organization of Military Hospitals and the details of field service.

Respectfully submitted,

R. C. WOOD,
*Acting Surgeon-General.*

DRAFT OF POWERS ASKED FROM THE GOVERNMENT BY THE SANITARY DELEGATION TO THE PRESIDENT AND THE SECRETARY OF WAR.

WASHINGTON, D. C., *May* 23, 1861.

To the Hon. SECRETARY OF WAR:

The Medical Bureau of the United States Army having asked for the appointment of a Sanitary Commission, in aid of its own overtasked energies, the Committee of the New York Delegation to the Government on Sanitary Affairs beg leave, at the request of the Medical Bureau, and as explanatory of its wishes, to state what precise *powers* are sought by the proposed Commission, and what specific *objects* are aimed at.

POWERS.

1. The Commission being organized for the purposes only of inquiry and advice, asks for no legal powers, but only the official recognition and moral countenance of the Government, which will be secured by its public appointment. It asks for a recommendatory order, addressed in its favor to all officers of the Government, to further its inquiries; for permission to correspond and confer, on a confidential footing, with the Medical Bureau and the War Department, proffering such suggestions and counsel as its investigations and studies may, from time to time, prompt and enable it to offer.

2. The Commission seeks no pecuniary remuneration from the Government. Its motives being humane and patriotic, its labors will be its own reward. The assignment to them of a room in one of the public buildings, with stationery and other necessary conveniences, would meet their expectations in this direction.

3. The Commission asks leave to sit through the war, either in Washington, or when and where it may find it most convenient and useful; but it will disband should experience render its operations embarrassing to the Government, or less necessary and useful than it is now supposed they will prove.

## OBJECTS.

The general object of the Commission is, through suggestions reported from time to time to the Medical Bureau and the War Department, to bring to bear upon the health, comfort, and *morale* of our troops, the fullest and ripest teachings of Sanitary Science in its application to military life, whether deduced from theory or practical observation, from general hygienic principles, or from the experience of the Crimean, the East Indian, and the Italian wars. Its objects are purely advisory.

The specific points to which its attention would be directed may here be partly indicated, but in some part must depend upon the course of events, and the results of its own observations and promptings, when fairly at work. If it knew precisely what the results of its own inquiries would be, it would state them at once, without asking for that authority and those governmental facilities essential to a successful investigation of the subject. As the Government may select its own Commissioners, — the persons named in the recommendation of the Medical Bureau being wholly undesirous, however willing, to serve, if other persons more deserving of the confidence of the Government and of the public can be nominated; — it is hoped that the character of the Commission will be the best warrant the Government can have that the inquiries of the Commission, both as to their nature and the manner of conducting them, will be pursued with discretion and a careful eye to avoiding impertinent and offensive interference with the legal authority and official rights of any of the bureaus with which it may be brought in contact.

## SPECIFICATIONS.

I. MATERIEL. — II. PREVENTION. — III. RELIEF.

I. *Materiel of the Volunteers.* — The Commission proposes a practical inquiry into the *materiel* of the Volunteer Force, with reference to the laws and usages of the several States in the matter of Inspection, with the hope of assimilating their regulations with those of the Army proper, alike in the appointment of medical and other officers and in the rigorous application of just rules and principles to recruiting and inspection laws. This inquiry would exhaust every topic appertaining to the original *materiel* of the army, considered as a subject of sanitary and medical care.

II. *Prevention.* — The Commission would inquire with scientific thoroughness into the subject of Diet, Cooking, Cooks, Clothing, Tents, Camping Grounds, Transports, Transitory Depots, with their exposures, Camp Police, with reference to settling the question, How far the regulations of the Army proper are or can be practically carried out among the Volunteer Regiments, and what changes or modifications are desirable from their peculiar character and circumstances? Everything appertaining to outfit, cleanliness, precautions against damp, cold, heat, malaria, infection; crude, unvaried, or ill-cooked food, and an irregular or careless regimental commissariat, would fall under this head.

III. *Relief.* — The Commission would inquire into the organization of Military Hospitals, general and regimental; the precise regulations and routine through which the services of the patriotic women of the country may be made available as nurses; the nature and sufficiency of Hospital supplies; the method of obtaining and regulating all other extra and unbought supplies contributing to the comfort of the sick; the question of ambulances and field service, and of extra medical aid; and whatever else relates to the care, relief, or cure of the sick and wounded — their investigations being guided by the highest and latest medical and military experience, and carefully adapted to the nature and wants of our immediate army, and its peculiar origin and circumstances.*

Very respectfully submitted, in behalf of the New York delegation.

HENRY W. BELLOWS, *Chairman.*
WILLIAM H. VAN BUREN, M. D.
JACOB HARSEN, M. D.
ELISHA HARRIS, M. D.

SANITARY COMMISSION ORDERED BY THE SECRETARY OF WAR, AND APPROVED BY THE PRESIDENT.

WAR DEPARTMENT,
*Washington, June* 9, 1861.

The Secretary of War has learned with great satisfaction that, at the instance and in pursuance of the suggestion of the Medical Bureau, in a communication to this office, dated May 22, 1861, Henry W. Bellows, D. D., Prof. A. D. Bache, LL. D., Prof. Jeffries Wyman, M. D., Prof. Wolcott Gibbs, M. D., W. H. Van Buren, M. D., Samuel G. Howe, M. D., R. C. Wood, Surgeon U. S. A., G. W. Cullum, U. S. A.,

* Looking back on these proposals, a feeling of wonder fills the mind that they could at that moment of inexperience have been formed to embrace nearly all that has since proved essential.

Alexander E. Shiras, U. S. A., have mostly consented, in connection with such others as they may choose to associate with them, to act as "A Commission of Inquiry and Advice in respect of the Sanitary Interests of the United States Forces," and without remuneration from the Government. The Secretary has submitted their patriotic proposal to the consideration of the President, who directs the acceptance of the services thus generously offered.

The Commission, in connection with a Surgeon of the U. S. A. to be designated by the Secretary, will direct its inquiries to the principles and practices connected with the inspection of recruits and enlisted men; the sanitary condition of the volunteers; to the means of preserving and restoring the health, and of securing the general comfort and efficiency of troops; to the proper provision of cooks, nurses, and hospitals; and to other subjects of like nature.

The Commission will frame such rules and regulations, in respect of the objects and modes of its inquiry, as may seem best adapted to the purpose of its constitution, which, when approved by the Secretary, will be established as general guides of its investigations and action.

A room with necessary conveniences will be provided in the City of Washington for the use of the Commission, and the members will meet when and at such places as may be convenient to them for consultation, and for the determination of such questions as may come properly before the Commission.

In the progress of its inquiries, the Commission will correspond freely with the Department and with the Medical Bureau, and will communicate to each, from time to time, such observations and results as it may deem expedient and important.

The Commission will exist until the Secretary of War shall otherwise direct, unless sooner dissolved by its own action.

SIMON CAMERON,
*Secretary of War.*

I approve the above. A. LINCOLN.
*June* 18, 1861.

All this was the result of the forces of patriotism and human love, which began to bear with strength upon the Government. For not only did the nation, in its merciful and patriotic instincts, need the Commission as its guide and means, but the Government needed the Commission to protect them against the vast tide of home-feelings, and the ardor of a people pouring down upon them in indiscriminate benevolence, and clogging the machinery, already too limited, through which alone the real good to the soldier could be applied. They needed, even if they did not wish, something to eke out and supplement the established system. It was small enough, to be sure, for it was a system made for a few thousand men, suddenly called on to provide for the wants of an army of several hundred thousand; but at least it was the organized nucleus of something larger. The Commission came in, with offers of obedience, to supplement and aid, by an organization running side by side with the military system in the difficult work before it.

And here it is important to understand the precise attitude assumed by the Government towards the Sanitary Commission at its inception. The Government, while to a certain extent aware of the necessities that might soon arise in the Medical Department, had what seemed so much more pressing demands upon their attention that they could not give very earnest heed to the suggestions which Dr. Bellows urged with piteous reiteration upon them. They saw the country heaving with sensibility to the probable wants of the sick and wounded, before any such existed. It seemed to them an idle forethought to make this great ado about a class which might never exist in any great proportion. The honest truth doubtless is this: that they supposed the sensibilities of women and clergymen and humane physicians had finally culminated in a sentimental scheme which had little solid foundation in practical sense and efficiency, and that they regarded the proposed Sanitary Commission with only as much interest as the pertinacity and respectability of its advocates compelled them to give to it. They did not understand the character of the men who were urging the plan upon them; far less did they comprehend that these men were prompted by the irresistible voice of the people; and thus they were excusable for suspecting that the scheme was a soft-hearted invention which would very poorly sustain the hard knocks which every accessory of war must be fitted to endure.

The Government frankly told the projector of the Sanitary Commission their doubts and misgivings as to the feasibleness of his plan: the President feared it might be "the fifth wheel of the coach," not only needless but embarrassing to the indispensable running gear; the Secretary of War very slowly and reluctantly gave up his objections; the Medical Bureau, won over to the plan only by the most gentle and cautious approaches, at length yielded their consent, and made application for the appointment of the Commission.* Even then a change in the head of the Medical Bureau perilled the ground thus laboriously gained; for the new Surgeon-General, Dr. Finlay, signified his consent with an expression of his total opposition to the plan, and

* This was due to the efforts of Dr. Van Buren, whose guiding wisdom in the rise and progress of the Sanitary Commission has been one of the chief sources of its strength and power.

merely from unwillingness to interpose himself against what was evidently becoming a powerful popular opinion in favor of the scheme.

These objections were all natural, honest, and even sagacious: nor has the Commission ever complained that it encountered them. In ninety-nine cases out of a hundred they would have been well-founded. But the course of the Commission has shown — what no foresight could have established — that the objections made to it were unfounded and needless. It is, however, due both to the Commission and to the People who created it, that the obstinate difficulties under which it came into existence should be known; and it must be added that it was treated for the first few months of that existence with jealous coldness on the part of the Government — a coldness gradually melting away as experience taught the various Bureaux to confide in it.

In all its intercourse with the Government the Commission has studied the strictest subordination, asked the fewest possible favors, conferred the largest assistance in its power, and claimed the least possible recognition of its services. Whilst the Government, whatever their actual sense of its labors may be, have seldom shown any sense of obligation to the Commission, yet it must be said that, from their various subordinates, it has received favors too numerous to detail, whilst the actual obstacles to its labors have been few indeed.

The best witness — the only competent judge of the Sanitary Commission — is the Army itself. The Generals recognize and facilitate its plans and movements from their own deep acquaintance with its work and their personal conviction of its importance; whilst the other officers, medical and military, strengthen it from a yet closer experience of its benefits. The real triumph of the Commission has been a triumph over the medical and military prejudices of the Army; and these have yielded, and yielded wholly, to the actual experience they have had of the beneficence and indispensableness of its work.

It was soon found necessary, for the practical working of the Commission, to add five other members to those already appointed; and these were again increased at a later period until the number of its members is now twenty-one. Their names are as follows: —

H. W. Bellows, D. D., *President*, — A. D. Bache, LL. D., *Vice-President*, — G. W. Cullum, U. S. A., — R. C. Wood, M. D., U. S. A., W. H. Van Buren, M. D., — Wolcott Gibbs, M. D., — S. G. Howe, M. D., — C. R. Agnew, M. D., — Elisha Harris, M. D., — George T. Strong, Esq., — Horace Binney, Jr., Esq., — Rt. Rev. T. M. Clark, D. D., — Hon. Joseph Holt, — Hon. R. W. Burnett, — Hon. Mark Skinner, — Rev. John H. Heywood, — Prof. Fairman Rogers, — J. Huntington Wolcott, Esq., — Fred. Law Olmsted Esq., — J. S. Newberry, M. D., — A. E. Shiras, U. S. A.

The Commission, being thus organized, fell at once to work, and before twenty-four hours had passed was involved in the leading practical questions of the business before it,—the Executive Committee meeting daily as it has continued to do from that time to the present day. On this Committee we may be suffered to pause for a moment. If others in the Commission are known in this story by their deeds, these men, who are the spirit that inspires and the mind that guides the whole, should be known by their character and attainments.

It has been shown how the inception and existence of the Sanitary Commission are due to Dr. Bellows; but his labors for it have not ended here. To it he has given the experience of a thoughtful life and the best hours of every day and night since it came into existence,—strengthening it with his power, and inspiring it with his enthusiasm.

Of Dr. Van Buren, whose eminent professional attainments have carried, with weight and conviction, the advice of the Commission to the Medical Bureau, it is not too much to say that the war in its medical history owes more to him of what is sound, progressive, and humane than to any other physician in the country:—while to Dr. Agnew, his colleague in the work, the Commission owes in a high degree, through his earnest and powerful administrative qualities, the practical and successful application of the wisdom of his friend. The attainments of the Commission in all matters of a scientific nature are due to its good fortune in having as active workers two men of the highest scientific character,—Prof. A. D. Bache and Prof. Wolcott Gibbs,—who have maintained a steady and practical supervision over all questions and affairs of this nature.

To its Treasurer, Mr. George T. Strong, the Commission owes a debt of gratitude which it is difficult to express in words. With the burden of much responsibility upon him of a private and public nature, he has yet found time and strength to give himself, with ceaseless industry and judgment, to the financial business of the Commission, which has been wholly conducted by him.

The last who shall be named here is one who is no longer in the active service of the Commission, but who was until recently its General Secretary,—Mr. Frederick Law Olmsted. He has left the work, called elsewhere by a duty which he could not disregard. The Sanitary Commission, owing its conception and life to others, owes in a chief degree its moulding and its practical success to him. He has gone from it, but his spirit within it will never die nor fail. He will return, for the country needs him. A man like him belongs before all else to the generation in which he is born. We want men of height and breadth and purity, and a Nation's wants produce their own fulfilment. He will return: meantime, wherever he is, God bless him.

In his place has been elected Dr. J. Foster Jenkins, long actively engaged as Associate Secretary of the Commission; and it is enough to say that no appointment to that place could have given more sincere satisfaction.*

The Commission, as we have said, went at once to work. Almost its first act was to solicit the coöperation of Associate Members throughout the country. They were asked to obtain for the Commission the means required to carry out its object; to inform the public fully (through the press and otherwise) of the existence and design of the Commission, and of the great and pressing danger which it was intended to avert; to promote the establishment of auxiliary associations; and so to direct the labors of associations already formed, that they might strengthen and support those of the Commission.

At the present moment there are more than five hundred Associate Members.

Of the multiplied subjects which first claimed the attention of the Commission, no record can be given here; but it should be told how the suggestion was made that it ought to look to the Government for the money it required, rather than to private liberality. The question was fully and deeply considered, and the conclusion was reached that it was inexpedient to appear before Congress as an applicant for pecuniary aid.

* See Appendix A.

The Commission had little or no official power, and could accomplish its objects only through whatever moral weight and influence it might possess. These would have been impaired, if not destroyed, in public estimation at least, were it to appear among the crowds which fill the lobbies of Congress. The mere suspicion that it was connected with political agencies would paralyze its usefulness. On this and other grounds, the Commission determined to rely for support on the community at large, and time has shown its wisdom in adopting that course.*

On the question of supplies, there could be no anxiety. Already, from the distant country villages, as from the cities and towns, they were flowing in. The Commission went forward to its first inquiries after need and suffering, backed by ample means to relieve them. The distribution of stores, clothes, bedding, etc., became at once a recognized function; and so, finding its way intelligently into every avenue of succor, the People's Commission went on.

## DEPARTMENT OF INSPECTION.

The order of the Secretary of War, by which the Sanitary Commission was appointed, invested it with the power of "inquiry and advice in respect to the Sanitary interests of the United States forces," — and specially directed it to

* See Appendix B.

"inquire into the principles and practices connected with the inspection of recruits and enlisted men; into the sanitary condition of the volunteers; into the means of preserving and restoring the health and securing the general comfort and efficiency of troops; into the proper provision of cooks, nurses, and hospitals; and into other subjects of a like nature." That a permission of this kind should have been given, inviting instruction and advice at the very commencement of the war, — not delaying until decimating evil and the anger of a people demanded it, — is one of those facts by which we judge the character of our nation; and as a people we may be grateful to the men who were wise enough to grant it.

If we think of the condition of the Army at that moment, we shall see at once the enormous value of the advice of the Commission, composed as it was of men who were all more or less experts in the work in which they were engaged. The Medical Bureau, organized with reference to the wants of an army of only a few thousand men, was likely to be seriously embarrassed in its operations, when called on to provide for a newly levied force of several hundred thousand; especially as both officers and men of the new levies were mostly without experience, and required immediate and extraordinary instructions and supervision to save them from the consequences of exposure, malaria, unwholesome food, and other perils of camp-life. What could these men, just from their home-life, know of this aspect of war?—they did not even know their own ignorance. War to them was battle and the art of it. Precautions for health; preventions of disease; the bodily well-being of the troops, — all that makes the enduring strength of an army,—scarcely entered, if it entered at all, their eager minds. The Sanitary Commission, by a gracious permission, was to teach them. Who shall say where the results of this teaching ended, or shall end?

The first step of the Commission was to survey its ground. The President, with another member, at once undertook a preliminary examination into the condition of the troops assembling at Cleveland, Alton, Cairo, St. Louis, Cincinnati, and other military centres in the West. A like preliminary examination was made, by other members of the Commission, into the state of the troops on the Potomac and at Fortress Monroe. Full reports of the results thus ascertained showed that the dangers of the Army from ignorance and neglect of sanitary precautions were in no degree exaggerated, and that a vast field of work was before the Commission. That work was twofold: 1st, Inquiry into the sanitary condition of the army; 2d, Advice as to its improvement. This latter function included, not only the duty of addressing to the Government, from time to time, such recommendations or suggestions as occasions and facts might suggest, but also that of keeping the volunteer officers, and the soldiers themselves, constantly and directly instructed and warned of the novel dangers to which they were exposed, of the necessary precautions against them, and of the means pointed out by experience as best calculated to preserve them in bodily health and vigor for the performance of their duty to their country.

It was obviously necessary to put experts upon the duty of inspection and inquiry, and for this purpose the Commission hastened to secure the services of a body of physicians specially fitted for this duty, and to send them into the field at various points, from Fortress Monroe to St. Louis. It was not easy to find at once a sufficient number of gentlemen of the requisite qualifications. It was indispensable that they should possess, not only scientific qualifications and a special acquaintance with sanitary laws, but sufficient tact to perform their duties as agents of an organization till then unknown to Army Regulations, without awakening jealousy of their interference as officious or seemingly intrusive. It was also necessary, in view of the fact that the Commission could afford to pay but moderate compensation to its employés, that they should be men actuated by a strong and disinterested desire to be of service to the country. Such men, however, were found; and it is proper to record the fact that in several instances they withdrew from positions far more remunerative, undertaking their new duties from motives of the highest benevolence and patriotism. Some have declined the office of Brigade Surgeon, tendered to them by the War Department, to enter on what they considered a wider field of usefulness in the service of the Commission. No one is now employed on this service who is not entitled by education, experience, and social standing to speak with some degree of moral authority; and whatever success the Commission may have obtained in the execution of its duties is believed to be due as much to the high character and intelligence of its Inspectors, as to any of the other advantages it has enjoyed.

The duties of the Inspectors, beyond what is necessarily trusted to their discretion, are minutely detailed in the printed instructions which are issued to them. They are enjoined carefully to avoid whatever can excite apprehension of a disposition to interfere with military authority. Before entering any camp, they are required to obtain the formal approval of the Major General, the Brigadier General, and the Medical Director, in whose military jurisdiction the camp is included; together with an introduction to the commanding officer of the regiment, and through him to the company officers. Having done this, they are required to make a minute investigation into every point bearing directly or indirectly on the sanitary condition of the camp. Among the subjects on which they are required to make written detailed reports are the quality of rations and water, the methods of camp-cooking, the ventilation of tents and quarters, the drainage of the camp itself, the healthfulness of its site, the administration of the hospital, the police of the camp, and all which that word includes; the quality of the tents, and the material used for flooring them; the quality of the clothing and the personal cleanliness of the men, &c., &c. Whatever deficiencies or evils they find to exist, by which the health, *morale*, or efficiency of the men may be endangered, they are instructed to indicate to the proper officers; at the same time offering advice, if it is needed, as to the best method of remedying them. Very few camps have been visited in which important improvements have not been ordered by the proper officers, at the suggestion and in the presence of the Inspector.

The influence, however, which officers unconsciously receive, through the mere direction of their attention to unknown or neglected duties, by the inquiries which the Inspectors necessarily address to them, constitutes one great value of the services of the Commission. The brigadier or colonel, who is asked whether military or sanitary considerations determined the selection of his camp-site, will not be likely, when next he chooses a camping-ground, to plant it, unless a military exigency so require, on the leeward side of a swamp or in a damp wood. The major, who is asked if the drains about the tents and through the camp are wide and deep and straight, and kept free from rubbish, will get an idea, if he never had one before, as to the importance of drainage. When the company captains are asked if they, or any of their subordinate officers, look after the ventilation of the tents at night, if they are struck at short intervals, for the thorough cleansing of both the canvas and the site, they are made to feel that *these* things are important; and when subaltern officers and privates see careful inquiry made as to their habits of personal cleanliness, and the cleanliness of their camps, regarding the water they drink, and the character and cooking of their food, concerning the sufficiency of their clothing and bedding, and the healthful conditions of their rest, they are incited to attend themselves to what seems to give so much concern to others, and henceforward can hardly fail to think more of the influences affecting health. All this, of course, cannot be specified, recorded, and presented under the head of facts; but it is to be dwelt on thoughtfully.

As every regiment brought to a high sanitary condition is found to be a radiating centre of good influences, it was thought that the labors of the Inspectors (their number being necessarily far too small) would be most effectively and economically applied, by making as thorough work as practicable in the inspection of each regiment visited, and in securing the efficient co-operation of its officers, rather than in superficial examination and hurried efforts for the benefit of a larger number. It must be said emphatically, and in justice to our volunteer officers, that the Inspectors of the Commission have seldom had occasion to complain in any way of the want of prompt, cordial, and intelligent co-operation on their parts. This was due partly to their honest sense of the real service rendered to them, and partly to that obedience to the spirit of the Commission's pledge of non-interference with the military service, which the wisdom of the General Secretary kept, by precept and example, before the mind of its employés.

Through its Inspectors the Commission has distributed gratuitously to the surgeons and officers of regiments eighteen concise treatises on the best means for preserving health in camp, and on the treatment of the sick and wounded in camp and on the battle-field. They were each prepared by a committee of gentlemen selected from the best medical talent of the country, with special reference to their peculiar acquaintance with the special subject intrusted to them. As the surgeons of the Volunteer Army are drawn almost wholly from civil practice, and as no books, nor even circulars of instruction in regard to their novel responsibilities were issued to them by Government, these medical monographs, although very modest in form, were found to contain an amount of information of such practical value that there is scarcely a surgeon in the Army who has not sent to the Commission to ask for fresh copies, when the casualties of war have caused the loss of those he had.*

After the inspection of a camp or post, the Inspector is required to make an elaborate report upon its condition. This report consists partly of written answers to printed questions, one hundred and eighty in number, covering every important point connected with the sanitary condition of the Army. These printed questions are used to secure information on essential points, but all personal observations are specially encouraged. More than one thousand four hundred and seventy of these reports have been received by the Commission. They are the guides to the advice offered by the Commission itself to the Heads of Departments. They are afterwards carefully tabulated, and suitable digests prepared by an accomplished actuary. It is much to be desired that, for the sake of the future, and in the cause of humanity, the Commission may be enabled to continue this work, and thus eventually to lay before the country a body of military medical statistics, more complete, searching, and trustworthy than any now in existence.

It will be seen that the primary business of

* See Appendix C.

Inspectors was not to take care of the sick and wounded, — that was the business of a force of men specially assigned to it, — but to keep the Commission in its central offices informed of the sanitary condition of the Army, and to advise it of excessive wants, excessive neglects, frauds, &c., affecting the sick and wounded. For the punctual and exact performance of this duty of the Inspectors, the Secretaries were held accountable to the Commission; as, for the duty based upon it, the Commission itself is primarily accountable to the President. This measure of the duty was fulfilled without breaking its unity, until the great services in the field, commencing in 1862, swept even the Inspectors away from their special responsibility into the work of actual succor and relief, — not, however, at any time arresting the work. The Commission is now about to bring back the Inspectors to their proper duties, and to keep them to the important and responsible work for which men of their acquirements were engaged. In the past they have taught the Commission what were the needs of an army in its infancy; it now becomes their duty to teach it the lessons that the Army should learn from a three years' experience, and thus step by step to rise to results which will be of immense benefit to the country should the war be prolonged.

There is no doubt that the public sympathy is not greatly enlisted in this department, but out of it comes the very strength of the work of relief and mercy, — *enlightenment*, — through which alone a practical, economical, and thorough use of the gifts of the people can be reached. Some definite results of this work in the shape of facts may be asked for. Many of these (and the most practical) will appear in the course of the narrative. Only one of them will be mentioned here.

The statistics of the British forces during the war against Russia show the following rates of mortality: —

On the arrival of the army in Turkey, (April, 1854,) to the embarkation for the Crimea, (September, 1854,) the annual death-rate was 129 per 1000 men. In July, August, and September, it was increased to 293 per 1000 men; for the next three months to 511 per 1000 men; and it culminated in January, 1855, when it reached the fearful amount of 1174 per 1000 men.* In other words, at this rate it would be necessary, in order to supply the loss occasioned by death alone, to replace the dead army by a new army of equal strength in about ten ($10\frac{1}{4}$) months. *Then it was* that the British Government established sanitary operations, and so soon as their influence began to be felt, (in April, May, and June, 1855,) the rate of mortality fell to 250 per 1000 men, and from that time gradually and rapidly diminished, until the annual death-rate

* Of which 97 per cent. was from disease.

for January, 1856, (one year from its culmination,) was 25 per 1000 men.

The mortality of the United States forces during the present war (exclusive of three-months men) is being tabulated by the Sanitary Commission from the records in the Adjutant-General's office. These tables show that from the commencement of the war to the latest time when they could be made, the annual death-rate of our forces has been 65 per 1000 men. From June 1st, 1861, to March, 1862, a period when our army lay comparatively inactive, we find the annual death-rate was 44⅓ per 1000 men. During the campaign on the Peninsula, when the effects of climate were to the full as deadly, if not more so, than those of the Crimea, when every breath drew in swamp poison, and our men advanced by forced marches through Virginia mire, and camped along the banks of malarious watercourses, the annual death-rate was 165 per 1000 men. To what was this owing? Not to the fact that our troops bring a greater amount of health into the service than those of other armies, for their mortality during the period of inaction was much greater than that of the British army during a like period.* It was owing in part, undoubtedly, to lessons learnt from the Russian war, and to the Amer-

* This is owing largely to the careless inspection of recruits, a subject to which the Sanitary Commission has never ceased to call the attention of the Government.

ican spirit of improvement, which has made our armies, let who will say to the contrary, a splendid spectacle of progress in many points of efficiency. But was it not in a chief degree owing to the Sanitary Commission? Has not the Sanitary Commission a right to point to that result, and say, "*It is mine?*"

A branch of Special Inspection was established by the Commission for a limited period of time, in September, 1862, to examine into the condition and wants of Army General Hospitals throughout the country. While the strength of the army had been nearly doubled, and the population in General Hospitals quadrupled, the Staff of Medical Inspection had not been increased. Under these circumstances, the Commission resolved to seek among the best and ablest members of the medical profession the services, for short periods, of men ready to help the national cause and the cause of humanity, by undertaking a course of Hospital Inspection.

An efficient corps of such Inspectors was organized under Dr. Henry G. Clark, of Boston, Inspector-in-Chief. The approval and authorization of the Surgeon-General were accorded to them, and their duty at once commenced; its distinct object being to secure to sick and wounded soldiers thorough and able hospital treatment, by the detection of all defects in administration or professional care susceptible of remedy or improvement. When the list of these Inspectors is read, showing names which command the highest respect in many large communities, and the fact is told that their suggestions with regard to defects and evils found to be existing in Army Hospitals have, when transmitted to the Surgeon-General, *invariably* received his immediate and effective attention, nothing more need be said upon this branch of the subject.*

The reports of all Inspectors are taken into the office of Statistics, presided over by an actuary of great attainments, Mr. E. B. Elliott. There they are recorded and tabulated: first, in what is called the "Abstract of Camp Inspection, classified by States"; secondly, in a more condensed table or abstract of the leading points about each regiment inspected.

With this current work much else is carried on. Data are being collected, and abstracts made from the rolls of the Adjutant-General's office, relating to certain points in the condition of the troops, out of which abstracts vast instruction for the future is derived. Of these rolls, 10,000 have been already examined, covering at least 900 regiments and 750,000 men. The enormous amount of labor necessary for this work cannot be comprehended by a mind not trained to such details.

Returns to this office from the Inspectors

* See Appendix D.

travelling with armies on the march, are also made, and there tabulated, showing the effect on men of long and continuous marches, &c., &c., and the influence of these causes on the health and endurance of the troops. Returns are also recorded and tabulated on wounds and injuries received in battle.

A Department of Vital Statistics has been commenced, which is yet in its infancy, but which has within its scope the prospect of results greater than any yet attained. And last, but not least in present results, is a series of diagrams prepared from the rolls of the Adjutant-General's office, showing the constant rates of mortality and sickness, with various particulars, throughout the army and in special portions of it.

All this work is of untold value, not only now, but to future ages; and if the Sanitary Commission had not promptly undertaken it, its practical results would have been greatly delayed; for the records in the government offices, owing to want of time and adequate clerks, are either not tabulated at all, or so slowly as to cause despair of their appearing in time to be useful to this generation.

Let us trust that the work may be enabled to go on to its end, so that the Sanitary Commission may give to future eras of suffering the experience and warnings of the present.

## THE BRANCHES.—SOURCES OF SUPPLY.

At the moment when the Sanitary Commission acquired its functions from Government, its relation to the women's work throughout the land changed, with the plastic ease which marks the change into things better and truer, especially in moments of trial. No longer a mere commission of inquiry, for the purposes of the Woman's Relief Societies, it became the head, the strength, the teacher, the central means through which the work of the women was to flow. And here it may be said that nowhere is the true relation of men and women to each other better worked out than in the service of the Sanitary Commission. And it may also be said that never before in the history of the world have women had such an opportunity to use themselves for a great purpose. In England, those women who, with Florence Nightingale, did their work in the Crimea, showed a courage in taking the initial step to which we can lay no claim. Our turn to take up the work came after the world had applauded it. They did not know whether they went to honor or to dishonor;—enough that they went to avert suffering. But they had no such *opportunity* as ours. They had no national channel through which every woman in the land could feel that she might work with the Government itself, and reach the very spot of need. Theirs was no national cause, in which the women were to rise as the men; and as the men went to their work in the national army, so the women were to go with them, in an organization running side by side with the army,—knowing its needs and meeting them,—yet all the while *at home*, in quietness nursing thoughts of those in the field, whilst their busy hands poured into the thousand channels supplies of relief and love. Supplies which, meeting in one great centre, were to take a wider flow, and, by instructed and authorized means, were to reach and relieve suffering wherever a regiment or company of soldiers could be found.

But all this had to be learnt; perhaps it is not wholly learnt yet. And the first step of the Woman's Central Association of Relief was to establish relations with other women, and so to learn and teach how to make the best of the opportunity given to them. Happily, women were found, in every part of the country, who comprehended at once the great principle of union and national working together, which is the foundation of the Sanitary Commission; and many who did not see it at once, soon came to it out of their very needs.

Preliminary steps were rapidly taken, and the tide of unorganized effort began to set into the great channel. Boxes, cases, packages, which before had gone independently, and often fruitlessly, on their tender and patriotic mission, and which, if not wholly wasted, fell far short of the generous good intended, now poured into the Central Depot, and went forward from there to the spot where the need of them was ascertained. From a variety of testimony which is overwhelming, the fact is known that the waste of the first unorganized work for the needs of the Army is scarcely to be estimated. But beyond the evil of the waste of goods was the waste of living energy and power; and far beyond that, again, was the spirit which began to spring up, innocently God knows, yet leading to that evil which has brought us to disunion and the rupture of our country,—the spirit of "our section," "our State," "our regiment." This spirit grew up in the commencement because no higher spirit was obvious. Boxes, love-freighted, were sent to "our regiment," because that was the only spot to which we knew how to send. No wilfully sectional motive had influence; it was simply ignorance of other methods which produced the sectional result. To be sure, love of friends and the satisfaction of knowing from them that the boxes had arrived, led to much of this unorganized work, although its evil results were so grave that many were disposed to condemn it in a spirit of greater severity.

Amongst these results, and setting aside the important question of waste, may be named that of the petty jealousies it was capable of fostering, and out of which, as we all know, comes emptiness of result. Not the great principle of Union, but rivalries among societies; "our regiment's better furnished than your regiment," answered by rivalries among the men themselves. "Our people love us better than your people, for look what they send!" or, perhaps, "Our people love us less than their people, for look what *they* send!" Ah! what is this but the germ of the principle which struck the blow at our country, and which, if carried out, would have paralyzed even the nationality of the loyal Army?

But the impression must not be given that the army, as a general thing, approved of this sectional method of aiding it. On the field, banded into one whole, fighting for the principle of Union, disunited and sectional bounty was against the grain of its daily feelings. The men themselves rebuked it; and there are many instances in which when the kind face looked into barn or tent or ward, and the kind voice said, as the basketful of relief was opened, "Any boy here from the State of . . . . ?" that the men of that State kept silence; — or, better still, they answered, "No! only United States soldiers!"

But all this had to be learnt, and had to be taught. It was believed from the very start, by those who brought to this war a living faith in the people, that they needed only to see the scheme of the Sanitary Commission in its great national relations and analogies, — only to have some proof that it would sustain its pledges, and be, as well as claim to be, the great effective channel of the people's love to the people's army, — to come to its support in loving ardor, and on the great principle for which husbands and sons were laying down their lives upon the battle-field. And this belief has been justified; if the people have not all come to the response expected, it is because the Commission has not had the time nor the means to teach its truths. Wherever its broad principles have been made known, wherever the proofs have been given of its actual work, the people have sprung to join it; not, let us say, for itself or for its agents, — they are nothing, — but for the sake of its great principles, and for the vast opportunities which a wise Government has given to it.

If the history which underlies all this could be given (and it never can be), what a record it would be of human nature! Let us follow home the cases that come into one large branch from a thousand villages: the people that packed them never saw a wounded soldier; they have no stimulants of excitement; *their* individual exertions are never known beyond their little village, and seem as nothing compared to the great whole. The people of cities give money without feeling it, but it is the farmers' wives and daughters who make the sacrifices; the materials are purchased by money earned by daily work; the time is taken out of the night's rest, and then, when the box is ready, they send it away to strangers, not knowing where it is to go, nor who it is that shall receive it. This is Faith, and it is human nature rising out of self — which is Christianity. Let us go into that house where a Soldiers' Aid Society is at work: it is in a little village in Connecticut, as neat as all New England villages are, but the people are very poor. As we examine a quilt which is on the frame, pieced out of an old dress, for materials are their greatest difficulty, the mistress of the house (she is a widow) says, in the simplest way, with a glance at the windows, "You see our window-curtains have gone." Before the war those curtains were the pride and pleasure of that neat New England home. And shall one of us, — we who work in sight, we who work with great results, we who take a pride in our faculties, and enjoyment in the use of them, — shall *we* dare to name our work in the same breath with the self-sacrifice of these women?

A Council of Representatives from the principal Aid Societies, from all parts of the loyal States, was held in Washington in November, 1862; out of this grew the effort, still in progress, to reach a more thorough organization, on the part of each Branch of that part of the country from which its supplies were drawn. This effort has been strengthened, as it was found that from obvious causes the hospital supplies of the Commission were beginning to fall off. The plan for this effort which was proposed by the Boston Branch of the Commission proved to be by far the best, and it has been adopted by many, if not by all, the branches. The system, in brief, was to divide the field of each branch into such sections as convenience and the facilities of transportation pointed out; each section with an Associate Manager of the Branch resident within it. In this way close relations could be established with all auxiliaries; truth could be broadly spread, and the country, in its remotest villages, could feel the impetus given by the central head.

Through these Associate Managers it could be said to the people: — The work of the Commission invites the closest scrutiny. It is because those who have investigated it most thoroughly — who have examined its books; followed its Inspectors into camp and hospital; its relief agents on to the battle-field, and its supplies to the soldiers — are its most earnest supporters, that we wish to say to those who stay at home, and by their unwearied labor and patriotic zeal keep this great machinery in motion: You cannot see what is going on, but you shall *know* all and everything. We want you to learn what we learn, and know what we know, and thus be able to determine fairly, for yourselves, whether the Commission is, or is not, worthy of your support and confidence. It is truth that we would give you,—truth that you shall have, if so be that you will take it.

As a preliminary measure, and to open a more general correspondence, a circular letter was sent by some of the Branches to the Secretaries of all their auxiliary societies. This will be found in the Appendix (E) and will show the principle on which the women's work throughout the country is being organized.

To form this network of organized effort throughout the land, the Branches have generally arranged to draw their supplies according to geographical limits;—in other words, geography being now determined by steam, they are to draw them according to the lines of transportation by rivers and railroads.

Brief mention of these Branches must be made here. In one sense they are independent of the Sanitary Commission, because they have a body of their own, laws and a system of their own; but all for *what?*—to pour, with power and economy, the vital strength into the central head and heart which guides them. The principle of their relation to the United States Sanitary Commission is best shown in the vote by which the first "Branch" came into existence.

"*Resolved*—That the Woman's Central Association of Relief, at New York, is hereby, at its own generous instance, constituted an auxiliary branch of the Sanitary Commission, retaining full power to conduct its own affairs in all respects independently of the Commission; neither the Commission nor the Association being in any way responsible for any pecuniary liabilities or obligations, except such as are contracted or incurred by itself or its authorized agents.

"*Resolved*—That the Corresponding Secretary of the Board communicate, in writing, semi-weekly, with the Woman's Central Association of Relief, keeping it regularly informed of the wants of the Army, and the expectations of the Commission from that source of supply."

The writer deeply regrets an inability to give, in this place, a proper sketch of several of the great Branches of the West; it has not been possible to obtain their reports,* and the reader must find them in their deeds as this narrative goes on: but the narrative also will be unsatisfactory and inadequate, and the reader must bear in mind that the Western Branches have been, from the first, in keeping with their western character for generosity and energy.

*Branch of the United States Sanitary Commission for Northern Ohio.*—The call to arms was sounded on the 15th of April, 1861; on the 20th of April the Soldiers' Aid Society in Cleveland, Ohio, was formed; and it has the honor—the great and lasting honor—of

* They were written for at the earliest moment, but have not been received. If possible, something upon the subject will be placed in Appendix F.

being the first society of women that met and was organized. With earnest hearts and busy but unskilful hands, went on the preparation of lint and bandages. The first service that it performed was to supply the wants of volunteers arriving at a Camp of Instruction near their city. Havelocks were made and furnished to the troops; and then the Society languished, not from lack of interest in the work, but simply from utter ignorance of what the work ought to be. It revived, from time to time, as openings to a real service were seen before it, and the idea presented itself to centralize at this depot the efforts of all women in that part of the State of Ohio. Meetings were regularly held, and a concerted action was obtained. Every one strove to do her part, but every one doubted as to the proper disbursement of the stores. Informal letters of inquiry were written, — one of them to the United States Sanitary Commission. In reply the advice was given, to confine their shipments, for the sake of economy and natural causes, to the armies then collecting at the West. But the hazard of transportation, and the difficulty of guarding against waste or misapplication of stores, were deeply felt; out of this feeling grew a proposal from the society to become, and it accordingly became, a Branch of the United States Sanitary Commission.

Strengthened in its work by the generous inflowing of its auxiliaries from all parts of its field, this Society has borne its part in the majestic work of the West. At the present day it sends a car-load to the Central Depot at Louisville every ten days; makes shipments at irregular intervals to Wheeling, Va., and to Kansas; besides occasionally sending in smaller quantities to other points where special need occurs. The Army of the Cumberland receives the bulk of its stores, but it has added largely to the lading of many Sanitary Commission boats for Vicksburg. With all this work accomplished, and amidst their rejoicings at the opening of the Mississippi, the hearts of these women went to that portion of the land then enduring special suffering. "We have gratefully watched," they say, "the course of our Army at the East, and only wished that we were not too far off to help the sufferers at Gettysburg. The Sanitary Commission has left a noble record upon that battle-field: we hear for ourselves the gratitude expressed for the Commission, its agents, and its supplies, from the wounded who come through this city from Vicksburg and the Army of the Cumberland. We hope that we may soon see the end of this war; but, lest that hope should make us impatient in our work, we temper it by constantly remembering that we are 'in for the war,' be the time what it may."

*Cincinnati Branch United States Sanitary Commission.* — The first meeting of the Cincinnati Branch of the United States Sanitary Commission was held Nov. 27, 1861, when steps were taken to form a working organization, to obtain a depot and an office, to issue a circular to the people of Southern Ohio, Indiana, and Northern Kentucky, and to open the work of inspection, and supply the wants of camp and hospital within these limits. A few days later, the "Woman's Central Soldiers'-Aid-Society" was under way, composed of delegates from twenty-four independent societies already at work since the commencement of the war in the city and county of Cincinnati; for it must not be supposed that, although the organization of the Board was deferred to November, the citizens of Cincinnati have looked idly upon the great struggle of the country for national existence and the integrity of territory and institution.

On the 13th of December, 1861, a circular was issued stating the position and purpose of the United States Sanitary Commission, and explaining in detail that system through which the liberal and patriotic, especially the women of the country, might coöperate with the Government. In all this the advice was taken of some of the older auxiliaries of the Commission. The strength of union was soon apparent. At the central office, the work of packing and forwarding supplies became so great as to require the labors of six men, and at the present day there is no point within the lines of the

Armies of the Mississippi which their abundant stores do not systematically supply.

Some general idea of the work of the Western Branches may be obtained from the following list of the issues of supplies from their depots from Sept. 1, 1861, to Sept. 1, 1863. The branches here represented are those of Chicago, Cincinnati, Cleveland, Louisville, Pittsburg, Buffalo, and New Albany. Detroit and Columbus not reported.

| Article | Quantity | Article | Quantity |
|---|---|---|---|
| Packages | 62,445 | Condensed Milk | 46,807 lbs. |
| Blankets | 10,911 | Crackers | 100,320 " |
| Comfortables | 38,957 | Dried Beef | 13,423 " |
| Bed-ticks | 24,898 | Tea | 5,779 " |
| Pillow-ticks | 10,421 | Sugar | 21,580 " |
| Pillows | 18,841 | Dried Fruit | 466,347 " |
| Pillow-cases | 153,017 | Light Groceries | 47,657 " |
| Sheets | 87,082 | Codfish | 50,862 " |
| Shirts | 192,712 | Cheese | 11,981 " |
| Drawers | 107,465 | Butter | 40,170 " |
| Dressing-gowns | 11,483 | Eggs | 38,633 doz. |
| Coats and Vests | 8,999 | Wine and Spirits | 29,378 bottles |
| Towels and Handk'fs | 270,276 | Apple-Butter | 2,160 galls. |
| Socks | 84,485 | Pickles | 27,471 " |
| Slippers | 15,207 | Sauer Kraut | 3,780 " |
| Mittens | 9,180 | Potatoes | 50,281 bush. |
| Nightcaps | 4,464 | Ale and Cider | 11,584 galls. |
| Bandages and Rags | 205,632 lbs. | Chickens | 4,114 |
| Sponges and Pads | 51,024 " | Crutches | 3,309 prs. |
| Pin-cushions | 27,182 | Miscellaneous articles | not stated |
| Fruit-cans | 97,642 | Hospital Furniture | not stated |
| Concen. Beef | 30,116 lbs. | | |

The Eastern Branches are those in New York, Boston, Philadelphia, Buffalo, and Pittsburg. The first derives its supplies (on the principle already named) from the States of

New York, Northern New Jersey, Rhode Island, and Connecticut; the second from Maine, Vermont, New Hampshire, and Massachusetts; the third from southern New Jersey, Delaware, and Pennsylvania; the fourth and fifth from the western parts of the States of New York and Pennsylvania. The first of these (10 Cooper Union, New York) led the way, as we have shown, April 25th, 1861. The second (22 Summer Street, Boston) followed in the autumn of 1861 with that earnestness of purpose, that steadiness of will, which are the birthright and the power of New England. The third (1307 Chestnut Street, Philadelphia) has come but recently into the Union work. For this reason some discouragement was felt as it entered upon its effort to turn the liberality of the State into the national channel. The delay, however, has proved an element in its favor. The zeal of the societies throughout the State had begun to languish, but the spirit and principles of the Sanitary Commission, when laid clearly before them, ran like fire through their veins, until, to-day, in act and promise, this Branch holds ground with all the others. The fourth (No. 2, Adams's Block, Washington Street, Buffalo) sprang up simultaneously with the second, in the autumn of 1861, through the influence of some associate members of the Commission. No branch has worked more faithfully to show the truth and instil the principles of the Sanitary Commission, learning them and teaching them with wisdom, faith, and patience. The fifth (59 4th Street, Pittsburg, Pa.) has brought to the Commission an ardor in its service, a faithfulness to its spirit, which have earned for it a noble response throughout the western part of the State of Pennsylvania. The two Branches last named send their supplies East or West as necessity demands, but chiefly to the Armies in the West.

These fields are again broken up into "Centres of Collection," in the cities, from which everything flows into the Branches, where the supplies are held at the disposal of the central head.

The work done by the gentlemen and the gentlewomen of the land, in the offices and storehouses of the Branch Commissions, is that of an immense shipping business. The boxes come in from every part of their tract of supply: from the centres of collection, from the villages and country towns.[1]

The goods are sorted and stamped "U. S. Sanitary Commission"; then each article, and each kind of article, is repacked in separate boxes, which are closed up and held ready on demand. Soon the demand comes. A telegram

[1] There is a pathos in these boxes, which none but those who have unpacked them can understand. But alas! too often no care has been taken to send a list within them, nor a letter by mail; and so they can never be identified, and the grateful hearts which are unpacking them must grieve over the impossibility of acknowledging their receipt.

arrives from Washington, "The transport —— sails to-day for Beaufort, S. C." The Branch knows what is needed in that region and that climate, and within an hour boxes of *thin* flannel shirts, *cotton* socks, *light* quilts, *single* wrappers, mosquito netting, fans, &c., &c., are on their way to the Government transport. Or, it may be that the season is winter, and the region a cold one; then go forth the stores of warm clothing (greatly needed just now by all the Branches): blankets, bedding, heavy quilts, &c. The thoughtfulness and tenderness of the Commission, in these little niceties, remind us of a mother's care, (little niceties we call them, but are they not the source of a large economy?) There is something inexpressibly touching in this looking at the masses as individuals, guessing and foretelling their necessities, as a mother sends to her absent one those comforts which her anxious thought tells her that *he* must need.

Every week, an account of stock on hand, and of the distribution, is sent from every Branch to the central office in Washington, and the Relief Agents who have received these supplies account for them weekly to the same office: so that a knowledge of all articles on hand, and of the distribution throughout the United States, is possessed at any moment by the central head.

A large number of cases, especially from the Boston Branch, go into the storehouses in Washington from which the Armies of Virginia receive their supply. These storehouses are five in number: one, the receiving building; the second for woollen goods (alas! too empty); the third for cotton goods; the fourth for edibles the fifth, miscellaneous.

Out of 20,000 cases sent to these warehouses, but one is known to have been lost. The letters announcing them are copied into a book; and an agent watches for them at the railroad, and keeps his book of their receipt: the agent at the warehouses, who receives and sorts them, keeps *his* book; the agent at the disbursing or distributing office keeps *his* book; and every day these several books are brought together at the Central Office, checking and balancing each other; and every morning a printed schedule-sheet is filled out, showing goods on hand, what, and how much, of each and every article.

We have now shown briefly how the people's gifts are collected and dealt with. Nothing, however, can ever show the loving confidence of the people in the Commission, growing and strengthening by tangible proof, day after day, month after month, year by year.

We must now follow those gifts along their wider flow, into the regions and places of suffering.

## PART II.

### GENERAL RELIEF.

THE opening work of the Sanitary Commission was naturally one of prevention rather than cure. Inspection and inquiry was its first object and its first labor. It was no sooner fairly in existence than the great flight of Bull Run occurred. An inquiry made into the causes of that disaster; its history from a sanitary point of view, — showing how far the flight and panic were due to the weary and exhausted preceding condition of the troops, — was, and still remains, one of the remarkable works of the Commission; and it was one which produced, even in other countries, a just sense of its character and value.

Out of that disaster the Commission, taught always by necessity, came into another field of work, which has since become one of its most beneficent; for the cup of cold water given to fainting men as they toiled back into Washington, was the earliest act in the history of Special Relief. Verily, it has in nowise lost its reward. A sketch of the history of this Relief will be given later. It may be said here that it was under way early in August 1861; its first object being to supply to the sick men of regiments arriving at Washington such medicines, food, and care, as it was impossible for them to receive from their own officers, in the confusion of their arrival, with the regimental medicine-chest inaccessible in the baggage-car, and the regimental surgeon and quartermaster obliged to leave the men and go to hunt up government officials in a strange city.

A few weeks later, we find a little record from which will date an enlargement of the work.

"August 25th, I went to the Paymaster's Department, by request of a sick man at the Station House, who had his papers, but said he was so weak he could not push up to the window and get his pay. I found about forty men waiting in the yard of the office, some apparently very feeble. This was on Tuesday afternoon. One man had been waiting since Saturday forenoon. He was lame and weak, and the other new-comers kept him back. Three others had waited since Monday morning; one who was there all day Saturday without getting his pay, had died on Sunday night, in a house near by. Seeing the case from the outside, which the officers within the building in their press of business did not observe, I stated the facts to the proper officers, and they immediately made arrangements by which the men most sick were paid off at once, and facilities secured for the future." — *From Mr. Knapp's First Report, p.* 8.

The story of relief which was thus produced will be found elsewhere.

During the winter of 1861–62, when the Army of the Potomac lay in cantonments in and around Washington, or remained comparatively inactive in Virginia, the Sanitary Commission began its system of current supply. This was done, either by means of the Inspectors, who ascertained the wants of the sick in camp or hospital, and reported them to those in charge of the work of relief, — or through the direct appeals to the Commission of surgeons and commanding officers for such supplies as they could not obtain, or knew not how to obtain from Government. The office-books of that period are very interesting, and show a little history of the condition of each regiment in the Army. Parallel with its work of Inspection, and of Relief to troops in camp or barracks, the Commission has, from the first establishment of General Military Hospitals at the base of the various armies, maintained its supervision over their inmates, and has bestowed on them the same inspection of their condition, and the same relief of their necessities which it gave to the sick in camp or post hospitals. It signified its sense of the importance of this special work by the appointment of a medical man as Inspector of General Hospitals in the summer of 1861, soon after the battle of Bull Run; and, in its instructions to General Inspectors, prominence has always been given to these duties.

With the improvements everywhere progressing in the condition and management of Hospitals, the need of inspection has been growing less; but there has been no suspension of the readiness of the Commission to bestow the people's gifts here, or wherever they are needed. Hospital Inspectors have given place to Hospital Visitors, who, at brief intervals, renew their visits to each hospital; ascertain by careful inquiry of surgeons, and of the most reliable ward-masters and nurses the wants, present and prospective, of the inmates; and give orders on the storehouses of the Commission for requisite articles not included in the government supplies.

The only important field-work with the Armies of Virginia, which occurred during the winter of 1861–62, was the relief sent to the wounded after the battles at Edward's Ferry, Ball's Bluff, and Drainesville. It will be seen, therefore, that, though the work of the Commission at this time was of the utmost importance, as supplying what may be called the routine needs of the Army and of the hospitals, yet no very salient point in its history occurred until the Army advanced to its first campaign in March, 1862.

In other fields, however, in the West and at the South, such work was already in progress, and an account of it will be found in its appropriate place. The history of the field-work with the Army of the Potomac will therefore open with the Peninsular Campaign of 1862.

### ARMIES OF VIRGINIA.—PENINSULAR CAMPAIGN.

The sudden transfer of the scene of active war from the high banks of the Potomac to a low and swampy region, intersected with a network of creeks and rivers, early in the summer of 1862, required appliances for the proper care of the sick and wounded, which the Government was not, at that time, prepared to furnish. Seeing this, and armed with the approval of the Medical Bureau, the Sanitary Commission applied to the Quartermaster-General for the use of some large steamers, to be fitted up as Hospital Transports, for the reception and conveyance of the sick and wounded. These steamers had been lately used in transporting troops to the Peninsula, and were then lying idle, at a cost of $800 or $1000 a day. The Secretary of War immediately ordered so many of them as would carry 1000 men, to be detailed to the Commission, which, on its part, entered into an agreement with the Quartermaster-General to take charge and proper care of at least that number of sick and wounded.

The first vessel, "The Daniel Webster," was assigned to the Commission, April 25th, 1862. A hospital company and stores were immediately embarked, and she reached the York River, April 30th, refitting as a hospital on the voyage down. The General Secretary, Mr. Olmsted, took charge of the expedition, and with it went several members of the Commission. The hospital company was composed of surgeons, dressers, and nurses, — some of the latter being women. The ship was at once reported ready for duty; her stores, of which she brought a large quantity over and above her own needs, were placed in a storehouse ashore, — additional supplies coming down in store-boats, — and the work of supplying the sick in camp and hospital at once began. Meantime (May 1st) patients wére received on board the "Webster," — fed, cleaned, and put to bed, in a droll state of grateful wonder.

"The Daniel Webster" was no sooner started on her voyage to New York than the work of all was concentrated on "The Ocean Queen," a magnificent vessel, capable of carrying one thousand sick, which the Quartermaster then detailed to the Commission. Of course she came into their hands naked, as it were, for their purpose, — not a bunk nor an article of food on board of her. But the anxiety of the surgeons ashore (a species of anxiety which the Commission, on serious grounds, had forever to contend with) pressed the sick and wounded on board; and tugs and lighters came off with their freights of misery to be thrown upon the "Queen." All hands went to work; the supply-boat found her corner along-side, and, as the poor fellows tottered on board the empty ship at one gangway, the stores were hastily brought in upon the other. Some of the party went ashore, shot a rebel cow at pasture, and brought off the beef. The women, meantime, had hunted out a barrel of Indian meal, forgotten and left behind in some dark corner of the big ship, and were already ladling out from the ship's buckets hot gruel which they had made of it.

It was a hard first experience, and how it was got through with, none of the party could ever tell; but they all had one definite idea:— namely, that every man had had a good place to sleep in, and something hot to eat, and that the very sick had had every essential that could have been given them in their own homes.

The last work of somebody was to capture two draught-oxen, left behind by Franklin's division, (fresh beef was a great essential,) meantime the vessel filled up to 900, mostly typhoid; and then, to prevent more from being forced on board, she was got under-weigh and went out to sea.

Meantime Yorktown was evacuated; the battle of Williamsburg had been fought; the Army was thrown forward in rapid pursuit, and the hospital party, having sent off the "Ocean Queen," started in a little boat called "The Wilson Small" for West Point, where a battle was reported to be in progress,—accompanied by the supply-boat "The Elizabeth," commonly called "The Fiend," from her habit of rushing up, shrieking and howling at all hours of the night, much to the disgust of the poor, tired hospital company, who had to wake up *fully* to the idea that she was going off on some nocturnal errand of mercy, before they could be comforted.

On this little boat—"The Wilson Small"—the Commission received almost its first *wounded* men. They consisted of picked cases of special danger,—several being amputations of a bad character. One of these seemed dying as he came on board; but the next morning, at sunrise, he opened his eyes, and, looking up at his nurse, said, "You have saved my life for my wife." These men were kept on board "The Small" until they could be safely transferred to a proper boat, which had to be found and fitted up. Meantime they were in the care of Dr. Robert Ware, and nursed by a company of men and women.

It is not the purpose here to speak of the services of individuals, nor to give praise of that small kind; but a record of this work would be incomplete if it made no mention of the conduct of the young men who were employed upon it. They were of all classes and all characters; chiefly students of medicine. They had but one spirit and one purpose, and they gave themselves gayly, without a sense of fatigue, discomfort, or reluctance, to any work which was assigned to them; their conduct will never be forgotten by those who saw it.

Dr. Robert Ware, an Inspector of the Commission, and long employed in its service, had joined the expedition as it passed Fortress Monroe, the point where he was stationed. This narrative, as it goes on, will show him to the reader, and if there be in it any truth or interest, it is dedicated to his memory.

At West Point the hospital company broke up for a time into parties of two and three, going upon the different boats crowded with wounded, which passed down the river and discharged their freight into the hospitals at Fortress Monroe. These boats, pressed into the service by the medical officers on the emergency of the moment, were bare of everything for hospital purposes; and if it had not been for the Commission stores, and the Commission people, hastily thrown on board of them as they passed, the men would have been scarcely better off than on the battle-field.

Meantime the Commission people, at Yorktown, were taking possession of "The Elm City" and "The Knickerbocker," North River steamers, made over to them by the Quartermaster. Both were splendid surgical boats, especially "The Knickerbocker," with her great main-deck running clear from stern to waist, giving an amount of "floor-room" appreciated by any one in the service. "The Small" returned to Yorktown with her freight of wounded, to meet the steamship "Daniel Webster," arriving from her first trip, and bringing the intelligence that "The Ocean Queen" had reached New York, but was withdrawn for the transportation of troops to the Gulf, and that "The S. R. Spaulding" could be taken in her place. This was rather hard, especially as "The Spaulding" was entirely unfitted for the purposes of a hospital ship. One of the great difficulties of the Commission throughout was, that the Government did not consider the boats detailed to it as *made over* for the time for its especial purpose. Signal instances occurred where immense labor, and even expense, were brought upon the Commission by this difficulty.

"The Daniel Webster," freighted with typhoid, left again the day after her arrival, and then came a little breathing-space. The surgical cases which had been a week on "The Small" were carefully removed to "The Elm City," which lay in the stream, and was being fed with sick and wounded coming off in lighters from various points along the shore; — sick and wounded, who, dropping from the army on its march, and getting to the shores of the river, were there picked up by little tugs and brought down to the Commission boats. When "The Elm City" had four hundred and forty on board, she weighed anchor and left for Washington, and the Commission turned its attention to the work of fitting up "The Spaulding," and making arrangements for future emergencies. All this time, however, the current work was going on; the hospitals at Yorktown were examined and supplied with stores; the hospital transports "Vanderbilt," "Louisiana," and "State of Maine," (not directly in charge of the Commission,) were fitted out with supplies; whilst the work of receiving and collecting straggling parties of wounded men, as they came down from the front, kept those on board the boats unceasingly busy. Take, for instance, the history of one day. A telegram from the Medical Director of the Army at Williamsburg comes to the quartermaster at Yorktown, demanding a boat to be ready to take on two hundred sick and wounded at Queen's Creek, "*within two hours; this,*" adds the telegram, "is of the utmost urgency. See the Sanitary Commission." So, with great exertions, and quite a little history of effort, up goes a small boat after the men. To be sure they were not to be found at the point indicated; the Director saying that he did not suppose his telegraphic order *could* be so promptly complied with, and so he had as yet taken no measures to send them down:—the landing was four miles from Williamsburg. However, they were obtained at last, and brought back out of their misery, and shipped on board the large steamer ready for them at Yorktown. Meantime another despatch has been received from somewhere else: "A hundred sick are left on the shore at Bigelow's Landing, in the rain, to die without attendance or food," — and another expedition goes off at night, and brings them back; and so on, and so on, through many such days and many such histories.

Meantime "The Knickerbocker" has been fitted up and has gone North. Things are doing, on the whole, pretty well at Yorktown, but evidently the future work is to be nearer the Army, now advancing along the Pamunkey River, close upon Richmond. Mr. Olmsted determines to go forward and see the ground for himself. In the meanwhile, however, the poor little "Small," kicked and cuffed and knocked round by all the big vessels (not to speak of "The Fiend") is *hors de combat*, and can't even get up steam. So the hospital party, reluctantly leaving for a time the dear little home in which they had lived a life which was life indeed, went on board "The Spaulding" and started for the Pamunkey.

It must here be explained that the Sanitary Commission corps naturally divided itself into certain fields of work. One portion of the party, composed equally of men and women, under the guidance of Mr. Olmsted, remained permanently at the scene of action; their work was anything that came to hand, but chiefly this:— to superintend the shipping of sick or wounded on board the boats which returned from the North for fresh loads; to fit up those boats, or others coming into the Commission's hands; to receive at the landing, to sort and to distribute, according to orders, the patients who arrived in freight-cars from the front; to feed, cleanse, give medical aid and nursing to all these men, and otherwise take care of them, before the vessels left again for the North; and finally to be ready for any great emergency, and, when it came, to do their utmost to meet it.

This was the work of the subordinates; the work of the chiefs was heavier far, and will be alluded to further on. Another portion of the hospital company took charge of the vessels when they left the landing, and fulfilled the great object of the Commission, in carrying their freights of sick and wounded, with tender care, to the Northern hospitals; returning in the ships, (which were cleansed and painted at the North,) and refitting them for the sick as they returned. In this history more reference is necessarily made to the company remaining at the scene of action; but it must be remembered that their work was not, in any degree, more important than the work of the others, though it was doubtless harder and more exciting. Perhaps the story will be more graphic if we let some of these people speak for themselves.

On the 16th May, 1862, the Army of the Potomac reached White House, a point twenty-five miles from Richmond, where the Richmond and York River Railroad crosses the Pamunkey. On the 19th it was on its way to the line of the Chickahominy, leaving nothing behind it but a barren plain, and its great "base of supplies."

"*Floating Hospital 'S. R. Spaulding,' White House, Pamunkey River, May* 18*th*, 1862. — Yesterday, after getting off 'The Knickerbocker' from Yorktown, with three hundred sick on board, we transferred our quarters to this vessel, and started to run up the Pamunkey. It was audacious in us to run this big ocean steamer up this little river, without a chart and without a pilot. In some places we brushed the trees as we passed; but we came safely up, and this morning when we came on deck, what a sight was there to greet us! The glow of the morning mist, the black gunboats, the shining river, with the gleam of the white sails and the tents along the shore, made a picture only to be painted by Turner. We ran up to the very head of the fleet, — to the very head-quarters of the Army, and to the burnt railroad-bridge, beyond which no one could go. After breakfast we went ashore with Generals —, —, —, and spent an hour at the White House. . . . . .

"We were going to Head-quarters, but refrained on consideration, and came back to 'The Spaulding,' through army wagons and pie-pedlers (we met one man eating six pies at once); and rewarded the three Generals who had come over to meet us with a few miscellaneous luxuries: — handkerchiefs and cologne to General M.; hair-pins to General P., — one button of whose cap was already screwed on by that female implement; linen thread and buttons to General F. The Harbor-Master wanting the room in the evening, we dropped down the stream and anchored by a feathery elm-tree."

Meantime, however, "The Daniel Webster," always prompt and true, with her manly captain, good sailor, and good man, — and in charge of Dr. Grymes and a capital hospital company of women and young men, — arrived May 19th, filled up, and sailed again on the 20th, — the "Elm City" and "Knickerbocker" arriving empty on the same day.

It is impossible to give, in a small compass, an adequate idea of the difficulties which the Commission had taken upon itself, and which now began to manifest themselves; — difficulties seeming small, perhaps, but which were terrible, because the lives of men frequently hung on their being overcome, and that instantly. Some of these difficulties may be briefly indicated, and that is all.

One thing clearly important was to gain a *sys-*

*tem* by which the work could be carried on, — the current work disposed of in such a way as that everything could be kept clear for an emergency. For this Mr. Olmsted toiled; building unweariedly upon shifting sands. Agreements to this end were no sooner made than they were suffered to be transgressed by the very wants against which they sought to guard. One of these was the anxiety to "get off the sick." It was known that hospital transports were lying in the river; and to that point the surgeons sought to send down their sick, which were cumbering the Army on its march, and requiring care which it was not possible for them to give under the circumstances. Men who ought never to have gone North — who could have got well in ten days, with care, in a good hospital at White House — were *rushed* upon the Commission. In vain did Mr. Olmsted protest, on every ground, national and expedient. In vain did he form plans, and make agreements, and ask persistently for the tents for a shore-hospital; striving to keep his boats for the *essential* work. At first his efforts seemed in vain. Some of his assistants themselves hardly understood them; — but after a while it was seen that, slowly, things were getting shaped according to his moulding, and the time came when the wisdom of it was acknowledged. The only thing regretted was that the means to carry out his system were not greater.

Among the minor difficulties may be counted, 1st. The conflicts of authority upon the ships hired by the Quartermaster's Department, the masters of which growled at going into hospital service, and, as the Commission's position was somewhat that of sufferance, they had to be forever coaxed and conciliated. 2d. The amount of work given by sudden orders to return such or such a boat at once to the Quartermaster's Department for special service. On one occasion, "The Spaulding" and "The Elm City" were lying together at White House; "The Elm City" was being used as a receiving ship, and was two thirds full; "The Spaulding" was shipping men from the shore, and from "The Elm City," intending to sail the next day. One hundred of these were very sick men. A telegraphic order is suddenly received to take "The Spaulding" from the Commission, and send her to Fortress Monroe on transport duty. The work is arrested; an explanation and entreaty sent: — "The men are very sick; shall the work go on, or must we stop it?" The answer comes, "Go on." So it recommences. An hour later, the Assistant Quartermaster comes on board: "I have received orders to have 'The Elm City' and every other available vessel ready at break of day, for special transport service." A long and hard day's work had just been got through with when this order came, but there was no help for it. So all hands went to work again. The sick were transferred to "The Spaulding"; some of them very sick. Two died during the night. Then all the stores had to be transshipped, and the vessel cleared and coaled. It was a pitch-dark night, but before daybreak the vessel was ready, and — it was all for nothing. A change in the plans of Government occurred. She was again assigned to the Commission, and so, after a hard day's work and a hard night's work, the next day was spent in replacing her just as she was before.

Another heavy labor and responsibility was that of attending to the stores; that is, to the supply of the thousand applicants coming ceaselessly for help from the regiments and field hospitals at the front; — in short, the Commissariat of the Commission. This was in charge of Mr. Knapp, — then Special Relief Agent, now Associate Secretary of the Commission. The unwearied labor of heart and body which he gave to it was too great for the frame or mind of any man to bear; and before the work ceased he was in the treadmill of typhoid delirium.

The difficulty of bringing the work, *as it was*, before the reader's mind, is really very great. Scenes jostle each other in the memory until it is very hard to be definite. Day and night had not at times their proper meaning; and every hour was crowded by something vivid which broke in upon the last thing on hand. Here is a little picture which will serve to illustrate part of the life: —

"The last hundred patients were brought on board" (imagine any of the ships, it does not matter which) "late last night. Though these night-scenes are part of our daily living, a fresh eye would find them dramatic. We are awakened in the dead of night by a sharp steam-whistle, and soon after feel ourselves clawed by little tugs on either side of our big ship, bringing off the sick and wounded from the shore. And, at once, the process of taking on hundreds of men — many of them crazed with fever — begins. There is the bringing of the stretchers up the side-ladder between the two boats; the stopping at the head of it, where the names and home addresses of all who can speak are written down, and their knapsacks and little treasures numbered and stacked; then the placing of the stretchers on the platform; the row of anxious faces above and below deck; the lantern held over the hold; the word given to 'Lower'; the slow-moving ropes and pulleys; the arrival at the bottom; the turning down of the anxious faces; the lifting out of the sick man, and the lifting him into his bed; and then the sudden change from cold, hunger, and friendlessness, into positive comfort and satisfaction, winding up with his invariable verdict, if he can speak, — 'This is just like home!'"

"We have put 'The Elm City' in order,

and she began to fill up last night. I wish you could hear the men after they are put into bed. Those who *can* speak, speak with a will; the others grunt, or murmur their satisfaction. 'Well, this bed is most *too* soft; I don't know as I shall sleep, for thinking of it.' 'What have you got there?' 'That is bread; wait till I put butter on it.' 'Butter, on *soft* bread!' he slowly ejaculates, as if not sure that he is n't Aladdin with a genie at work upon him. Instances of such high unselfishness happen daily, that, though I forget them daily, I feel myself strengthened in my trust in human nature, without making any reflections about it. Last night, a man comfortably put to bed in a middle berth (there were three tiers, and the middle one incomparably the best) seeing me point to the upper berth as the place to put the man on an approaching stretcher, cried out: 'Stop! put me up there. Guess I can stand h'isting better 'n *him*.' It was agony to both.

"I have a long history to tell you, one of these days, of the gratefulness of the men. I often wish, — as I give a comfort to some poor fellow, and see the sense of rest it gives him, and hear the favorite speech: 'O, that 's good! it 's just as if mother was here,' — that the man or woman who supplied that comfort were by to see how blessed it is. Believe me, you may all give and work in the earnest hope that you alleviate suffering, but none of you realize what you do; perhaps you can't conceive of it, unless you could see your gifts *in use*. . . . .

"We are now on board 'The Knickerbocker,' unpacking and arranging stores, and getting pantries and closets in order. I am writing on the floor, interrupted constantly to join in a laugh. Miss —— is sorting socks, and pulling out the funny little balls of yarn, and big darning-needles stuck in the toes, with which she is making a fringe across my back. *Do* spare us the darning-needles! Reflect upon us, rushing in haste to the linen closet, and plunging our hands into the bale of stockings! I certainly will make a collection of sanitary clothing. I solemnly aver that yesterday I found a pair of drawers made for a case of amputation at the thigh. And the slippers! Only fit for pontoon bridges!"

This routine of fitting up the ships as they arrived, and of receiving the men on board as they came from the front, was accompanied by constant hard work in meeting requisitions from regiments, with ceaseless battlings for transportation to get supplies to the front for camps and hospitals; and was diversified by short excursions, which we will call "special relief"; such, for instance, as the following: —

"At midnight two steamers came along-side 'The Elm City,' each with a hundred sick, bringing word that 'The Daniel Webster No. 2' (a sidewheel vessel, not a Commission boat) was aground at a little distance, with two hundred more, having no one in charge of them, and nothing to eat. Of course they had to be attended to. So, amidst the wildest and most beautiful storm of thunder and lightning, four of us pulled off to her in a little boat, with tea, bread, brandy, and beef-essence. (No one can tell how it tries my nerves to go toppling round at night in little boats, and clambering up ships' sides on little ladders.) We fed them, — the usual process. — Poor fellows! they were so crazy! — And then 'The Wissahickon' came along-side to transfer them to 'The Elm City.' Only a part of them could go in the first load. Dr. Ware, with his constant thoughtfulness, made me go in her, to escape returning in the small boat. Just as we pushed off, the steam gave out, and we drifted end on to the shore. Then a boat had to put off from 'The Elm City,' with a line to tow us up. All this time the thunder was incessant, the rain falling in torrents, whilst every second the beautiful crimson lightning flashed the whole scene open to us. Add to this, that there were three men alarmingly ill, and (thinking to be but a minute in reaching the other ship) I had not even a drop of brandy for them. Do you wonder, therefore, that I forgot your letters?"

Or, again, the following: —

"Sixty men were heard of as lying upon the railroad without food, and no one to look after them. Some of us got at once into the stern-wheeler 'Wissahickon,' which is the Commission's carriage, and, with provisions, basins, towels, soap, blankets, &c., went up to the railroad bridge, cooking tea and spreading bread and butter as we went. A tremendous thunder-storm came up, in the midst of which the men were found, put on freight-cars, and pushed to the landing;—fed, washed, and taken on the tug to 'The Elm City.' Dr. Ware, in his hard working on shore, had found fifteen other sick men without food or shelter,—there being 'no room' in the tent-hospital. He had studied the neighborhood extensively for shanties; found one, and put his men in it for the night. In the morning we ran up on the tug, cooking breakfast for them as we ran, scrambling eggs in a wash-basin over a spirit-lamp:—and such eggs! nine in ten addled! It must be understood that wash-basins in the rear of an army are made of *tin*."

And here is one more such story: "We were called to go on board 'The Wissahickon,' from thence to 'The Sea-shore' and run down in the latter to West Point, to bring off twenty-five men said to be lying there sick and destitute. Two doctors went with us. After hunting an hour for 'The Sea-shore' in vain, and having got as low as Cumberland, we decided (*we* being Mrs. —— and I, for the doctors were new and docile, and glad to leave the responsibility upon us women) to push on in the tug, rather than leave the men another night on the ground, as a heavy storm of wind and rain had been going on all day. The pilot remonstrated, but the captain approved; and, if the firemen had not suddenly let out the fires, and detained us two hours, we might have got our men on board, and returned, comfortably, soon after dark. But the delay lost us the precious daylight. It was night before the last man was got on board. There were fifty-six of them, ten *very* sick ones. The boat had a little shelter-cabin. As we were laying mattresses on the floor, whilst the doctors were finding the men, the captain stopped us, refusing to let us put typhoid fever below the deck, on account of the crew, he said, and threatening to push off, at once, from the shore. Mrs. —— and I looked at him! I did the terrible, and she the pathetic, — and he abandoned the contest. The return passage was rather an anxious one. The river is much obstructed with sunken ships and trees; the night was dark, and we had to feel our way, slackening speed every ten minutes. If we had been alone it would n't have mattered; but to have fifty men unable to move upon our hands, was too heavy a responsibility not to make us anxious. The captain and pilot said the boat was leaking, and remarked awfully that 'the water was six fathoms deep about there'; but we saw their motive and were not scared. We were safe along-side 'The Spaulding' by midnight; but Mr. Olmsted's tone of voice, as he said, 'You don't know how glad I am to see you,' showed how much he had been worried. And yet it was the best thing we could have done, for three, perhaps five, of the men would have been dead before morning. To-day (Sunday) they are living and likely to live. *Is* this Sunday? What days our Sundays have been! I think of you all at rest, and the sound of church-bells in your ears, with a strange, distant feeling."

This was the general state of things at the time when the battle of Fair Oaks was fought, June 1, 1862. All the vessels of the Commission except "The Spaulding" — and she was hourly expected — were on the spot, and ready. "The Elm City" happened to be full of fever cases. A vague rumor of a battle prevailed, soon made certain by the sound of the cannonading; and she left at once (4 A. M.) to discharge her sick at Yorktown, and performed the great feat of getting back to White House, cleaned, and with her beds made, before sunset of the same day. By that time the wounded were arriving. The boats of the Commission filled up calmly. The young men had a system by which they shipped their men; and there was neither hurry nor confusion, as the vessels, one by one, — "The Elm City," "The Knickerbocker," "The Daniel Webster," — filled up and left the landing. After them, other boats, detailed by the Government for hospital service, came up. These boats were not under the control of the Commission. There was no one specially appointed to take charge of them; no one to receive the wounded at the station; no one to see that the boats were supplied with proper stores. A frightful scene of confusion and misery ensued. The Commission came forward to do what it could; but it had no power, only the right of charity. It could not control, scarcely check, the fearful confusion that prevailed, as train after train came in, and the wounded were brought and thrust upon the various boats. But it did nobly what it could. Night and day its members worked: not, it must be remembered, in its own well-organized service, but in the hard duty of making the best of a bad case. Not the smallest preparation was found, on at least three of the boats, for the common food of the men; and, as for sick-food, stimulants, drinks, there was nothing of the kind on any one of the boats, and not a pail nor a cup to distribute food, had there been any.

No one, it is believed, can tell the story, *as it occurred*, of the next three days; — no one can tell distinctly what boats they were, on which they lived and worked through those days and nights. They remember scenes and sounds, but they remember nothing as a whole; and, to this day, if they are feverish and weary, comes back the sight of men in every condition of horror, borne, shattered and shrieking, by thoughtless hands, who banged the stretchers against pillars and posts, dumped them anywhere, and walked over the men without compassion. Imagine an immense river-steamboat filled on every deck: — every berth, every square inch of room, covered with wounded men, — even the stairs and gangways and guards filled with those who were less badly wounded; and then imagine fifty well men, on every kind of errand, hurried and impatient, rushing to and fro, every touch bringing agony to the poor fellows, whilst stretcher after stretcher comes along, hoping to find an empty place; and then imagine what it was for these people of the Commission to keep calm themselves, and make sure that each man, on such a boat as that, was properly refreshed and fed. Sometimes two or even three such boats were lying side by side, full of suffering and horrors.

This was the condition of things with the subordinates. With the chiefs it was aggravated by a wild confusion of conflicting orders from head-quarters, and conflicting authority upon the ground, until the wonder is that *any* method could have been obtained. But an earnest purpose can do almost everything, and out of the struggle came daylight at last. The first gleam of it was from a hospital tent and kitchen, which, by the goodness and thoughtfulness of Capt. (now Col.) Sawtelle, Assistant

Quartermaster, was pitched for the Commission, just at the head of the wharf, and near the spot where the men arrived in the cars. This tent (Dr. Ware gave to its preparation the only hour when he might have rested through that long nightmare) became the strength and the comfort of the Commission people. As the men passed it, from cars to boat, they could be refreshed and stimulated, and from it meals were sent to all the boats at the landing. During that dreadful battle-week, 3000 men were fed from that tent. It was not the Vale of Cashmere, but many dear associations cluster round it.

After the pressure was over, the Commission went back to its old routine, but upon a new principle. A member of the Commission came down to White House for a day or two, and afterward wrote a few words about that work. As he saw it with a fresh eye, his letter will be given here. He says: —

"I wish you could have been with me at White House during my late visit, to see how much is being done by our agents there to alleviate the sufferings of the sick and wounded soldiers. I have seen a good deal of suffering among our Volunteers, and observed the marvellous variety and energy of the beneficence bestowed by the patriotic and philanthropic in camp, in hospital, and on transports for the sick; but nothing has ever impressed me so deeply as this. Perhaps I can better illustrate my meaning by sketching a few of the daily labors of the agents of the Commission as I saw them. The sick and wounded were usually sent down from the front by rail, a distance of about twenty miles, over a rough road, and in the common freight-cars. A train generally arrived at White House at 9 P. M., and another at 2 A. M. In order to prepare for the reception of the sick and wounded, Mr. Olmsted, with Drs. Jenkins and Ware, had pitched, by the side of the railway, at White House, a large number of tents, to shelter and feed the convalescent. These tents were their only shelter while waiting to be shipped. Among them was one used as a kitchen and workroom, or pantry, by the ladies in our service, who prepared beef-tea, milk-punch, and other food and comforts, in anticipation of the arrival of the trains. By the terminus of the railway the large Commission steamboat 'Knickerbocker' lay in the Pamunkey, in readiness for the reception of 450 patients, provided with comfortable beds and a corps of devoted surgeons, dressers, nurses, and litter-bearers. Just outside of this vessel lay 'The Elizabeth,' a steam-barge, loaded with the hospital stores of the Commission, and in charge of a storekeeper, always ready to issue supplies. Outside of this again lay 'The Wilson Small,' the head-quarters of our Commission. As soon as a train arrived, the moderately sick were selected and placed in the tents near the railroad and fed; those more ill were carried to the upper saloon of 'The Knickerbocker,' while the seriously ill, or badly wounded, were placed in the lower saloon, and immediately served by the surgeons and dressers. During the three nights that I observed the working of the system, about 700 sick and wounded were provided with quarters and ministered to in all their wants with a tender solicitude and skill that excited my deepest admiration. To see Drs. Ware and Jenkins, lantern in hand, passing through the trains, selecting the sick with reference to their necessities, and the ladies following to assuage the thirst, or arouse, by judiciously administered stimulants, the failing strength of the brave and uncomplaining sufferers, was a spectacle of the most touching character. If you had experienced the debilitating influence of the Pamunkey climate, you would be filled with wonder at the mere physical endurance of our corps, who certainly could not have been sustained in the performance of duties, involving labor by day and through sleepless nights, without a strong sense of their usefulness and success.

"At Savage's Station, too, the Commission had a valuable depot, where comfort and assistance was dispensed to the sick when changing from the ambulances to the cars. I wish I could do justice to the subject of my hasty narrative, or in any due measure convey to your mind the impressions left on mine in observing, even casually, the operations in the care of the sick at these two points.

"When we remember what was done by the same noble band of laborers after the battles of Williamsburg and Fair Oaks, in ministering to the wants of *thousands of wounded*, I am sure that we shall join with them in gratitude and thankfulness that they were enabled to be there."

But the end of it all was at hand; the "change of base," of which the Commission had some private intelligence, came to pass. The sick and wounded were carefully gathered up from the tents and hospitals, and sent slowly away down the winding river — "The Wilson Small" lingering as long as possible, till the telegraph wires had been cut, and the enemy was announced, by mounted messengers, to be at "Tunstall's"; in fact, till the roar of the battle came nearer, and we knew that Stoneman with his cavalry was falling back to Williamsburg, and that the enemy were about to march into our deserted places.

"All night we sat on the deck of 'The Small' slowly moving away, watching the constantly increasing cloud and the fire-flashes over the trees toward the White House; watching the fading out of what had been to us, through these strange weeks, a sort of home, where we had all worked together and been happy; a place which is sacred to some of us now for its intense living remembrances, and for the hallowing of them all by the memory of one who, through months of death and darkness, lived and worked in self-abnegation; lived in and for the suffering of others, and finally gave himself a sacrifice for them." *

"We are coaling here to-night ('Wilson Small,' off Norfolk, June 30th, 1862). We left White House Saturday night, and rendezvoused at West Point. Captain Sawtelle sent us off early, with despatches for Fortress Monroe; this gave us the special fun of being the first to come leisurely into the panic then raging at Yorktown. 'The Small' was instantly surrounded by terror-stricken boats; the people of the big 'St. Mark' leaned, pale, over their bulwarks, to question us. Nothing could be more delightful than to be as calm and monosyllabic as we were. . . . We leave at day-

* ROBERT WARE,

WHO DIED AT WASHINGTON, N. CAROLINA, DURING THE SIEGE, OF DOUBLE-PNEUMONIA BROUGHT ON BY EXPOSURE AND TOO GREAT DEVOTION IN THE SERVICE OF THE 44 REGT. MASS. VOLS., OF WHICH HE WAS THE SURGEON.

GREATER LOVE HATH NO MAN THAN THIS, THAT A MAN LAY DOWN HIS LIFE FOR HIS FRIENDS.

break for Harrison's Bar, James River, where our gunboats are said to be; we hope to get further up, but General Dix warns us that it is not safe. What are we about to learn? No one here can tell. . . . (Harrison's Bar, July 2d.) We arrived here yesterday to hear the thunder of the battle,* and to find the army just approaching this landing; last night it was a verdant shore, to-day it is a dusty plain. . . . . 'The Spaulding' has passed and gone ahead of us; her ironsides can carry her safely past the rifle-pits which line the shore. No one can tell as yet what work there is for us; the wounded have not come in." . . . .

"*Hospital Transport 'Spaulding,' July 3d.*— Reached Harrison's Bar at 11 A. M., July 1st, and were ordered to go up the James River, as far as Carter's Landing. To do this we must pass the batteries at City Point. We were told there was no danger if we should carry a yellow flag; *yellow flag* we had none, so we trusted to the *red* Sanitary Commission, and prepared to run it. 'The Galena' hailed us to keep below, as we passed the battery. Shortly after, we came up with 'The Monitor,' and the little captain, with his East India hat, trumpet in hand, repeated the advice of 'The Galena,' and added that, if he heard firing, he would follow us. Our cannon pointed its black muzzle at the shore, and on we went. As we left 'The Moni-

* Malvern Hill.

tor,' the captain came to me, with his grim smile, and said, 'I'll take those mattresses you spoke of.' We had joked, as people will, about our danger, and I had suggested mattresses around the wheel-house, never thinking that he would try it. But the captain was in earnest; when was he anything else? So the contrabands brought up the mattresses, and piled them against the wheel-house, and the pilot stood against the mast, with a mattress slung in the rigging to protect him. In an hour we had passed the danger and reached Carter's Landing, and there was the Army, 'all that was left of it.' . . . . Over all the bank, on the lawns of that lovely spot, under the shade of the large trees that fringed the outer park, lay hundreds of our poor boys, brought from the battle-fields of six days. It seemed a hopeless task even to feed them. We went first into the hospital, and gave them refreshment all round. One man, burnt up with fever, burst into tears when I spoke to him. I held his hand silently, and at last he sobbed out, 'You are so kind, and — I — am so weak.' We were ordered by the Surgeon in charge to station ourselves on the lawn, and wait the arrival of the ambulances, so as to give something (we had beef-tea, soup, brandy, &c., &c.) to the poor fellows as they arrived. . . . . Late that night came peremptory orders from the Quartermaster, for 'The Spaulding' to drop down to Harrison's Landing. We took some of the wounded with us; others went by land or ambulances, and some — it seems incredible — walked the distance. Others were left behind and taken prisoners; for the enemy reached Carter's Landing as we left it."

The work of the Commission upon the hospital transports was about to close. That work had been undertaken as supplemental to the Government, — to work a system which the Government had not at first been ready to take up. Until the Government could do what it *should do* for its sick and wounded, the Commission stood ready to throw itself into the breach, as it did during that dreadful battle-week, — as it does, more or less, all the time. But if in this supplemental work it may chance to point to better things, and *lead the way*, it does not ask, nor is it willing, to remain in it. The thing it asks is, not the gift of power, but that the Government should come forward and take the work away from it by doing it thoroughly. Let this be remembered. When the work of gathering up the wounded at Harrison's Landing commenced, it was found that the Medical Bureau was at least more prepared for it than it was on the Pamunkey; and, true to its proper character, the Commission withdrew to its proper work. "The Elizabeth" found her berth at the landing, and from that time till the evacuation kept up the work of supply.* Three able Inspectors,

* See Appendix G.

Drs. Douglas, Steiner, and Crane, remained with the Army; but the transports were given back into the hands of the Government, and the campaign of the hospital party was over. Whatever may have been the ultimate results of that campaign, or its influence on future work, at least those employed in it could look back upon the lives saved to the country with satisfaction. We speak of *lives* saved only; the amount of *suffering* saved was incalculable.

But before it was all over, the various vessels had made several trips in the service of the Commission, and one voyage of "The Spaulding" must not pass unrecorded.

"We were ordered up to City Point, under a flag of truce, to receive our wounded men who were prisoners in Richmond. . . . . At last the whistle sounded and the train came in sight. The poor fellows set up a weak cheer at the sight of the old flag, and those who had the strength hobbled and tumbled off the train almost before it stopped. We took four hundred and one on board. Two other vessels which accompanied us took each two hundred more. The rebel soldiers had been kind to our men,— so they said,— but the citizens had taken pains to insult them. One man burst into tears as he was telling me of their misery: 'May God defend me from such again.' God took him to Himself, poor suffering soul! He died the next morning, — died because he would not let them take off his arm. 'I was n't going to let them have it in Richmond; I said I *would* take it back to old Massachusetts.' Of course we had a hard voyage with our poor fellows in such a condition, but, at least, they were cleaned and well fed."

This closes the three-months history of the Sanitary Commission transports, and of its hospital company. If it has interested the reader enough to make him desirous to know more, he is informed that he will find the subject expanded in a series of letters lately published, under the title of "Hospital Transports," * to which this narrative is indebted for some assistance.

After the evacuation of Harrison's Landing the steam-barge "Elizabeth" served as the principal depot of the Commission for the region adjacent to Hampton Roads; and most opportunely was she placed there, for the hospitals of that vicinity, containing over 8000 patients at that time, were unusually dependent on the current assistance of the Commission. An Inspector was placed in charge of the work at that point. Norfolk became his head-quarters, and the chief depot of supplies from which, through the ensuing year, the United States forces in and around Yorktown, Gloucester

* Messrs. Ticknor & Fields, Boston.

Point, Williamsburg, Fortress Monroe, Portsmouth, and Suffolk, (numbering in all nearly 50,000 men,) received what supplemental aid they needed. In August, 1863, thirty thousand men having been withdrawn from those regions, and the work no longer needing an Inspector, this depot was left in charge of the Relief Agents.

During the Peninsular campaign, the ceaseless letters of inquiry from the friends of the sick, the wounded, and the dead, brought the Commission to a sense that it must endeavor to meet the want thus indicated; * and thus commenced the "Hospital Directory," of which an account will be found elsewhere.

The pause of the operations in the field which followed the evacuation of Harrison's

* These letters will never cease to be a tender, sad memory to those who received them: — "I think you will know my boy; he is fair-haired, straight, and slender, with a fair skin and delicate hands." — Poor mother! could she have seen him then! — "Tell me he is living, and has done *well*, and I care for nothing else." The mother's love always seemed more lofty, in one sense, than the wife's. "Give him back to me or I die," was the sound of the wife's cry. "Give him back to me dead, if he *is* dead, for I *must see him*," were the words of one such letter. Some one recollected his death, (his name was in the little note-book,) and that he had been buried ashore one Sunday evening. So one of us went up and found him under the shadow of the feathery elm-tree; and a little sketch was made of his quiet resting-place, and sent to her. All we could send, poor soul!

Landing was first broken by Stonewall Jackson's attack on General Banks at Cedar Mountain. Two Inspectors of the Commission, with a Relief Agent, were at once despatched to the scene of action. The lack of supplies of all kinds, in the field and the hospitals, proved to be very great. In one instance, stimulants were so imperatively needed that a surgeon sent for them by private hand to Washington, rather than see the suffering of his men. At this moment the Commission came in. When the Government supplies were exhausted, and the people of the entire region, stripped of their substance, were unable to give even the necessaries of life to the wounded soldiers, — when starvation added its horrors and fed upon the flesh of mangled men, — the Commission was there to render succor. With medicines, morphine, and chloroform, it saved as many lives as by stimulants and food. The Commission Corps fell back with the retiring columns, and finally took charge of the trains of wounded men sent back to Washington.

A few days later, the Medical Department found itself overwhelmed by the demand made upon it by the disasters of General Pope at Bull Run. The lowest estimate of the killed and wounded was 8000. General Halleck placed it at double that number. With an emergency of this sort, the Medical Department was, of course, unable to cope; but a great misfortune maimed the work it was prepared to do. Forty-three wagon-loads of supplies were sent forward by the Surgeon-General, and, relying on the representations of General Pope that he had no intention of retreating, they took up a position which when the army *did* retreat on the following day, led to their capture by the enemy.

When the news of the battle reached Washington, two Inspectors and some Relief Agents, with two wagon-loads of supplies, started for the battle-field, and reached it before the close of the action of the second day. During the succeeding two days, sixteen wagon-loads arrived safely. The sufferings of the wounded after this battle have probably not been equalled, at least not exceeded, during this war.

The Inspectors of the Commission assisted for a time in dressing the wounds, — the force of surgeons being greatly overworked, — and then followed a flag of truce which entered the enemy's lines for the purpose of obtaining those of our wounded (and that the chief body of them) who had remained on the battle-fields of the previous days. Many of them had been lying forty-eight hours on the field, and had as yet received no assistance. The sights of that field of carnage must not be told. Here, in the rear of it, were little groups, under a tree, or in slight depressions of the ground; these were the wounded, who had crawled or been borne to this scanty shelter. In one such group, there was no one still living; in another, a single poor fellow, with his head pillowed on a rock, looked around him on the bodies of four or five comrades, whom he had seen die off beside him. A little on one side of the field were a number of the living, gathered on the edge of a grove, most of whom had their canteens filled with water by their foes, who had killed an ox and a sheep for them, and had given them a portion of their own scanty supply of bread.

On the third day, the wounded were released on parole, and were slowly gathered into the hospitals at Centreville, guided and aided on their way by the Sanitary Commission. Here its agents gave out a constant supply of hot beef-tea, soup, brandy and water, and biscuit, to the exhausted inmates of the ambulances which poured in through the long days and longer nights, — together with shirts, drawers, and blankets. All the wounded came in within a week, and the work of the Commission was ended, except so far as its supplies were needed in the hospitals.

A few days later, the scene of the war was transferred by the rebels themselves into Maryland. General McClellan, recalled to the command, advanced upon the invaders; and a jaded army, wearied by forced marches, disheartened by its loss of *prestige*, and broken by defeat, followed its noble Leader to a field of victory.

*Battle of Antietam.* — The advance, led by Generals Franklin, Hooker, and Reno, came up with the enemy, Sept. 14th, under General Lee, drawn up in line of battle at South Mountain, and won the day, — the enemy hastily retreating upon Sharpsburg. On the evening of the 16th, our troops again came up with the lines of the enemy, ranged in force along the banks of Antietam Creek, reinforced by General Jackson from Harper's Ferry.

At daylight on the 17th, the battle of Antietam was opened.

Alas! that we must turn back at once to the dark side of war. In putting together a history like this, the accumulation of misery and suffering, the anguish that each page and each record brings back to the mind that knows it, is worse, — yes, it *is* worse, than the pain of any experience, however terrible, on the field.

The history of what was done by the Sanitary Commission at and after the battle of Antietam will be found abridged in the following letters: —

"WASHINGTON, *Sept.* 23.

"TO DR. BELLOWS, PRESIDENT. — SIR: —

"I inclose Dr. Agnew's letter. We have sent him since the Army of Virginia went to meet the invaders, that is, within ten days, 28,763 pieces of dry goods, shirts, towels, bedticks, pillows, &c.; 30 barrels old linen, bandages, and lint; 3188 pounds of farina; 2620 pounds condensed milk; 5000 pounds beef-stock and canned meats; 3000 bottles of wine and cordials, and several tons of lemons and other fruit; crackers, tea, sugar, rubber-cloth, tin cups, and hospital conveniences.

"We are sending forward more, constantly. Four thousand sets of hospital clothing will (by special train from New York) get through to Frederick to-morrow, if money and energy can break through the obstructions of this embarrassed transportation. Your daily supplies from New York reach us regularly.

"Respectfully yours,

"F. L. Olmsted,

"*General Secretary.*"

* "I cannot now give you a report of all our doings since last Wednesday night, but it will give you joy to know that we have given some aid and comfort to *over five thousand wounded.* I left Washington, as you know, on Wednesday at midnight. Arriving at the break in the railroad at Monocacy, Dr. Harris and I walked on to Frederick, where I found Dr. Steiner, our Inspector, working with great zeal and efficiency. The demand for our supplies was so pressing that it was thought best to open a storehouse at once, and Dr. Steiner procured one near the railroad station, in anticipation of the resumption of steam transportation. Fred-

* Dr. Agnew's letter.

erick will be the great depot for the wounded, whence they will be distributed to Washington and Baltimore; and hence the necessity of giving Dr. Steiner large supplies of hospital stores. . . . . . No additional medical supplies having arrived for Dr. Thompson, acting Medical Director at Middletown, I desired him to take such as he needed from the Sanitary Commission wagons as they came. He had previously obtained many essential articles of food, &c., from our advanced train. I left him twenty-five dollars, to be used in purchasing such things as we had not, to replenish his deficient stores. Early on Friday morning I went to Keedysville, and to General McClellan's head-quarters; about noon, (Friday 19th,) Dunning arrived with his wagons; on Saturday morning, Dr. Brink and Mr. Peverly arrived, and now our stores of stimulants, condensed food, bandages, &c., became abundant. Dunning and I went out with stores of beef-stock, stimulants, and surgical dressings, as soon as he arrived, and visited barns and farm-houses within a mile and a half of head-quarters, and carried some relief to nearly two thousand wounded. Everywhere we were asked for chloroform and opiates, instruments and bed-pans, and everything, in fact, required for the wounded, except the coarser food furnished by the Commissary, and the comforts provided to the extent of their ability by the inhabitants, who had been previously nearly stripped by the rebels.

"It should be remembered that so rapid was the movement of the Army through Washington after the disaster and losses of the Virginia campaign, that the regimental and brigade and division medical officers could not, to any considerable extent, replenish their exhausted supplies.

"The medical supplies sent to meet the emergency on Wednesday did not begin to arrive on the battle-field until Saturday afternoon, and then in small quantity, and entirely inadequate. Many of the same supplies are still here (at Frederick) awaiting transportation, while the Commission has at least four wagon-trains sent to the front that left Washington subsequently to Wednesday afternoon, in addition to two sent before in anticipation of the battle. You can estimate at your office the number of wagons we have sent forward, including Hay's trains, which will be on the battle-field this afternoon. As soon as Brink and Mitchell and Parsons arrived on the battle-field, I sent them over radii previously ascertained to be within the circle of the late battles. They will be able to state personally the fields of their operations, as I desired them to keep notes. I left Dunning's wagons — in fact, all the two-horse wagons and ambulances of our train — constantly going, and carrying relief to thousands of wounded.

"The wounded were mainly clustered about barns, occupying the barn-yards and floors and stables; having plenty of good straw well broken by the power threshing-machine. I saw fifteen hundred wounded men lying upon the straw about two barns, within sight of each other! Indeed, there is not a barn, nor farm-house, nor store, nor church, nor school-house, between Boonsborough, Keedysville, and Sharpsburg, nor between the latter and Smoketown, that is not gorged with the wounded — rebel and Union. Even the corn-crib, and in many instances the cow-stables, and in one place the mangers, were filled. Several thousand lie in the open air upon straw, and all are receiving the kind services of the farmers' families and the surgeons.

"I hope I never shall forget the evidences everywhere manifested of the unselfish and devoted heroism of our surgeons, regular and volunteer, in the care of both Federal and rebel wounded. Wherever I went, I encountered surgeons and chaplains who had given themselves no rest, in view of the overwhelming claims of suffering humanity. General McClellan's Medical Director had several times been over the field, and given personal direction to the labors of the surgeons; and Dr. Rauch, U. S. A., and others were everywhere actively engaged.

"Having studied the field and the relations of the clusters of wounded to a central point, I took on Saturday a store at Sharpsburg, hiring it of a Union citizen of the name of Cronise.

On Saturday evening, I brought up the mule teams of Peverly to Sharpsburg. On Sunday morning, Dunning, Mitchell, Parsons, and I unpacked the boxes, and filled the shelves and bins. I took charge of the wagons on Saturday night, because Dunning, Brink, and Mitchell were out with relief, to the right and left, for about three thousand wounded; and Parsons had gone back, under instructions from Medical Director Letterman and my approval, to Birkettsville, with relief to five hundred and forty wounded.

"Our plans, so far, are working splendidly,—thanks to the vigor with which you at Washington have crowded forward supplies, and the aid given by Dr. Letterman and his medical officers. We have been ahead of all supplies, and at least two days ahead of those of the Medical Bureau; the latter fact due to its want of independent transportation. A single item will show the value of our supplies; we have given out over thirty pounds of chloroform within three days after the battle. The medical authorities had not one hundredth part of what was needed; and in many places important operations were necessarily neglected, and life lost. *Our chloroform saved at least fifty lives, and saved several hundred from the pain of severe operations.*

"The want of chloroform was the most serious deficiency in the regular medical supplies, and, as the result, amputations which should have been primary will now be secondary or impossible, and the mortality from secondary amputations is much greater than from primary.

"I venture to say that nearly every barn and hospital and cluster of wounded, over the wide extent of the late military operations, embracing a circle of nearly thirty miles, was receiving most essential relief from the Commission, while the regular medical stores lay at Monocacy Bridge. I affirm that great loss of life has occurred, and will occur, among the wounded, as the direct result of an inability on the part of the medical authorities to furnish, by rapid and independent means of transportation, the surgical and medical appliances needed within the two days *immediately subsequent* to the battles.

"When will our rulers learn wisdom and humanity? I do not ask for the Medical Bureau means of transportation entirely independent of and above those of the quartermaster's department; but I do demand such conveyances as shall enable the medical officers moving with an army, in line of battle, to carry forward surgeons and such surgical materials as chloroform, opiates, stimulants, and the primary dressings. A few supply-carts, in addition to the ordinary medicine wagons, would meet almost any emergency. Let such carts be light one-horse wagons upon springs, so constructed as to be easily drawn past or through the army trains that seriously obstruct the approaches to battle-fields. Had Dr. Letterman had under his control one dozen one-horse supply-wagons, he could have sent to every part of the field the supplies most in demand. If Government will not give to the Medical Bureau such a train, I insist that *we* must do it. The Commission can have no higher object than to strengthen the hands of our army surgeons, *who now strive so hard* to perform the most exhausting duties with so few appliances.

"We now need hospital clothing more than anything else. I should say, Send two thousand shirts and drawers to Frederick, fifteen hundred to Boonsborough, and four thousand to Sharpsburg. As to other supplies, await telegraphic orders. We have now, I think, with the wagons met last night, enough for several days of food, stimulants, and surgical dressings. I shall never cease saying, God bless you for all your efforts in sending forward relief to the wounded.

"I cannot close this hasty letter without expressing my sense of obligations to Dr. Letterman for unusual facilities, and to all the surgeons with whom I came in contact for their uniform courtesy and confidence. The country should be proud of those faithful men, who labored day and night to alleviate the sufferings of the battle, without hope of 'honorable mention' or a 'brevet' in this world. May they have their reward in the next world, where the fact of having given a cup of cold water to a suffering human being will be made the occasion of a never-fading record and an exhaustless blessing.

"I beg to add that I saw at Hagerstown and Sharpsburg, and at the hospitals on the field of Antietam Creek, the most abundant and gratifying evidences of the activity with which our Inspectors and agents were doing their duty, and of the essential service they were rendering the Army."

The great extent of country over which the Army now spread itself required two stationary depots of the Sanitary Commission. One was already established at Sharpsburg, another was placed at Harper's Ferry. The march of a great army, let it be remembered, is marked by the emptying from the regiments of the sick men, and the dropping out of the feeble. All these the Commission assists to gather up and succor. The sick of one corps alone, left behind on its march from the Potomac across the Shenandoah into the Valley of the Blue Ridge, amounted to eighteen hundred men. By degrees, and owing to care in which the Commission may claim to have assisted largely, one thousand of these were returned to duty.

To meet sudden emergencies, a depot for the Commission was established at Manassas Junction, as soon as it became safe to advance so far, and from thence, by army stages, it reached Acquia Creek and Fredericksburg. During the march the relations of the Commission to the officers of the Army remained as intimate and cordial as ever. The General commanding expressed his hearty appreciation of its success, and intimated a desire that the principal depot of its field supplies should be stationed near his head-quarters. But, nevertheless, the reader will gather from all this very little real idea of the amount of current work which the Commission was doing on this field at this very time.

*Battle of Fredericksburg.* — The report of the battle of Fredericksburg, December 13, reached Washington the same night. A propeller was chartered, laden with stores, and with a special relief party, under the charge of Dr. Douglas, started for the front. The steam-barge "Elizabeth," with an efficient crew and well provided with stores, was at the Acquia Landing when the battle commenced, and the regular corps of Inspectors and Relief Agents, marching with the Army, had been reinforced by others from various points even before the arrival of the special relief party. As soon as the movement to cross the river was made, they had proceeded to the front from Acquia, visited the field-hospitals on the Falmouth side of the river, which had been organized in expectation of a battle, and distributed several wagon-loads of stores.

The special relief party reached Acquia Landing, with the extra supplies, at daybreak on Monday, and a large part of it immediately went forward to Fredericksburg, arriving there in time to assist in the removal of the wounded to the field hospitals. Two wagons, which had been brought from Washington, were filled and pushed on. Owing to the condition of the roads, the entanglement of the wagons in an ambulance train, and the overturning of one of them, night found this last half of the party still upon the road. They were obliged to bivouac, and did not reach the front till the next morning, in the midst of a severe rain-storm. It was during this stormy night that the Army, with a small remaining portion of the wounded, was withdrawn from Fredericksburg.

On the arrival of Dr. Douglas a thorough inspection of the whole field was undertaken. The labor was divided, and an especial duty assigned to each individual of the party. By noon, all the hospitals where the wounded were congregating had been visited, and the surgeons informed of the presence of the Sanitary Commission, and the location of its depot of supplies, from whence, until the wounded were all removed to general hospitals, the issue of stores was steady and unremitting.

We will here leave Dr. Douglas to tell his own story: —

"The scene at our field station was a busy

one. Could the contributors to the stores and the treasury of the Commission have heard the fervent expressions of grateful relief; could they have seen the comfort which their bounty afforded our brave wounded; could they realize by actual intercourse with the wounded the suffering from, for instance, cold, alleviated by the abundant supply of blankets which their bounty had provided; could they have observed the change produced when the soiled and bloody garments were replaced by clean and warm clothing which they had sent, — they would be eager to replenish our storehouses and keep our hands filled with the means to accomplish these purposes.

"Early Tuesday morning the rain subsided, the sun appeared, and the weather became clear and cold. The wounded were for the most part placed in hospital tents, upon a plentiful supply of hay. Blankets had to repair the absence of stoves, which, by some singular mistake, had arrived in a condition not to be used, — the necessary stove-pipe not being included in the shipment. The supply in the hands of the Purveyor soon became exhausted from the unusual demands made upon him, on account of the severity of the weather. Fortunately we were enabled to supplement his stores, and to answer his calls upon us from the reserve, of 1800 blankets and over 900 quilts, which we had sent forward. Many of these were employed in covering the wounded during the period of their transportation by car and steamboat from the field hospitals to the general hospitals at Washington.

"It is with a deep feeling of gratitude that I have also to report that the last sad office could be paid to the dead with an approach to the ceremonies of civil life, through the stores placed by us at the disposal of the surgeons of the hospitals.

"The comfort of the wounded, and the result of the treatment of their wounds, were materially affected by the change of clothing provided by us. We had been able to get up to our field station 5642 woollen shirts, 4439 pairs woollen drawers, 4269 pairs socks, and over 2500 towels, among other articles. These were liberally distributed wherever the surgeons of hospitals indicated that there was a need. Certain articles of hospital furniture, of which there was a comparatively greater want than of anything else, were freely obtained by all surgeons at our station. Stimulants, I am happy to say, were in great abundance among the Purveyor's stores, so that the calls upon us were few. The same was generally true of food, and positively so of all kinds of medicinal articles which at other battles have been furnished by us. Nothing of the kind was asked for. In the article of food alone, we issued in one week, solely to hospitals, sixteen barrels of dried fruit, ten boxes of soda biscuit, six barrels of crackers, and nearly 1000 pounds of concentrated milk. The beef-stock we had brought up was, I am again happy to say, not needed, there being a bountiful provision among the hospital stores, and fresh beef at command at all times, and in any quantity.

"As rapidly as the wounded were attended to, and put in a condition for safe transportation, they were removed from the field hospitals to the general hospitals in Washington and Point Lookout. The removal was effected by ambulance or stretcher to the cars, by car to the landing at Acquia Creek, and thence to Washington by steamboat. The principal battle occurred on the 13th December, and on the 25th the last of the wounded were removed. The floors of both cars and boats were well covered with fresh hay, and in addition to this, the severely wounded had mattresses or bed-sacks.

"In order to meet whatever demands might arise for the proper sustenance of the wounded while on this trying journey, Mr. Knapp, our Special Relief Agent, was despatched from Washington to Acquia Creek, to provide suitable accommodations for furnishing food or shelter at that point. A kitchen was improvised upon the Landing, and the first night meals were provided for 600 wounded brought down by the cars. Mr. Knapp was cordially assisted in this humane work by several members of the Christian Commission who were present at that place. Through the cordial coöperation of the Quartermaster of the post, Mr. Knapp had a building erected adjoining our portable store-house, which affords shelter and a good bed to nearly 100 every night.

"Our field operations have gradually diminished with the removal of the wounded. Our supplies were brought up from Acquia Creek in every case in charge of a special messenger. By the schedule, it will be seen that all the division hospitals were visited and supplies furnished to them on requisition. Besides this, supplies were also issued to a number of brigade hospitals, and to over fifty regimental hospitals, previous to my leaving on the 24th December. The issue to regimental and brigade hospitals was continued by Dr. Andrew after my departure, an account of which will be hereafter furnished.

"I cannot close my report without referring with admiration to the plan of organization for the Medical Corps of the Army just introduced by Dr. Letterman, (Medical Director Army of the Potomac). The manner in which it was carried out was to the honor of the Medical Corps, for the advancement of science, and to the credit of humanity. . . . .

"In most instances the wounded were accompanied to Washington by their own surgeons. This was particularly true of the more serious cases. At Acquia Creek, Dr. Warren Webster, U. S. A., had charge of the transportation, and everything was done by him to secure the well-being of the wounded. Extra clothing from our storehouse was placed at his disposal to meet any deficiencies.

"The watchful care, the cautious solicitude of the surgeons, and the general kind attention of nurses and attendants, should not be passed without notice. Individual cases there were, where, from constitutional indifference or inherent slothfulness, the medical officers or the attendants were derelict of duty; but these instances were rare, — so infrequent, indeed, as not to affect the general opinion that no battle since the war commenced has found the medical corps so fully prepared for every emergency, or has witnessed such prompt, careful, and judicious performance of the necessary operations; such comparative immunity from suffering occasioned by a deficiency or absence of supplies. Too much credit cannot be accorded to Surgeon Letterman for the persistency with which he has inaugurated and carried out the present efficient plan of field division hospitals after a battle.

"Much has been said of the demoralization of the Army. I have seen no evidence of it. It does not exist in the constitution of the men of our climate to be turned back from any undertaking by one check, nor to be disheartened even by a series of obstacles. Their temperament as men is not changed by their discipline as soldiers. If signs are to be believed, the

Army of the Potomac to-day is, in firmness of purpose, in discipline, in soldierly qualities, stronger than ever, and more determined to merit by its deeds the high trust and confidence reposed in it by the country."

But not all the care now given to the Army, not all the appliances now lavished on it for its efficiency and comfort, could keep it from the gloomy influences of that repulse. We look in vain for something cheerful to break the record of that winter, and find only this:—"Signs and rumors of another crossing. Pontoon movements of great obscurity. Ambulance inspections. Ammunition supplies." "Marching orders have come for 8 A. M. to-day. A most dispirited army is moving forward, and dragging itself along over bad roads, with every prospect of a speedy return. We ride among the soldiers, and look in vain for any trace of hope or cheerfulness. They are all of the same spirit—sad and dejected." This was the dismal mud march from which, thank God, they returned without a battle.

But the Commission followed it on the *qui vive*, and the report goes on to say how, here and there, its sentinels of relief were posted. One little record is gracious and gratifying:—"A verbal report made to Dr. Letterman of neglected duties in the ambulance corps. He issues orders for inquiry and correction, and expresses his appreciation of such reports through the Sanitary Commission."

Meanwhile the current work went on, and every corps, regiment, and company of the entire Army was visited, examined, and aided.

*Battle of Chancellorsville.*— On the morning of the 27th of April, 1863, orders were issued that the Army of the Potomac should be in readiness to move at an hour's notice; and before night the main body of it was already on its march, under the pressure of orders to move rapidly. With each corps went a representative of the Commission, furnished with sufficient stores for its current necessities, and for the first demands of an emergency. These stores were replenished from time to time with fresh supplies, sent forward on mules.

During the fatal week which saw the battle of Chancellorsville and the storming of the heights of Fredericksburg, over those heights and upon that field the agents and stores of the Commission were rendering all the assistance which was needed. At no previous period of the war had medical and surgical appliances been so accessible to the surgeons. They were obtained readily, without perplexity or delay, and the work of the Commission became therefore strictly supplemental.

When the wounded were removed to the Falmouth side of the river, for temporary lodgment in field hospitals or for transportation to corps hospitals scattered between the Potomac and Acquia Creeks, the Commission agents who had remained at Acquia were able to render much manual assistance; whilst their stores were of great value, from the fact that on that side of the river no such large numbers of the wounded were expected, and the preparations for them were not sufficient.

From that time until the wounded were all brought in, the toil was very great; there were many thousands of them, and their numbers were increased by the addition of those who had been prisoners, and who were released by the enemy on parole, eight days after the battle. Meantime arrangements were made to transport the majority of them to the hospitals at Washington; and owing to the wise care of the medical officers, Dr. Brinton at Falmouth, and Dr. Taylor at Acquia, this was done as expeditiously and comfortably to the poor fellows as the gigantic proportion of the work would allow.

Nevertheless there was much need of the assistance of the Commission. At first the transports were found to be in good order, and well supplied for the relief and comfort of the men; but soon the immense number of wounded who poured in obliged the medical officers to take the common transports into their service. To supply these transports, to shelter and feed the unhappy sufferers who were brought down to the Landing, and often compelled to wait many hours before they could be shipped, became at once the recognized work of the Commission,—a work which had, however, existed, though in a lesser degree, during the greater part of the winter. For, from the battle of Fredericksburg, in December, 1862, until the Army evacuated Falmouth and Acquia Creek to meet the second great invasion of Maryland, in June, 1863, lodges and homes had been maintained by the Commission near the Army at these points. These lodges were on the system of those already under way with vast results in Washington; but their fields were even more varied. The chief of them was the lodge at Acquia Creek, where the disabled and discharged soldiers were sheltered and sent on their way, comforted, if not rejoicing; and where the very sick and wounded were received whilst waiting for the boats at the Landing, fed, lodged, nursed, and medically cared for. In many instances, also, the unhappy friends of wounded and dead or dying men were received, sheltered, and assisted in their inquiries.

What became of the men who thus passed through this Lodge is told elsewhere, and nothing but a few little incidents connected with it can be mentioned here.

Its daily routine was as follows:—By the evening it was filled to overflowing with pale and weary soldiers, who arrived too late to be taken in the boats which had left for Washington, many on stretchers, and some accompanied by parents and friends. A large quantity of milk-punch was always on hand, and a liberal draught given to call up their flickering strength. A table was spread for the least suffering, who were served with good hot coffee, biscuit, and butter.

In the evening the physician passed through and prescribed for those in need of him, and then they were put to rest for the night. At eight o'clock next morning the line was formed for the boat, each man with a *blue ticket* for "The Home," or a *red ticket* for "The Lodge" in Washington, and in many cases a bottle of milk-punch or beef-essence, to keep up their strength on the way. Out of a thousand incidents occurring, each of equal interest, it is hard to select any to place here. The following are chosen as the shortest that can be found. "Seventy-five men were reported, at 10 A. M., as needing our care, having been left at the railroad without shelter or food. Nine were taken to the Lodge, and a permit was obtained for the remainder to go to the 'Soldiers' Rest.' At 8 P. M. they were again reported as having been in a car since two o'clock without food. Our force was again called out, and we supplied them with what they needed." "A man, shoeless, shirtless, and stockingless, feet frost-bitten, and mind deranged, was brought to our Lodge, as the only refuge for the wanderer. We kept him nine days, ascertained his regiment, and returned him for discharge." "A soldier picked up — typhoid fever — flighty. With the best of care, he died the next day." "At daylight another poor fellow fainted on the wharf, and fell into the water. When rescued he was nearly dead, — respiration and pulsation apparently ceased. Did everything possible, — rewarded by his recovery. He was dried, cleaned, and put into new warm under-clothes. Third case of the kind within a week."

From December 25th, 1862, to April 1st, 1863, lodgings and food and succor were given at the Acquia Creek Lodge to over three thousand men.

During all this winter "The Elizabeth" was plying between Washington and Acquia, carrying up requisitions, and returning loaded with supplies. When this base of the Army was abandoned in the following June, and the Government stores were brought off or destroyed, the Commission agents worked with a devotion which the country ought to know of, in bringing safely off the country's gifts. They worked without rest for forty consecutive hours, with the great reward of knowing that not an article was lost.

*Second Invasion of Maryland and Pennsylvania.* — The Army of the Potomac broke camp on the Rappahannock June 12th, 1863, the effective troops moving northwards by forced marches, and the sick and wounded being removed by rail to Acquia Creek, and thence to Washington.

A small part of the Commission's Potomac Relief Corps marched with the Army. They were frequently replenished with supplies from the depot at Washington, and daily rendered valuable assistance to the surgeons having the care of men wounded in the skirmishes and in the cavalry engagements, as well as of those falling ill under the fatigues and privations of forced marches, undertaken in the heat of midsummer, in a dry and desolated region.

On the retreat of General Milroy from Winchester, it was found that the supply of hospital stores at Harper's Ferry was very limited, and a relief agent was sent there with a wagon-load of supplies. This was got safely through, but the wagon on its return was captured by Stuart's cavalry. The Relief Agent, having remained at Harper's Ferry, escaped. The Commission's stores at Frederick were safely concealed during its occupation by the enemy, but so soon as the Army of the Potomac reached the city, the depot was again opened and the stock increased. Responsible and experienced officers of the Commission were stationed at Harrisburg, Philadelphia, Baltimore, and Frederick, and a systematic daily communication was established between them and the agents moving with the different columns of the Army. Supplies were accumulated, and held ready for movement at different points in the circumference of the seat of war, and care was taken to have ample reserves at the branch offices ready for shipment.

*Battle of Gettysburg.*—With the first news of the battle of Gettysburg, Westminster, the nearest point of railroad communication to the battle-field, was fixed upon as the point of approach, and authority to run a car daily to that station was asked for and obtained.

Two wagon-loads of battle-field supplies had been distributed to meet deficiencies in the stores of the surgeons, shortly before the battle commenced. These wagons returned for more loads; two others, fully loaded, arrived from Frederick at the moment of the assault of Longstreet upon the left wing of the loyal Army, and were pushed forward *under fire*, to reach the collections of wounded in its rear. As one of them came up to a point where several hundred sufferers had been taken from the ambulances and laid upon the ground, behind a barn, less than five hundred yards in the rear of our line of battle then fiercely engaged, a surgeon was seen to throw up his arms exclaiming, "Thank God! here comes the Sanitary Commission; now we shall be able to do something." His supplies were exhausted, and the chloroform, lint, bandages, sponges, brandy, and beef-soup, which were at once given to him, were undoubtedly the means of saving many lives. The empty wagons which had gone back to Frederick were reloaded, and left again the same day. Dr. McDonald, Chief Commission Inspector on the field, conducted one of them by Emmetsburg; the other was sent by Winchester.

The latter got safely through; but the former, with Dr. McDonald and the Rev. Mr. Scandlin, Relief Agent, fell into the hands of the enemy. These gentlemen were marched to Richmond as prisoners of war.* This misfortune, and the fact that Dr. McDonald was charged with all the field arrangements, caused some temporary embarrassment; but supplies of the Commission arrived from other directions before the close of the battle.

A school-house centrally situated was taken as a depot, and thence eleven wagon-loads of special supplies were distributed to the corps hospitals, and to scattering groups of wounded on the field, long before any supplies arrived by railroad. As soon as the railroad was so far repaired as to allow a train to approach within a mile of the town, two car-loads of most valuable goods were sent to the Commission, and two more by each succeeding train for a week.

The wounded now began to be brought from the field to the railroad, for removal to fixed hospitals elsewhere. The Commission at once established a complete Relief Station on a large scale, at the terminus of the railroad; — and here shall be given intact the story of "WHAT WE DID AT GETTYSBURG," written by the woman best fitted for the work, and best fitted to tell of it. She is now in a far distant hospital, and it is therefore not improper that this allusion to her

* See Appendix H.

should be made. Her sense, energy, lightness and quickness of action; her thorough knowledge of the work, her amazing yet simple resources, her shy humility which made her regard her own work with impatience, almost with contempt,—all this and much else has made the memory of —— a source of strength and tenderness which nothing can take away.

"*July*, 1863.

"DEAR ——:

"*What we did at Gettysburg*, for the three weeks we were there, you will want to know. 'We,' are Mrs. —— and I, who, happening to be on hand at the right moment, gladly fell in with the proposition to do what we could at the Sanitary Commission Lodge after the battle. There were, of course, the agents of the Commission, already on the field, distributing supplies to the hospitals, and working night and day among the wounded. I cannot pretend to tell you what was done by all the big wheels of the concern, but only how two of the smallest ones went round, and what turned up in the going.

"Twenty-four hours we were in making the journey between Baltimore and Gettysburg, places only four hours apart in ordinary running time; and this will give you some idea of the difficulty there was in bringing up supplies when the fighting was over, and of the delays in transporting wounded. Coming toward the town at this crawling rate, we passed some fields where the fences were down and the ground slightly tossed up: 'That's where Kilpatrick's Cavalry men fought the rebels,' some one said; 'and close by that barn a rebel soldier was found day before yesterday, sitting dead'—no one to help, poor soul,—'near the whole city full.' The railroad bridge broken up by the enemy, Government had not rebuilt as yet, and we stopped two miles from the town, to find that, as usual, just where the Government had left off the Commission came in. There stood their temporary lodge and kitchen, and here, hobbling out of their tents, came the wounded men who had made their way down from the corps-hospitals, expecting to leave at once in the return-cars.

"This is the way the thing was managed at first: The surgeons left in care of the wounded three or four miles out from the town, went up and down among the men in the morning, and said, 'Any of you boys who can make your way to the cars can go to Baltimore.' So off start all who think they feel well enough; anything better than the 'hospitals,' so called, for the first few days after a battle. Once the men have the surgeons' permission to go, they are off; and there may be an interval of a day, or two days, should any of them be too weak to reach the train in time, during which these poor fellows belong to no one,—the hospital at one end, the railroad at the other,—with far more than chance of falling through between the two. The Sanitary Commission knew this would be so of necessity, and, coming in, made a connecting link between these two ends.

"For the first few days the worst cases only came down in ambulances from the hospitals; hundreds of fellows hobbled along as best they could in heat and dust, for hours, slowly toiling; and many hired farmers' wagons, as hard as the farmers' fists themselves, and were jolted down to the railroad, at three or four dollars the man. Think of the disappointment of a soldier, sick, body and heart, to find, at the end of this miserable journey, that his effort to get away, into which he had put all his remaining stock of strength, was useless; that 'the cars had gone,' or 'the cars were full'; that while he was coming others had stepped down before him, and that he must turn all the weary way back again, or sleep on the roadside till the next train 'to-morrow'! Think what this *would* have been, and you are ready to appreciate the relief and comfort that *was.* No men were turned back. You fed and you sheltered them just when no one else could have done so; and out of the boxes and barrels of good and nourishing things, which you people at home had supplied, we took all that was needed. Some of you sent a stove (that is, the money to get it), some of you the beef-stock, some of you the milk and fresh bread; and all of you would have been thankful that you had done so, could you have seen the refreshment and comfort received through these things.

"As soon as the men hobbled up to the tents, good hot soup was given all round; and that over, their wounds were dressed, — for the gentlemen of the Commission are cooks or surgeons, as occasion demands, — and, finally, with their blankets spread over the straw, the men stretched themselves out and were happy and contented till morning, and the next train.

"On the day that the railroad bridge was repaired, we moved up to the depot, close by the town, and had things in perfect order; a first-rate camping-ground, in a large field directly by the track, with unlimited supply of delicious cool water. Here we set up two stoves, with four large boilers, always kept full of soup and coffee, watched by four or five black men, who did the cooking, under our direction, and sang (not under our direction) at the tops of their voices all day, —

> 'Oh darkies, hab you seen my Massa?'
> 'When this *cruel* war is *over*.'

Then we had three large hospital tents, holding about thirty-five each, a large camp-meeting supply-tent, where barrels of goods were stored, and our own smaller tent, fitted up with tables, where jelly-pots, and bottles of all kinds of good syrups, blackberry and black currant, stood in rows. Barrels were ranged round the tent-walls; shirts, drawers, dressing-gowns, socks, and slippers (I wish we had had more of the latter), rags and bandages, each in its own place on one side; on the other, boxes of tea, coffee, soft crackers, tamarinds, cherry brandy, &c. Over the kitchen, and over this small supply-tent, we women rather reigned, and filled up our wants by requisitions on the Commission's depot. By this time there had arrived a 'delegation' of just the right kind from Canandaigua, N. Y., with surgeon's dressers and attendants, bringing a first-rate supply of necessities and comforts for the wounded, which they handed over to the Commission.

"Twice a day the trains left for Baltimore or Harrisburg, and twice a day we fed all the wounded who arrived for them. Things were systematized now, and the men came down in long ambulance trains to the cars; baggage-cars they were, filled with straw for the wounded to lie on, and broken open at either end to let in the air. A Government surgeon was always present to attend to the careful lifting of the soldiers from ambulance to car. Many of the men could get along very nicely, holding one foot up, and taking great jumps on their crutches. The latter were a great comfort; we had a nice supply at the Lodge; and they travelled up and down from the tents to the cars daily. Only occasionally did we dare let a pair go on with some very lame soldier, who begged for them; we needed them to help the new arrivals each day, and trusted to the men being supplied at the hospitals at the journey's end. Pads and crutches are a standing want, — pads particularly. We manufactured them out of the rags we had, stuffed with sawdust from brandy-boxes; and with half a sheet and some soft straw, Mrs. —— made a poor dying boy as easy as his sufferings would permit. Poor young fellow, he was so grateful to her for washing and feeding and comforting him. He was too ill to bear the journey, and went from our tent to the church hospital, and from the church to his grave, which would have been coffinless but for the care of ——; for the Quartermaster's Department was overtaxed, and for many days our dead were simply wrapped in their blankets and put into the earth. It is a soldierly way, after all, of lying wrapped in the old war-worn blanket, — the little dust returned to dust.

"When the surgeons had the wounded all placed, with as much comfort as seemed possible under the circumstances, on board the train, our detail of men would go from car to car, with soup made of beef-stock or fresh meat, full of potatoes, turnips, cabbage, and rice, with fresh bread and coffee, and, when stimulants were needed, with ale, milk-punch, or brandy. Water-pails were in great demand for use in the cars on the journey, and also empty bottles to take the place of canteens. All our whisky and brandy bottles were washed and filled up at the spring, and the boys went off carefully hugging their extemporized canteens, from which they would wet their wounds, or refresh themselves till the journey ended. I do not think that a man of the sixteen thousand who were transported during our stay, went from Gettysburg without a good meal. Rebels and Unionists together, they all had it, and were pleased and satisfied. 'Have you friends in the Army, madam?' a rebel soldier, lying on the floor of the car, said to me, as I gave him some milk. 'Yes, my brother is on ——'s staff.' 'I thought so, ma'am. You can always tell; when people are good to soldiers they are sure to have friends in the Army.' 'We are rebels, you know, ma'am,' another said. 'Do you treat rebels *so?*' It was strange to see the good brotherly feeling come over the soldiers, our own and the rebels, when side by side they lay in our tents. 'Hullo, boys! this is the pleasantest way to meet, is n't it? We are better friends when we are as close as this than a little farther off.' And then they would go over the battles together, 'We were here,' and 'you were there,' in the friendliest way.

"After each train of cars daily, for the three weeks we were in Gettysburg, trains of ambulances arrived too late, — men who must spend the day with us until the 5 P. M. cars went, and men too late for the 5 P. M. train, who must spend the night till the 10 A. M. cars went

All the men who came in this way, under our own immediate and particular attention, were given the best we had of care and food. The surgeon in charge of our camp, with his most faithful dresser and attendants, looked after all their wounds, which were often in a shocking state, particularly among the rebels. Every evening and morning they were dressed. Often the men would say, 'That feels good. I have n't had my wound so well dressed since I was hurt.' Something cool to drink is the first thing asked for after the long, dusty drive; and pailfuls of tamarinds and water, 'a beautiful drink,' the men used to say, disappeared rapidly among them.

"After the men's wounds were attended to, we went round giving them clean clothes; had basins and soap and towels, and followed these with socks, slippers, shirts, drawers, and those coveted dressing-gowns. Such pride as they felt in them! comparing colors, and smiling all over as they lay in clean and comfortable rows, ready for supper, — 'on dress parade,' they used to say. And then the milk, particularly if it were boiled and had a little whisky and sugar, and the bread, with *butter* on it, and *jelly* on the butter: how good it all was, and how lucky we felt ourselves in having the immense satisfaction of distributing these things, which all of you, hard at work in villages and cities, were getting ready and sending off, in faith.

"Canandaigua sent cologne with its other supplies, which went right to the noses and hearts of the men. 'That is good, now'; — 'I'll take some of that'; — 'worth a penny a sniff'; 'that kinder gives one life'; — and so on, all round the tents, as we tipped the bottles up on the clean handkerchiefs some one had sent, and when they were gone, over squares of cotton, on which the perfume took the place of hem, — 'just as good, ma'am.' We varied our dinners with custard and baked rice puddings, scrambled eggs, codfish hash, corn-starch, and always as much soft bread, tea, coffee, or milk as they wanted. Two Massachusetts boys I especially remember for the satisfaction with which they ate their pudding. I carried a second plateful up to the cars, after they had been put in, and fed one of them till he was sure he had had enough. Young fellows they were, lying side by side, one with a right and one with a left arm gone.

"The Gettysburg women were kind and faithful to the wounded and their friends, and the town was full to overflowing of both. The first day, when Mrs. —— and I reached the place, we literally begged our bread from door to door; but the kind woman who at last gave us dinner would take no pay for it. 'No, ma'am, I should n't wish to have that sin on my soul when the war is over.' She, as well as others, had fed the strangers flocking into town daily, sometimes over fifty of them for each meal, and all for love and nothing for reward; and one night we forced a reluctant confession from our hostess that she was meaning to sleep on the floor that we might have a bed, her whole house being full. Of course we could n't allow this self-sacrifice, and hunted up some other place to stay in. We did her no good, however, for we afterwards found that the bed was given up that night to some other stranger who arrived late and tired: 'An old lady, you know; and I could n't let an old lady sleep on the floor.' Such acts of kindness and self-denial were almost entirely confined to the women.

"Few good things can be said of the Gettysburg farmers, and I only use Scripture language in calling them 'evil beasts.' One of this kind came creeping into our camp three weeks after the battle. He lived five miles only from the town, and had 'never seen a rebel.' He heard we had some of them, and came down to see them. 'Boys,' we said,—marching him into the tent which happened to be full of rebels that day, waiting for the train,—'Boys, here 's a man who never saw a rebel in his life, and wants to look at you'; and there he stood with his mouth wide open, and there they lay in rows, laughing at him, stupid old Dutchman. 'And why have n't you seen a rebel?' Mrs. —— said; 'why did n't you take your gun and help to drive them out of your town?' 'A feller might 'er got hit!' — which reply was quite too much for the rebels; they roared with laughter at him, up and down the tent.

"One woman we saw, who was by no means Dutch, and whose pluck helped to redeem the other sex. She lived in a little house close up by the field where the hardest fighting was done, — a red-cheeked, strong, country girl. 'Were you frightened when the shells began flying?' 'Well, no. You see we was all a-baking bread round here for the soldiers, and had our dough a-rising. The neighbors they ran into their cellars, but I could n't leave my bread. When the first shell came in at the window and crashed through the room, an officer came and said, "You had better get out of this"; but I told him I *could not* leave my bread; and I stood working it till the third shell came through, and then I went down cellar; but' (triumphantly) 'I left my bread in the oven.' 'And why did n't you go before?' 'Oh, you see, if I had, the rebels would 'a' come in and daubed the dough all over the place.' And here she had stood, at the risk of unwelcome plums in her loaves, while great holes (which we saw) were made by shot and shell through and through the room in which she was working.

"The streets of Gettysburg were filled with the battle. People thought and talked of nothing else; even the children showed their little spites by calling to each other, 'Here, you rebel'; and mere scraps of boys amused themselves with percussion-caps and hammers. Hundreds of old muskets were piled on the pavements, the men who shouldered them a week before lying underground now, or helping to fill the long trains of ambulances on their way from the field. The private houses of the town were, many of them, hospitals; the little red flags hung from the upper windows. Beside our own men at the Lodge, we all had soldiers scattered about whom we could help from our supplies; and nice little puddings and jellies, or an occasional chicken, were a great treat to men condemned by their wounds to stay in Gettysburg and obliged to live on what the empty town could provide. There was a colonel in a shoe-shop, a captain just up the street, and a private round the corner whose young sister had possessed herself of him, overcoming the military rules in some way, and carrying him off to a little room, all by himself, where I found her doing her best with very little. She came afterward to our tent and got for him clean clothes, and good food, and all he wanted, and was perfectly happy in being his cook, washerwoman, medical cadet, and nurse. Beside such as these, we occasionally carried from our supplies something to the churches, which were filled with sick and wounded, and where men were dying, — men whose strong patience it was very hard to bear, — dying with thoughts of the old home far away, saying, as last words, for the woman watching there and waiting with a patience equal in its strength, 'Tell her I love her.'

"Late one afternoon, too late for the cars, a train of ambulances arrived at our Lodge with over one hundred wounded rebels, to be cared for through the night. Only one among them seemed too weak and faint to take anything. He was badly hurt, and failing. I went to him after his wound was dressed, and found him lying on his blanket stretched over the straw, — a fair-haired, blue-eyed young lieutenant, with a face innocent enough for one of our own New England boys. I could not think of him as a rebel; he was too near heaven for that. He wanted nothing, — had not been willing to eat for days, his comrades said; but I coaxed him to try a little milk gruel, made nicely with lemon and brandy; and one of the satisfactions of our three weeks is the remembrance of the empty cup I took away afterward, and his perfect enjoyment of that supper. 'It was *so* good, the best thing he had had since he was wounded,' — and he thanked me so much, and talked about his 'good supper' for hours. Poor fellow, he had had no care, and it was a surprise and pleasure to find himself thought of; so, in a pleased, childlike way, he talked about it till midnight, the attendant told me, as long as he spoke of anything; for at midnight the change came, and from that time he only thought of the old days before he was a soldier, when he sang hymns in his father's church. He sang them now again, in a clear, sweet voice. 'Lord, have mercy upon me'; and then songs without words — a sort of low intoning. His father was a Lutheran clergyman in South Carolina, one of the rebels told us in the morning, when we went into the tent, to find him sliding out of our care. All day long we watched him, — sometimes fighting his battles over, often singing his Lutheran chants, till, in at the tent-door, close to which he lay, looked a rebel soldier, just arrived with other prisoners. He started when he saw the lieutenant, and quickly kneeling down by him, called 'Henry! Henry!' But Henry was looking at some one a great way off, and could not hear him. 'Do you know this soldier?' we said. 'Oh, yes, ma'am; and his brother is wounded and a prisoner, too, in the cars now.' Two or three men started after him, found him, and half carried him from the cars to our tent. 'Henry' did not know him, though; and he threw himself down by his side on the straw, and for the rest of the day lay in a sort of apathy, without speaking, except to assure himself that he could stay with his brother, without the risk of being separated from his fellow-prisoners. And there the brothers lay, and there we strangers sat watching and listening to the strong, clear voice, singing 'Lord, have mercy upon me.' The Lord *had* mercy; and at sunset I put my hand on the lieutenant's heart, to find it still. All night the brother lay close against the coffin, and in the morning went away with his comrades, leaving us to bury Henry, having 'confidence'; but first thanking us for what we had done, and giving us all that he had to show his gratitude, — the palmetto ornament from his brother's cap and a button from his coat. Dr. W. read the burial service that morning at the grave, and —— wrote his name on the little head-board: 'Lieut. Rauch, 14th Regt. S. Carolina Vol.'

"In the field where we buried him, a number of colored freedmen, working for Government on the railroad, had their camp, and every night they took their recreation, after the heavy work of the day was over, in prayer-meetings. Such an 'inferior race,' you know! We went over one night and listened for an hour, while they sang, collected under the fly of a tent, a table in the middle where the leader sat, and benches all round the sides for the congregation, — men only, — all very black and very earnest. They prayed with all their souls, as only black men and slaves can; for themselves and for the dear, white people who had come over to the meeting; and for 'Massa Lincoln,' for whom they seemed to have a reverential affection, — some of them a sort of worship, which confused Father Abraham and Massa Abraham in one general cry for blessings. Whatever else they asked for, they must have strength and comfort and blessing for 'Massa Lincoln.' Very little care was taken of these poor men. Those who were ill during our stay were looked after by one of the officers of the Commission. They were grateful for every little thing. Mrs. —— went into the town and hunted up several dozen bright handkerchiefs, hemmed them, and sent them over to be distributed the next night after meeting. They were put on the table in the tent, and, one by one, the men came up to get them. Purple and blue and yellow the handkerchiefs were, and the desire of every man's heart fastened itself on a yellow one; they politely made way for each other, though,—one man standing back to let another pass up first, although he ran the risk of seeing the particular pumpkin-color that riveted his eyes taken from before them. When the distribution was over, each man tied his head up in his handkerchief, and they sang one more hymn, keeping time all round, with blue and purple and yellow nods, and thanking and blessing the white people in 'their basket and in their store,' as much as if the cotton handkerchiefs had all been gold leaf. One man came over to our tent next day, to say, 'Missus, was it you who sent me that present? I never had anything so beautiful in all my life before'; and he only had a blue one, too.

"Among our wounded soldiers, one night, came an elderly man, sick, wounded, and crazy, singing and talking about home. We did what we could for him, and pleased him greatly with a present of a red flannel shirt, drawers, and red calico dressing-gown, all of which he needed, and in which he dressed himself up, and then wrote a letter to his wife, made it into a little book with gingham covers, and gave it to one of the gentlemen to mail for him. The next morning he was sent on with the company from the Lodge; and that evening two tired women came into our camp, — his wife and sister, who hurried on from their home to meet him, arriving just too late. Fortunately we had the queer little gingham book to identify him by, and when some one said, 'It is the man, you know, who screamed so,' the poor wife was certain about him. He had been crazy before the war, but not for two years, now, she said. He had been fretting for home since he was hurt; and when the doctor told him there was no chance of his being sent there, he lost heart, and wrote to his wife to come and carry him away. It seemed almost hopeless for two lone women, who had never been out of their own little town, to succeed in finding a soldier among so many, sent in so many different directions; but we helped them as we could, and started them on their journey the next morning, back on their track, to use their common sense and Yankee privilege of questioning.

"A week after, Mrs. —— had a letter full of gratitude, and saying that the husband was found and secured for *home*. That same night we had had in our tents two fathers, with their wounded sons, and a nice old German mother with her boy. She had come in from Wisconsin, and brought with her a patchwork bed-quilt for her son, thinking he might have lost his blanket; and there he laid all covered up in his quilt, looking so homelike, and feeling so, too, no doubt, with his good old mother close at his side. She seemed bright and happy, — had three sons in the Army, — one had been killed, — this one wounded; yet she was so pleased with the tents, and the care she saw taken there of the soldiers, that, while taking her tea from a barrel-head as table, she said, 'Indeed, if *she* was a man, she'd be a soldier, too, right off.'

"For this temporary sheltering and feeding of all these wounded men, Government could make no provision. There was nothing for them, if too late for the cars, except the open field and hunger, in preparation for their fatiguing journey. It is expected when the cars are ready that the men will be promptly sent to meet them, and Government cannot provide for mistakes and delays; so that, but for the Sanitary Commission's Lodge and comfortable supplies, for which the wounded are indebted to the hard workers at home, men badly hurt must have suffered night and day, while waiting for the 'next train.' We had on an average sixty of such men each night for three weeks under our care, — sometimes one hundred, sometimes only thirty; and with the 'delegation,' and the help of other gentlemen volunteers, who all worked devotedly for the men, the whole thing was a great success, and you and all of us can't help being thankful that we had a share, however small, in making it so. Sixteen thousand good meals were given; hundreds of men kept through the day, and twelve hundred sheltered at night, their wounds dressed, their supper and breakfast secured — rebels and all. You will not, I am sure, regret that these most wretched men, these 'enemies,' 'sick and in prison,' were helped and cared for through your supplies, though, certainly, they were not in your minds when you packed your barrels and boxes. The clothing we reserved for our own men, except now and then when a shivering rebel needed it; but in feeding them we could make no distinctions.

"Our three weeks were coming to an end; the work of transporting the wounded was nearly over; twice daily we had filled and emptied our tents, and twice fed the trains before the long journey. The men came in slowly at the last, — a lieutenant, all the way from Oregon, being among the very latest. He came down from the corps hospitals (now greatly improved), having lost one foot, poor fellow, dressed in a full suit of the Commission's cotton clothes, just as bright and as cheerful as the first man, and all the men that we received had been. We never heard a complaint. 'Would he like a little nice soup?' 'Well, no, thank you, ma'am'; hesitating and polite. 'You have a long ride before you, and had better take a little; I'll just bring it and you can try.' So the good, thick soup came. He took a very little in the spoon to please me, and afterwards the whole cupful to please himself. He 'did not think it was this kind of soup I meant. He had some in camp, and did not think he cared for any more; his "cook" was a very small boy, though, who just put some meat in a little water and stirred it round.' 'Would you like a handkerchief?' and I produced our last one, with a hem and cologne too. 'Oh yes; that is what I need; I have lost mine, and was just borrowing this gentleman's.' So the lieutenant, the last man, was made comfortable, thanks to all of you, though he had but one foot to carry him on his long journey home.

"Four thousand soldiers, too badly hurt to be moved, were still left in Gettysburg, cared for kindly and well at the large, new Government hospital, with a Sanitary Commission attachment.

"Our work was over, our tents were struck, and we came away after a flourish of trumpets from two military bands who filed down to our door, and gave us a farewell 'Red, white, and blue.'"

During the battle all the wounded were gathered into field hospitals, as most convenient. Soon they were divided into corps hospitals in the field, from which those who were able to be removed to a distance were brought to the railroad depot, where the Sanitary Commission had large tents erected for their reception and refreshment during the interval of the departure of trains morning and evening.

Large store-tents of the Commission were also at hand, filled to repletion with all manner of supplies. A cook-house was put up with caldrons and stoves and a steam apparatus, all of which were in full blast, day and night. Ten cooks and some thirty attendants were occupied in preparing and dealing out to each sufferer such nourishment as the case allowed. Clothes, shoes, crutches, canes, pads, pillows, splints, lint, bandages, and every kind of stimulant, and anodyne, and every appliance which long experience and thoughtful care could anticipate for so extreme a necessity, were dealt out with unsparing diligence and attention, day and night. Not the least important part of the work which the Commission performed at this Depot-Lodge was the dressing of wounds, preparatory to a removal in the cars. In this department a surgeon and a corps of dressers were employed, who devoted their entire attention to the examination of each case, applying fresh dressings and preparing the wounded to sustain the journey to the best advantage.

The trains were despatched either to Elizabethport (their living freight to take boat there for David's Island) or direct to Baltimore. With each train went a surgeon and attendants in charge of the wounded. Large cans of iced water, bags of crackers, stimulants, &c., were placed on board the cars to supply every necessity. Generally, before leaving, each canteen was filled with water, and each man furnished with an extra cup of coffee, or soup, or with broth, as they desired. This system was continued from the 9th of July till the corps hospitals were relieved of all who were able to be removed to a distance. Those that remained, therefore, were only the desperate cases of amputation, compound fracture, and penetrating wounds of the chest and pelvis. These were collected with the utmost care, many of them on stretchers, from miles around, and placed under the three hundred tents which constitute Camp Letterman Hospital; which contained, in truth, the very dregs of battle from two armies.

The Sanitary Commission station, under the charge of one who, whether as pastor or in the field, works with strength and a single mind, was here established. The large tents of his mission were spread beneath tall oaks and hickorys. One of them was the lodging-place of thirty persons; the rest, some six or eight, were occupied as store-tents and offices. There was also a kitchen from which many of the sick and wounded received the lighter diet which was prescribed or allowed by the surgeons. This was under the direction of ladies, two of whom remained there for several months.

The surgeons of this post, deeply impressed with the services of the Sanitary Commission, have given a marked testimony of their feelings to the Rev. Dr. Winslow, the Inspector who is stationed there: —

"CAMP LETTERMAN HOSPITAL, GETTYSBURG,
"*August 20th*, 1863.

"The undersigned, Surgeons and Assistant-Surgeons of the General Hospitals near Gettysburg, take pleasure in expressing our gratification at the manner in which the affairs of the United States Sanitary Commission have been managed since the late battle. The supplementary articles for the sick and wounded have been abundant, comprising every requisite which the exigency demanded, and which nothing but a well-regulated system, with much experience and forethought, could have secured.

"We are furthermore convinced that the system adopted by the Commission, of disbursing their supplies only on the requisition of a surgeon, is the only proper and safe method. Any other method necessarily supposes an extra force, which is calculated to cumber the hospital with irresponsible attendants, distract the public benefactions, if not divert them, from a just and equal distribution among the patients for whom they were intended.

" Henry Janes, *Surg*. U. S. V., in charge Hospitals at Gettysburg.

E. W. Chamberlain, *Surg*. U. S. V., in charge General Hospital.

S. W. Oakley, *Surg*. U. S. A., Medical Purveyor.

Albert B. Stonelake, *Surg*. U. S. A., in charge 7th Division.

J. D. Osborne, *Surg*. U. S. V., 4th Regt. N. Jersey Vols.

W. F. Bradley, *Asst. Surg*. 16th Regt. Mich. Vols.

H. C. May, *Asst. Surg*. 145th Regt. N. Y. V.

J. B. Sturtevant, *Asst. Surg*. Penn. Vols.

| | | |
|---|---|---|
| Charles D. Gauntt, M. D., | A. A. S., | U. S. A. |
| B. F. Butcher, M. D., | " | " |
| S. A. McArthur, M. D., | " | " |
| W. L. Hayr, M. D., | " | " |
| H. H. Sutton, M. D., | " | " |
| E. P. Townsend, M. D., | " | " |
| D. R. Good, M. D., | " | " |
| P. S. Leisenring, M. D., | " | " |

This is the last record of a great field-work still going on with the Army which is so dear to us — the noble Army of the Potomac! — but to-day the Sanitary Commission is in closer relations with that Army than ever before.

Immediately after the battle of Gettysburg,

the General Secretary prepared a plan for a "Field Relief Corps," which has since been admirably organized by the Chief Inspector, Dr. Steiner, and the Field Superintendent, Mr. Johnson. Each army corps is supplied with a relief agent, who lives with it and moves with it. He has a four-horse wagon, amply supplied and kept supplied with stores, travelling usually with the ambulance train. These stores are issued, as usual, to the field hospitals, on the requisitions of the medical officers. The relief agents are men of high character: one of them has been well known and valued as a colonel in the army, another as a clergyman in California, who resigned his work to give himself to his country through that channel which his heart and mind most approved. These agents are welcomed as co-laborers in the great war of Law and Right, by the officers of the army, medical and military. They furnish the needed articles just where and as they are needed, and often personally superintend their distribution, keeping an eye on the proper use of what they have issued. While laboring for the good of the whole Army, each feels some special pride in seeing that his own special corps or family is kept in the best possible condition. The oneness of the Commission with the Government, — its thorough coöperation with the officers of the Army—working *with* them, — gives to its agents power and facilities which cannot be detailed here. They know what is needed, and, knowing it, they supply it. Any one who has seen, as the writer has, the waste of indiscriminate giving, will readily understand the cheapness and directness of this work of the Commission.

Another feature is its promptness and its availability. The requisitions of surgeons will show that, at the battle of Gettysburg, the Commission distributed its stores *under fire;* but it does not need the incitement of such scenes. Life and suffering are to be saved incessantly. The work of the battle-field can be told to the country, as the routine work cannot; but the ardor of the Commission agents is the same in both, for the incitements of humanity are the same. The following extract, which is in point, is from a report of the Agent of the 2d Army Corps, which held the advance in a late movement on Culpepper. He says:—"During the last two weeks of movement, I have the satisfaction of knowing that my wagon was always ahead of any other means of relief, and therefore doing a work which could not otherwise have been done. I dispensed relief to wounded cavalry from the front, within an hour after their wounds were received; and gave out stores at Culpepper long before other supplies had arrived. As we were in motion, I passed out articles to surgeons coming down with ambulances from the front. I believe this was the case with the relief agents of other corps. I am satisfied that the Commission on the late march was brought to the notice of some as a working institution, who never saw it before."

The Medical Inspector of the Army of the Potomac says: — " We could not do without the Sanitary Commission"; — and the Medical Director of that Army adds, " It gives no trouble, — there is no interference." That, indeed, is its strength. It is *supplemental* in spirit and in act. Thus it has a position of its own; it has become an indispensable portion of the organization of the Army, working at its proper task, avoiding all interference with rules and regulations, — nay, respecting and maintaining them. Has it, or has it not, fulfilled its pledges to the Government? And has it, or has it not, won a position in the confidence of the officers, which has given it a usefulness it *could not otherwise* have obtained?

By a system of weekly reports to the Chief Inspector for the Army of the Potomac, the latter is able to control the whole movement of the Field Relief Corps, and to keep up a complete knowledge of the perfection or imperfection of the machinery employed.

In concluding this little sketch, the belief must be expressed that in this field the Commission is doing all that could be expected of it. Its officers are working with a quiet enthusiasm which could not be obtained by money nor by any other reward. Each one knows that he is working in something which has become indispensable to the country and to the war; and each one employed feels that he shall look back hereafter with incalculable pleasure to the fact that he once labored in its ranks.

But this portion of the story must close. The reader is assured that the character and efficiency of the work have been no more than indicated. And yet, from what is here told perhaps the question can be answered, Has the Sanitary Commission justified the confidence of the people? or has it not?

### ARMIES OF THE WEST.

The insufficiency of the following sketch of the work of the Sanitary Commission in this Department is felt so keenly, that the reader is requested to bear in mind that it gives no just idea of what has been done; it is, in fact, a mere sketch of fragments of the work, — a mere allusion to the vast and manifold sources of supply. The reason for this must be found in the fact that the subject has not been fully reported in detail to the central government of the Commission. When those details have been collected, and the history of the Sanitary Commission shall have been written, it will be seen how the West has borne her magnificent part in the national work of relief and mercy.

It has already been shown that the women in

that division of our country were among the first to rise in the common cause, as they were among the first to recognize with those at the East the wants of their ignorance, and to seek and accept the Sanitary Commission. From their geographical position they have enjoyed one great advantage over their Eastern sisters. They have been personally, as it were, in the very centres of the suffering which they sought to relieve. From this cause it may be that there have been amongst them less doubt of the good; less disposition to put faith in stories which have hindered that good; less deliberation in giving themselves to the cause; a heartier energy in the work. From the same cause may have proceeded some deficiencies in working out the great Federal principle of the Commission,—in detail of work, however, not in the spirit of Union; which is to the full as strong in the Valley of the Mississippi as in the Atlantic regions.

The Mississippi River, the channel between the northern Lakes and the Gulf of Mexico, has been the great object of the struggle between the loyal and disloyal armies of the West.

Illinois, by her geographical position, was the chief State to profit by that bountiful provision of nature which united Lake Michigan to the

Gulf of Mexico, and brought the city of Chicago into close relationship with the city of New Orleans. This State, alive to the importance of securing a communication of so much consequence to her wealth and enterprise, eagerly endeavored to prevent the rupture of the Federal Union. Her troops accepted the call to arms, and soon held in force the little city of Cairo, at that time the most important strategic point at the West. It stands on the extreme south of Illinois, at the confluence of the Ohio and Mississippi rivers, as Chicago stands nearly due north at the other extremity of the State, upon the shores of Lake Michigan. Cairo thus commands the navigation of both rivers. It was the key to the Northwest, and the chief source of our power in the struggle which was to take place in Missouri; but it was thrust like a wedge into the heart of doubtful districts, and there was great danger that the disloyal in Missouri, Kentucky, and Tennessee might gain possession of it. Here, then, the shadows of war began to fall, and the Sanitary Commission, quickly upon their track, began its work. Within a week after the organization of the Commission, its President started for this and other military centres in the West, on a mission of preliminary inspection. Before the end of June other inspections had been made in a thorough manner, under the direction of Dr. Aigner, showing a great and unexpected need amongst the troops; and the

Branch Commissions at Chicago in Illinois, and Cleveland in Ohio, so soon as they were formed, began to distribute stores to the sick in camp and hospital at Cairo, Paducah, Mound City, Bird's Point, St. Louis, and at other places in the interior of Missouri.

It is interesting to notice in the reports of these societies that the first actual work brought out the instinct of central organization, to collect stores and economize the efforts of their States, and then the instinct to reach out into something Federal.

In the history of the rebellion, Missouri was one of the last among the insurgent States to lift her hand against the Federal Government. The clouds which gathered here in the early spring, rose and broke into a storm in May, 1861, when the attack was made on the arsenal at St. Louis; and Captain Lyon was ready for the emergency. This was the beginning of active military operations; the rebel General Price retreating finally towards Booneville, where a stand was made, and a battle fought and won by General Lyon. Meanwhile another division under General Sigel met the enemy at Carthage, after which occurred the battle of Wilson's Creek, where General Lyon was killed, and General Sigel took command of the Army. Later came the siege and fall of Lexington, which ended the campaign; and then the Federal troops were at once disbanded.

General Fremont assumed command of the Department and organized a new army in the autumn of 1861. He left St. Louis, compelled Price to evacuate Lexington, and marched southward, day and night, towards Springfield, — a forced march which had a terrible and fatal effect upon the health of the troops. Here General Hunter superseded General Fremont, and, after remaining at Springfield until Nov. 13, the army marched back over the same road it had just so laboriously and fruitlessly passed. At this point the United States Sanitary Commission began its work in this Department, of which General Halleck had taken the command, General Hunter being sent to Kansas.

The Inspectors of the Commission, Drs. Douglas and Warriner, found the Army in and around St. Louis. The condition of the troops, and the influences affecting that condition, which were found in Camp Benton, in Benton Barracks, in Camp Lamine, at Rolla, and elsewhere, are carefully and vividly portrayed in the reports of the Inspectors. The troops had returned from their fruitless marches, wearied, exhausted, disheartened, and distrustful; and in this condition they fell a prey to disease, especially to measles, — some regiments being almost wholly upon the sick-list. The wants of these men were very great. No sheets, pillow-cases, nor hospital shirts were supplied, until the Sanitary Commission arrived. Soon afterwards, however, their condition greatly improved, and their wants were fully inquired into and relieved by the "United States Sanitary Commission," and by the "Western Sanitary Commission,"—a society not at all connected with the United States Sanitary Commission, and founded at St. Louis, in Sept. 1861.* There were at this time fifteen general and post hospitals in and around that city. These were all visited, inspected, and aided with advice and supplies. The military hospitals in the city of St. Louis had been, as it were, founded by the Western Commission, with the approval and coöperation of the United States Medical Director then at the head of that Department. These hospitals were fully equipped by that society, aided by abundant supplies received from the East, and to them the sick were daily brought from camps and post hospitals. The latter, which extended along the whole line of the late marches, were very destitute, and to them the United States Sanitary Commission turned its attention, supplying at once their immediate wants, which were found to be very great indeed. The system of the Sanitary Commission,

* Although the "United States Sanitary Commission" had some reason to complain of the manner in which the "Western Sanitary Commission" assumed its name, and used advantages which belonged to it, yet nothing has ever influenced it to hold back from a warm acknowledgment of the great work which the Western Commission has performed on its own field.

in the field, is to give supplies in small quantities as they are needed. Surgeons in the field carry but little, or they are seriously embarrassed. If they have much on hand, it must be left behind as the Army advances. Just as these regiments were thus supplied, their needs began to be known abroad, and independent supplies came down to them. At this moment the Army moved, and a great deal of property was therefore lost, or returned to its donors. But the Sanitary Commission had the satisfaction of knowing that its supplies, judiciously timed and judiciously measured, had not met with any such waste or disappointment.

The sickness throughout the winter was of a depressing kind, and the mortality alarming. The inspections of the Commission show clearly that this resulted from the disheartening influences of retreat, malarious camp-sites, absence of proper camp police, badly ventilated tents, barracks, &c., &c. An entire revolution, however, took place in the post hospitals at Tipton, Syracuse, Otterville, and Sedalia, after the arrival of the Commission. When the Army began its movement into the interior of the State, the agents of the United States Commission, furnished with supplies from the Eastern Branches, went with it. They found it necessary to take precautions that those supplies should not go to places already abundantly provided. This caused some special and even laborious inspection and work; but they were successful enough to say, "We have the satisfaction of knowing that every article has been placed by us where it was needed. To such places as would not otherwise have been reached, we have during this month issued 6000 articles. . . . . We have been treated with the greatest courtesy, our suggestions have been listened to, and, where we advised, our advice has been acted upon."

In Western Virginia, that portion of the State bounded on the east by the Alleghany mountains, on the north and west by the free States of Pennsylvania and Ohio, and on the South by the Kanawha Valley, watered by the river of that name which empties into the Ohio,— were many geographical and social characteristics which allied it to the North, and kept it in the commencement of the struggle from sympathy with secession. The people strove to establish their territory as a State, separated from the seceded Old Dominion. They assembled at Wheeling, and Union military companies were formed throughout the loyal district, prepared to resist the advance of troops in arms for the rebellion. The first encounter took place at Clarksburg, — a bloodless opening to the bloody history of war upon the soil of the grand old State, whose hereditary instincts should have kept her safe from joining in outrage upon her country.

To sustain Western Virginia in her struggle of principle, the Army then collecting in Ohio under General McClellan moved into her borders, effected a junction with her troops at Grafton, and then opened that successful campaign, which, in a military point of view, was the first and perhaps the most brilliant glory of our arms. Here, too, the Sanitary Commission was present. Inspectors and supplies came from the East and the West. Its first depot was at Wheeling, Virginia, under charge of Dr. Griswold; and in September every camp and hospital in the department (Cheat Mountain excepted) had been inspected, reported on, and systematically supplied, according to their needs, from the central depot at Washington, and from the branch depots at Cincinnati and Cleveland. On the records of the latter branch we find how the grateful acknowledgments received for this aid stimulated the work, and steadily increased the interest of those from whom it collected its supplies.

The work performed by the Commission in this campaign was well done. It was not upon the scale of the great relief which afterwards marched on, but from the following item it will be seen that its work was responsible and systematic. A despatch comes from General Rosecrans to the quartermaster at Wheeling, to prepare a hospital for 500 men. The quartermaster telegraphs at once, "Send on the sick";

and then, without further anxiety, he turns over the General's despatch to the Sanitary Commission. There was no alternative but for the Inspector to do his best. The battle at Gauley was imminent; communication was cut off; and duty to the Commanding General, as well as to humanity, required that every effort should be made. He went to work, procured a building, furnished it, and in three days received his patients into comfortable beds, supplied them well with everything except sufficient medical care, (he was the only available medical officer,) and, on the second day after their arrival, he writes, "To-night the hospital is as cheerful as a large hotel."

The battle of Gauley Bridge and the defeat of Floyd by General Rosecrans ended the campaign, and the Army soon after went into winter quarters. Our troops continued to hold Cheat Mountain, but the greater part of them were sent under General Reynolds to Kentucky, or to service on the Potomac.

Kentucky, in her efforts to withstand the tide of disloyalty, which disgraced, alas! even her noble manhood, came into the struggle of arms first under General Anderson, and next under General Buell.

If our hearts bleed as we remember the traditions of Virginia, disowned and disgraced, much more are they wrung by the living anguish of Kentucky. Son against father, and father against son, — perhaps no people have given to their country sacrifices like hers.

Troops poured in to her assistance from Illinois, Indiana, Wisconsin, Michigan, Ohio, and the loyal districts of Tennessee. Under General Buell they advanced in five divisions, each with a special purpose, until they concentrated on the Cumberland River. Careful inspection was made of each division; supplies for the sick and wounded reached them from the Branches at Cleveland, Columbus, Cincinnati, and Detroit; and, at the battle of Mill Spring, the Sanitary Commission found its appropriate work upon the "dark and bloody ground."

The defeat of the enemy in Kentucky opened the way to those combined expeditions by land and water which had been long maturing at St. Louis, Cairo, and Paducah, under the direction of General Halleck.

The enemy had striven to secure command of the Mississippi, Tennessee, and Cumberland rivers, by the construction of forts upon their banks. Of these, Columbus on the Mississippi, Fort Donelson on the Tennessee, and Fort Henry on the Cumberland, were the most formidable. The last of these was captured without loss early in the month of February, 1862; and on the 15th of February, Fort Donelson, after a bloody resistance, fell into our hands.

The history of the Sanitary Commission at Fort Donelson is this:—

When the news reached Cincinnati, a steamer was promptly transferred to the Commission by General Buell. In two hours, three thousand dollars were spontaneously given to pay her expenses; and she started with nurses and supplies to the relief of the wounded. At Louisville, the Associate Secretary for the West, Dr. J. S. Newberry, joined the expedition; and this relief was swelled by more coming down from other branches of the Commission at Cleveland, Chicago, and other points.

This was almost the first field experience of many who were here engaged, but the relief which they brought was timely and well given. The large hospital steamers were amply equipped with stores from the Commission; the regimental surgeons thronged to its boat and obtained liberal supplies; and as each vessel left, loaded with wounded, it took with it the means of comfort for the men on board. The branch at Cincinnati had telegraphed to General Halleck, expressing the desire to take charge of some of the sufferers at Fort Donelson. The next morning the reply came, stating that five hundred men were on their way, and enjoining upon the Commission (could that be necessary?) to treat friend and foe alike. A large five-story building was obtained and fitted up; a second was soon after required and employed in the same way. It may here be mentioned, that, when the war began, the use of a United States Marine Hospital in Cincinnati had been obtained, and it had been furnished, organized, and opened for the reception of sick and wounded soldiers. It became so successful, that eventually the Government adopted it for its own, and the money paid by them for its furniture, &c., was kept as a little fund to meet the expenses of disabled men endeavoring to reach their homes.

Whilst the naval and military forces were assembling at Cairo, an Associate Secretary of the Commission, Dr. Douglas, who had been employed in a careful survey of the condition and need of the troops west of the Mississippi, reached that city. He there made to General Grant the first suggestion of the floating hospitals, destined afterwards to play an important part in the work of relief. The Government adopted the idea, detailed the large steamer "City of Memphis," carrying eight hundred men, for that service; and she was equipped, or nearly so, by the Sanitary Commission. In her the Commission moved up to Paducah in time to assist the wounded from Fort Donelson as they came down the river. Dr. Douglas left at Cairo, in a building given by the commander of the post, a depot well supplied with every necessary, in charge of the Chicago Branch of the Sanitary Commission.

This sketch may, perhaps, have given a general idea of the opening work of the Sanitary Commission at the West. The story must now be confined to a brief mention of the leading points of its subsequent work.

The fall of Fort Donelson opened the Cumberland River, first to Clarksville and then to Nashville, at which point a depot of the Commission was quickly established.

The enemy were everywhere falling back before the advance of our forces under Generals Grant and Buell and Admiral Foote. Their stronghold, Columbus, on the Mississippi, was first abandoned; then New Madrid; then Island No. 10; until they intrenched themselves at Corinth, on the Northeastern border of Mississippi and Tennessee.

General Grant, able, under cover of the gunboats, to advance his army up the Tennessee River, took possession of Savannah, and threw forward his main body of sixty thousand men to Pittsburg Landing, (an insignificant place of some few houses and a wharf, eight miles above Savannah,) with the view of advancing against Corinth. But a portion of the enemy, under General Johnson, which had retreated before Buell's columns from Nashville to Chattanooga, formed a skilful junction with the Army under Beauregard at Corinth, which marched out and gave battle to our forces on the rolling plains of Shiloh, before Pittsburg Landing. Defeated and forced back to the river on the first day, General Buell's timely reinforcements enabled us on the second day to resume the offensive and win a victory.

*Battle of Shiloh.* — From the depots at Cairo and Paducah and Savannah, the Sanitary Commission sent forward assistance. Dr. Douglas and Dr. Warriner, with a delegation and supplies from the Chicago and other branches, went up on the transport "Louisiana." As they reached the Landing, they passed steamer after steamer filling up with wounded. The wild confusion of that scene cannot be expressed; the hurry, the excitement, and the miseries of war all mingled together in that narrow space. Men and munitions of war were being landed, the wounded embarked, and the dead trampled over as of no account in that struggle for life. The night was spent by the Commission in going from boat to boat with assistance. Not a boat was omitted, and the surgeons from the field, hearing that the Commission was present, came eagerly for help. On the second day, fresh supplies arrived from the Cincinnati Branch of the Commission, in two first-class steamers, "The Tycoon" and "Monarch," furnished with every comfort, and with a corps of surgeons and nurses. These boats discharged their stores, and took in cargoes of wounded for the hospitals on the Ohio River. Other boats came up and did the same service, — especially from the depots at Paducah and Savannah. The Governor of Ohio sent the noble steamer "Magnolia" in charge of the Surgeon-General of the State, and fitted out by the Sanitary Commission at Cleveland and Columbus. A number of other boats were sent up from the different surrounding States; and a fact mentioned incidentally by the Associate Secretary for the West, Dr. Newberry, who was present on the field, speaks so forcibly to a certain point, that it must be given here. "We took on board," he says, "a large number of wounded men, who were mostly from Michigan regiments, — there being many more from that State requiring removal than from any other. This was due to the fact that steamers sent from Ohio, Illinois, Indiana, and Kentucky had taken away the wounded of those States nearly as fast as they gathered there." How sad that is! Think of those poor Michigan boys left languishing and watching for the Good Samaritan to pass their way! Had they no sense, as they lay there in their blood shed for their country, of the unnatural wickedness and selfishness of section? Thank God for the Sanitary Commission at that moment, if at no other.

After the battle, the Commission established a depot at the landing, by invitation on board the boat of the Medical Purveyor. From the

25th of May to the 1st of July the stores issued from this depot amounted in all to 160,143 articles, of which the following are items: — Shirts, 11,448; drawers, 3686; socks, 3592; bedsacks, 2777; pillows, 5434; brandy, whisky, wine, 1045 bottles; ale, 799 bottles; lemons, 941; dried fruits, 20,316 lbs.; canned fruit, 5770 cans; farinaceous food, 15,323 lbs. During the period that this depot was kept open, a great service was rendered to the Sanitary Commission by two women who volunteered for the work, and to whom its thanks are due.*

After the battle, both armies were reinforced; General Pope came up from the Mississippi, and we advanced to invest Corinth by Monterey, Farmington, and Hamburgh. At these places large general hospitals were established: those at Monterey for the troops of General Grant; those at Farmington for those of Pope, — General Buell's hospitals being nearest to the front. This is the true principle of the hospital system, —to establish large receiving hospitals in the rear of an army, and then, as the men become convalescent, they are easily returned to duty, and they are also more willing to go. To promote the establishment of such hospitals, the Associate Secretary of the Commission already named (Dr. Douglas) presented a plan to the Medical Director of the Army, which was immediately

* One of whom is familiarly known among the soldiers as "The Cairo Angel."

adopted in the construction of the hospital of General Buell's division. The plan was "simple but ingenious," and consisted of a framework made of trees, the roof covered with tarpaulins, (of which there happened to be four hundred lying unused at the commissary's,) and the sides made of old tent canvas, which by a simple arrangement were drawn up during the day. These buildings were a great success; for, from their size, perfect ventilation, (being opened at the sides and ends at will,) and from the cleanliness of the beds and the abundance of clothing on hand, they proved to be the best form of hospital, in such a climate, during the warm months of summer. This hospital, containing 1500 beds, and the other general and corps hospitals, received what assistance they needed from the supplies of the Commission on a liberal scale. In addition to these issues, regimental hospitals were supplied at the rate of fifteen hospitals a day.

Another suggestion, made by Dr. Douglas at the time, has since been adopted throughout the Army, East and West. It was that of cooking-caldrons, made upon the plan of those used on farms for boiling the food of cattle. Some were to be put on wheels, so that, in the event of a battle, they might be taken to the field, and soup prepared and served to the wounded and exhausted. This idea has also been adopted.

Perhaps at no time in the history of our armies has such wise and thoughtful care been taken by the medical officers, in anticipation of sickness and battle. To the Medical Director of that Army, Dr. McDougall, the praise for this is chiefly due.

At this point the armies rested for a while. The Sanitary Commission established a depot at Hamburgh, and soon after at Corinth; and then Dr. Douglas returned to Cairo to watch for the opening of the Mississippi down to Memphis, where a depot was established so soon as that city fell into our hands.

From this point the writer feels so incapable of indicating, with any justice, the work of the Commission at the West, that several months will here be passed over in silence, — months of steady and systematic work, such as the history of the Commission already given may partially illustrate. The personal service of the Commission agents must not, however, pass unrecorded. Life and health were sacrificed, hardships endured, and dangers braved by them. No money could have bought such services as these men gave. Through them we measure, from one point of view, the value of our Nation in the hearts of her sons.

The only point on which the narrative will touch during several ensuing months, will be the work of the Sanitary Commission after the battle of Perryville; stating merely that, throughout the summer, the wise and faithful Inspector of the Army of the Tennessee (Dr. H. A. Warriner, whose wife had already laid down her life in the cause) had, with unceasing energy, thrown forward ample stores in a circle round the central points of the Army at Corinth, Memphis, Jackson, Hamburgh, &c. On the other side, Dr. Read, Sanitary Commission Inspector for the Army of the Cumberland, then under General Buell, was preparing for the work which was about to cry out for hands to do it. When the news of the battle of Perryville reached Louisville, three wagons and twenty-one ambulances started with supplies from the Commission; but when the Inspector reached the field, he found that there had been almost no preparation for the care of the wounded, and, as a consequence, that the suffering for want of help of all kinds, as well as for proper accommodations, food, medicines, and hospital stores, was excessive. For this state of things, however, the surgeons were not to blame. Both those in authority and those in attendance were doing all in their power to mitigate the suffering which prevailed. The Sanitary Commission at once established its quarters near the field. The ambulances and the wagons arrived, loaded with stores, and attended by several efficient agents. Surgeons were notified that stores could be had, and the work of issuing them was rapidly carried on.

There were at this time, in and around Perryville, Danville, and Harrodsburg, 3000 wounded men, and more were coming in. They were all very dirty, lying in their bloody clothing; few had straw or other bedding, some were without blankets, others had no sheets; and some whose wounds had not been dressed were brought in, five days after the battle, from places of temporary shelter. The surgeons were laboring with their usual devotion; but they were shorthanded, overworked and had little to work with. Leaving agents to attend to the wants at Perryville, the Inspector, Dr. Read, went forward to Danville. Here the wants of the sufferers were as urgent as at Perryville,—more so perhaps. The Court-house was literally packed;—many had eaten nothing during the day. The Inspector asked if soup could be made. The surgeons feared not, but gladly gave him permission to make it if he could. Some Union men in the place assisted him. It was nearly evening; there was no *beef*, but a man offered to shoot a bullock and have it ready in two hours. There was no *water*,—the wells were all dry; but the same good man hauled water in barrels from a distance. Then there were no *kettles* to be had, —the rebels had taken them all; but at last one was found in a private family, and another was discovered two miles out of the town, owned by a man who sent it in, saying he should not want it till hog-killing time. Finally, no *pails* were to be had, for love or money; and how was the soup, when made under all these savage difficulties, to be distributed without them? But, by good luck, covered *firkins* with handles, *also a wash-tub*, were to be bought in a shop; and at last the Inspector, rejoicing in everything, digging the trench and laying the stones with his own hands, set both the precious kettles over a fire made of old boards picked up in the Court-house yard, and, by ten o'clock at night, distributed sixty-five gallons of good soup to the exhausted and starving men. Not that he did this last himself, poor fellow; for, by the time the soup had triumphed over its difficulties, it need scarcely be said that he was utterly exhausted. As many of the wounded were without shelter, the Inspector looked about for some place where they might at least have a roof over their heads. A carriage-shop was found; the owner, with ready kindness, removed the carriages; and there, on two loads of straw which the Inspector had hastily procured, two hundred men found rest and shelter.

Returning to Perryville, he had the great satisfaction of finding the condition of the wounded much improved, thanks to the untiring exertions of the surgeons in charge, and to the stores of the Sanitary Commission. Up to this time no medical stores of any kind had been received from Government; none were on the ground except those of the Commission. Ten tons more of supplies, in five large wagons, arrived soon afterwards from the storehouse of the Commission at Louisville. The Confederate prisoners were mostly in hospital at Harrodsburg, where such aid as was really required was sent forward by the Commission. A number of them had been taken into private families, and those in hospital were, to a certain extent, receiving aid from the secession citizens of Harrodsburg and Lexington. Several of these prisoners wore clothing taken from the Federal troops, and some complaint was made that, in certain instances, this had been done forcibly. One bright young fellow, with a good coat of his own and a United States overcoat under his head, was asked to say where he got the latter. He answered promptly that he came honestly by it; and said, further, that when he was lying wounded on the battle-field, a cold rain had come on, and a Federal soldier coming up to him asked him some questions, and, seeing how much he suffered, took off his coat and put it over him. "I shall never shoot *that* man," said he, as he finished his story.

The destitute and comfortless condition of the wounded at all these points may, perhaps, be guessed from such details as the following: — Hospital No. 1. — A church; seventy-eight patients lying on the floor and benches, on a moderate supply of straw; no bed-sacks, no pillows, several without blankets; no change of clothing; cooking done in three little kettles out of doors. No. 2.— A church; eighty-five men lying on a little straw; some lying together to make one blanket cover two; no bedding nor change of clothing; cooking done in one kettle and a stewpan. And so on through the whole list. This will show the terrible necessity for all kinds of hospital furniture, not to speak of supplies and stores for the men. A little incident occurred in one of these hospitals which is worth relating here. The Wisconsin State Agents were distributing relief to the Wisconsin boys only. One of them, lying seriously wounded, received some of it, but he afterwards said, "I did n't like it; it made me feel bad to have things given to me and not to the boy lying next to me. But I made it all right, for I divided with him."

So soon as the sick in all these hospitals, at Perryville, Danville, and elsewhere in the vicinity, were able to bear the journey, they were sent off to the large cities. Lebanon was the first railroad point from the battle-ground (from Danville it was twenty miles), and it became the rendezvous for the poor fellows. It was from here, and at this time, that the *Hospital Cars* of the Sanitary Commission commenced their Western service. An account of the Commission upon this field cannot be closed without alluding to the hearty appreciation which it called forth from army officers, who seem to have taken pains to bring before the Commission and the public their sense of the benefits they had received. A few of their letters are printed here:

"Dear Sir:

"Permit me through you to acknowledge my obligations to the United States Sanitary Commission for the very efficient aid which it has rendered to me, in furnishing supplies for the sick and wounded soldiers under my charge, at a time when they could not be obtained through any other source. When the hospitals were first established in this district, we were almost entirely destitute of hospital and medical supplies, including almost every article for the comfort of the sick. With an unusually large number of sick and wounded on our hands, we were compelled to see them suffer, without the proper means of affording them relief.

"The condition of things was immediately telegraphed to the Medical Purveyor in Louisville, and that officer, with his usual promptness, at once furnished everything necessary to render our sick comfortable; but from some cause the supplies were detained several weeks on the road, and were not received until long after those arrived that were sent by the Sanitary Commission.

"Considering the large number of the sick and wounded in the district (between six and seven thousand), and the almost total absence of everything necessary to make them comfortable, I have no doubt that the timely aid afforded by the Commission in this single instance has been the means of preventing much suffering, as well as of saving many valuable lives.

"I trust that the Commission will be able to continue in its good work, and that it may have, as it certainly deserves, the thanks of every friend of humanity.

"I am, dear sir, very respectfully,

"GEO. G. SHUMARD, *Surg. U. S. A.*,

"*Medical Director Danville District.*"

"TO DR. J. S. NEWBERY.

"SIR:—It is but just to the United States Sanitary Commission to say that the aid they have rendered to the wounded in the battle of Chaplin Hills has been indispensable. No one but an eye-witness can estimate the great advantage their supplies have been to the wounded. When the Government supplies shipped to us were detained in Bardstown and other places several weeks, theirs, by extraordinary efforts, were put promptly through, and came to our aid when we were perfectly destitute.

"A large proportion of the wounded coming from the battle-field were stripped of their clothing. The bedding, clothing, and dressings furnished by the Commission were of inestimable advantage. Considering the great help rendered by this Commission, it is to be hoped that the people will be stimulated to greater efforts to aid them in their benevolent mission.

"Very respectfully, your obedient servant,

"JAMES G. HATCHETT,

"*Surgeon U. S. Volunteers,*

"*In charge of Hospitals at Perryville.*"

"HEAD-QUARTERS THIRD DIVISION,
"TWENTIETH ARMY CORPS.

"TO DR. CASTLEMAN,

"*Inspector United States Sanitary Commission.*

"SIR:— Allow me through you to return the sincere thanks of the medical officers of this division to the United States Sanitary Commission, for their uniform promptness and attention to the wants of the sick and wounded soldiers.

"It has been my lot to be with this division as medical director through two hard-fought battles (Perryville and Stone's River), where we had many wounded men, with only limited means of ministering to their comfort. Consequently, I have had a good opportunity to judge of the efficiency of your organization, and the benefits derived from it. . . . . To it we are indebted also for many valuable suggestions which have added much to the comfort of camp-life.

"With the most sincere hope that the Commission may receive the continued support it deserves, I am,

"Very respectfully,

"D. V. GRIFFITH, *Medical Director.*"

"HEAD-QUARTERS THIRD DIVISION,
"TWENTIETH ARMY CORPS,
"*Murfreesboro, May* 4, 1863.

"I take great pleasure in indorsing every word of the within letter, and desire to return, through the Medical Inspector, my sincere thanks to the United States Sanitary Commission, for their almost invaluable services to my wounded men at Perryville and Stone's River. J. H. SHERIDAN, *Major General*."

Early in May, 1863, the Army of the Tennessee leaving its base of supplies, and carrying almost nothing but its munitions of war, struck out boldly into the heart of the enemy's country. After a rapid march upon the capital of Mississippi, it turned westward, and by a series of battles, each one of which was crowned with success, closed its victorious columns upon the rebel stronghold which had so long sealed the navigation of the great river. Letters and reports from Dr. Warriner, Inspector of the Sanitary Commission, whose duty lay with the march of this Army, came up from every advanced point gained upon the Mississippi, from Bolivar, Columbus, Young's Point, Haines's Bluff, Milliken's Bend, and at last Yazoo River, near Vicksburg. As the Army advanced it accumulated its sick and wounded, until an estimate made June 5th placed the amount at 5300. The Medical Director at Memphis speaks with enthusiasm of the manner in which the men rallied from the depressing influence of wounds and amputations. This could not be attributed to the effect of climate, which was clearly becoming more and more adverse to it. There is no doubt that it resulted from a change of diet, procured for the Army, in a great measure, by the exertions of the Sanitary Commission.

In the Spring an urgent call had been made for vegetables; and it was stated that many wounds, which, in a healthy condition of the system, were unattended with danger, would, in the present condition of the men, (scurvy having appeared,) prove fatal. Mention of this matter will be made further on; but it may be said here, that the remarkably healthy condition of the sick around Vicksburg is largely owing to the avalanche of vegetables with which the Sanitary Commission had supplied the Army of the Tennessee.

In March, 1863, General Grant issued a special order requiring the quartermaster's department to provide a suitable steamboat, to be called "The United States Sanitary Store Boat," and to put the same in charge of the United States Sanitary Commission, to be used exclusively for the conveyance of goods calculated to prevent disease, and supplemental to the Government supply of stores for the relief of the sick and wounded. With this boat, "The Dunleith," loading with stores at Cincinnati, Louisville, and Cairo, Dr. Warriner was able to throw forward his supplies at will, preceding and following them with his duties of inspection. The sick along the line, at Helena, Memphis, Jackson, Lagrange, Corinth, &c., &c., *all were* reached by her supplies. Sometimes the stores of the Sanitary Commission were increased by gifts from the "Western Sanitary Commission"; and at one time, by order of General Grant, one hundred tons of Government ice were turned over to it for distribution, — a wayside compliment which was appreciated. The supplies which it issued to the Army before Vicksburg during the months of May and June, were as follows:— Quilts, 1504; pillows, 2220; sheets, 1840; drawers, 5376; towels, &c., 7484; farina, &c., 266 lbs.; sago, &c., 1044 lbs.; bed-sacks, 758; pillow-cases, 2830; shirts, 7909; dressing-gowns, 422; socks, 2453 pairs; slippers, 1190 pairs; corn starch, 275 lbs.; cloths and bandages, 50 bbls.; fruit, 5114 cans; concentrated beef, 771 cans; dried fruit, 16,430 lbs.; dried beef, 888 lbs.; groceries, 1882 lbs.; wines and liquors, 1979 bottles; butter, 3557 lbs.; apple-butter, 30 gallons; eggs, 2401 doz.; pickles, 2376 gallons; molasses, 85 gallons; sour krout, 1532 gallons; potatoes, 5762 bushels; ale and cider, 1031 gallons; ice, 27,367 lbs.; crackers, 6898 lbs.; codfish, 6777 lbs.; cornmeal, 2485 lbs.; tea, 532 lbs.; pickles, 301 bottles; lemons, 13,200; hospital furniture, 1747 articles; fans, 2347; crutches, 65 pairs; cots and mattresses, 199; spices, 2006 papers; quinine, 200 oz.

When the great stronghold of Vicksburg fell into our hands, early in July, 1863, a portion of our Army moved, at full speed, in pursuit of the enemy, leaving behind them their sick and wounded, swelled by a large number of the rebel sick. The latter were in, a state of great destitution. They made beseeching appeals to the Sanitary Commission which were regarded. One of the best Government Surgeons was put in charge of their hospitals, and requisitions made for them at the North were not made in vain. As soon as it could be done with safety, the sick and wounded of both armies were sent away in special transports,—ours up the river to Northern hospitals, and theirs down the river to their own homes. In one month after the surrender of Vicksburg, everything was going on as well as could be reasonably expected; and it is a satisfaction to know from authority of the highest kind, that the services of the Sanitary Commission in leading to this result were well appreciated.

A general quiet prevailed in the Army of the Tennessee after the capture of Vicksburg, but the means of the Commission were fully employed in supplying the wants of a large and increasing number of sick (multiplying by the advance of the season) in every corps of General Grant's Army. The great privileges granted to the Commission by the Commanding General have opened wider, and still wider, doors of usefulness, so that the distributions at Memphis, Helena, and Vicksburg have been greater than ever before. It will give a strong picture of the work done and the hardships endured in that fearful climate, when we state that there is not a single agent of the Commission with that Army who has not been sooner or later prostrated by disease; there is not one of them who is not now performing his duty at the peril of life or health. The sickness at Vicksburg has been steadily on the increase. The autumn months of that climate are cursed with malarious fever and dysentery, which have assumed of late a malignant form. Yet, God be thanked, yellow fever has not appeared,—wonderful and blessed fact that, West or South, it has not appeared! It would seem as though this mighty scourge of earth felt eclipsed and put aside by the mightier scourge of War, not daring, or not needed to make a "holiday in hell."

From Vicksburg and the Mississippi River supplies have been thrown forward to many points. Boats have been sent to General Steele's advance on the White River, in Arkansas, and, for some time past, liberal supplies, under the charge of Mr. J. R. Brown, Inspector and Relief Agent, have gone forward into Kansas. The troops at Fort Leavenworth, Fort Scott, and other points in the Indian Territory, have been so situated as to be cut off from Government supplies, and urgent appeals were made to the Sanitary Commission in their behalf. Mr. Brown and his companion, Dr. C. C. Slocum, have been indefatigable in their efforts to reach even the most distant frontier with a train of supplies.

On the opening of the Mississippi, an agent of the Western Department of the U. S. Sanitary Commission, Dr. Fithian, was despatched to Port Hudson, meeting there the agents of the Eastern Department, who were, at that time, amply furnished with stores and assistance. Dr. Warriner has lately sent down fresh supplies, and is coöperating with those already stationed there for the expedition now preparing under General Banks.

Thus has the Sanitary Commission thrown out her arms until the "white hands of healing" meet and clasp around the whole palpitating mass of human suffering in the National Army.

We will now turn back to the Army of the Cumberland. The work here has been under the immediate supervision of Dr. A. N. Read, a veteran Inspector, whose efforts for months and years have been characterized by energy and wisdom. He is ably seconded by Dr. Castleman and others.

In no department of the whole Army has the

work been more thoroughly and systematically performed. The praise, however, must not be allowed to rest on the Commission alone; it must be given also to the military and medical authorities, all of whom, from the Commanding General down, have steadily and cordially co-operated; not only granting cheerfully all reasonable requests, but often spontaneously offering aid which the Commission was about to need.

In the Spring of 1863, as we have said, the great need of fresh vegetables for the armies of those regions began to appear, in the silent warning of here and there a case of scurvy. The United States Medical Inspector of the Army of the Cumberland was early aware of the fact, and of the great deficiency in the supply. The matter was seriously announced by the directors of several army corps; and the Medical Inspector, on his return to Nashville, brought the subject in its magnitude before the Sanitary Commission, which had, however, already done something in that direction. Under the supervision of Dr. Read, large shipments of vegetables to the Army of General Rosecrans were promptly made by boat and railroad; and, by order of that General, hospital gardens of forty acres were planted at Nashville and at Murfreesboro, under the care of the Sanitary Commission, to be in readiness for the season when the supplies from the North should fail. The gardens at Murfreesboro furnished, up to

August 30th, 248 barrels of assorted vegetables, and the gardener estimated that during the remainder of the season it would yield about 800 bushels of tomatoes; 1200 bushels of Irish potatoes; 1200 bushels of sweet potatoes; 25,000 heads of cabbage; besides large quantities of beans, melons, turnips, &c. Meantime the shipments made by the Commission to the Army of the Tennessee and to the Army of the Cumberland, amounted to more than 6000 barrels of assorted vegetables. Thanks to this care, the scurvy disappeared. This feature of the work called forth hearty thanks and appreciation. It was detailed in the official report of the Medical Inspector to General Rosecrans; and a request for the publication of a portion of the report called out the following letter from the Medical Inspector: —

"DEAR SIR: —

"Since it meets the approval of General Rosecrans, I am very willing to allow you to make such extracts from my report as had special reference to the Sanitary Commission. As you have read my report, you need not be informed of my opinion of the necessity of your work. I am scarcely able to give it the prominence it deserves.

"It is to this Army what I have found it to be everywhere in the armies of the United States: one of its most important means of support, and without which its efficiency would be greatly diminished. No one who has watched its work in the field, in the general hospitals, on the road toward home of discharged and disabled soldiers, but will agree with me in saying that it is doing a vast deal, both in the cause of our country and in the cause of humanity; and so long as the nation sends its soldiers to the field, the Sanitary Commission must continue its work. The agents, so far as I have seen them, are intelligent, faithful, and zealous, and the public has nothing to fear in trusting to them its gifts.

"Would to God that every one at the North could see and understand as well as we do the value and *necessity* of the work.

"Very respectfully yours,

"FRANK H. HAMILTON,

"*Medical Inspector, U. S. A.*"

It was computed and said at the time, that one shipment of vegetables from Pittsburg alone had done more to increase the effective fighting strength of the Army than would have been done by raising a full regiment of new recruits.

In looking through the records of the first six months of 1863, we find the old story of current supply — grown almost *monotonous* to us in the telling. Sketches of the "Homes" and the "Hospital Directory" come in like little golden arabesques to vivify the sober background of quiet mercy, and, here and there, we fall upon some blessed words of appreciation, which have done more to strengthen and support the Sanitary Commission than can ever be known or told. Can we measure the life and strength given by such words as these, taken at random:

"Your liberal shipment received; it will do more good than shipments from the Purveyor, for it *meets our need.* . . . . The benefit and good done by the Sanitary Commission has never been acknowledged. I hope I may live to see it. J. R. BLACK,

"*Medical Director.*"

"MEDICAL DIRECTOR'S OFFICE,
"DEPARTMENT OF THE CUMBERLAND,
"*Nashville, Tenn.*

"TO DR. NEWBERRY.

"SIR: — I understand that it is your intention to organize another Sanitary train for the transportation of the sick and wounded. I sincerely hope you may, for experience has shown me that the first was of the greatest benefit to the sick and wounded. The rapid transportation, the care exercised over the patients, and the competent attendants sent with each train have, I am convinced, been the means of saving many lives. I, personally, as well as the sick and wounded soldiers, am under many obligations to the Sanitary Commission; but in my opinion the 'Sanitary train' does more than aught else for the comfort of the sick.*

"A. Henry Thurston,
"*Asst. Med. Director Department Cumberland.*"

And last and best, that testimony from a great and good General, which is a trophy to the Commission:—

"Head-quarters Department of the Cumberland,
"Murfreesboro, *February* 2, 1863.

"The General Commanding presents his warmest acknowledgments to the friends of the soldiers of this Army, whose generous sympathy with the suffering of the sick and wounded has induced them to send for their comfort numerous sanitary supplies, which are continually arriving by the hands of individuals and charitable societies. While he highly appreciates and does not undervalue the charities which have been lavished on this Army, experience has demonstrated the importance of system and impartiality, as well as judgment and economy, in the forwarding and distribution of these supplies. In all these respects, the United States Sanitary Commission stands unrivalled. Its organization, experience, and large facilities for the work are such that the General does not hesitate to recommend, in the most urgent manner, all those who desire to send sanitary supplies, to confide them to the care of this Commission.

* See Appendix I.

"They will thus insure the supplies reaching their destination without wastage, or expense of agents or transportation, and their being distributed in a judicious manner without disorder or interference with the regulations and usages of the service.

"This Commission acts in full concert with the Medical Department of the Army, and enjoys its confidence. It is thus enabled with a few agents to do a large amount of good at the proper time, and in the proper way. Since the battle of Stone's River, it has distributed a surprisingly large amount of clothing, lint, bandages, and bedding, as well as milk, concentrated beef, fruit, and other sanitary stores, essential to the recovery of the sick and wounded.

"W. S. ROSECRANS,
"*Major-General Commanding Department.*"

In the middle of July the Army moved. With each division went an ambulance, filled with the stores of the Commission. Two Inspectors marched with the Army, accompanied by special messengers, to be sent back to the storehouses of the Commission when the supplies on hand should begin to give out. The history is the same as ever. As the Army starts the sick are left behind, or they fall out of the ranks as it moves on. Messengers are going back, and supplies are moving forward. General Rosecrans's headquarters are at Tullahoma;

a battle is expected, and things must be in readiness for it. So the telegraph keeps saying, "Bring stores by the next train." "Send forward, without delay, two ambulances with plenty of stimulants, morphine, and quinine." "We have clothing, but are nearly out of articles of diet, and they are in great demand," etc., etc.

The health of the Army on the 15th of August is reported as unusually good. "The 14th Army Corps has but 160 men unable to do duty." "At Winchester and Tullahoma there are but few sick, the worst cases have been sent to general hospitals." "Our cavalry command is distributed over a large territory; its left and right wings being not less than 120 miles apart. They are employed in scouting, have a sufficient number of good shelter-tents; cook by companies, even when scouting; and the surgeons inspect the food to see that it is well cooked. There has been no issue of fresh vegetables for a long time, but many are obtained from the country around. The clothing is sufficient, and of good quality. All have blankets of cloth or india-rubber. Each regiment has one hospital tent. The report of the sick in the whole command, in hospital and quarters, is 225, — mostly slight cases. There is one ambulance to each regiment, with a reserve supply well furnished with medical stores and instruments. The hospital record is properly kept, and there is a hospital fund. Diarrhœa and malarial fevers are the prevailing diseases."

So it appears that the Inspector is doing his duty in the advance, and discovers that others are doing the same. His little memorandum says much for the officers of that cavalry command.

At last from Chattanooga come the heavy laden words, "We are expecting a great battle." "Dr. Barnum came last night,—was very energetic in getting through. Mr. Crary came yesterday with seven loads of stores. Mr. Redding and his companion were left at Bridgeport, expecting to come on as soon as possible. They are wanted now at Bridgeport and at Stevenson more than here. I shall try to communicate with them to-day by telegraph. Stores designed for this place must be sent to Bridgeport at once, so as to be ready for the trains. They can be stored in tents, which have been furnished to us. We are practically farther from Bridgeport than Bridgeport is from Louisville; and we regard ourselves as exceedingly fortunate to get goods through as we have, but it is very difficult to communicate with those here. I will telegraph you of any special changes."

"STEVENSON, ALA., *Sept.* 24, 1863.

"I reached this point on the first of September, in company with my brother, Dr. A. N. Read, who had visited the place repeatedly before, and established a depot of stores here. The immediate demand for supplies was then not large, as much of the Army was inaccessible, and was so situated that vegetables and other supplies could, in part, be drawn from the country. All the sick who could be reached from the different stations along the road, were liberally supplied with stores, and vegetables were furnished to such regiments as seemed most needy.

"Arrangements were made with the medical director of the department, by whom we were to be notified by telegraph or courier of any probable engagement with the enemy; the notice to be accompanied by an order for the requisite transportation.

"As our troops passed further from the river, and began to concentrate around Chattanooga, it seemed best to have a personal inspection of the wants of the Army, and of the routes by which stores could reach the different divisions from Stevenson or Bridgeport. Accordingly, we purchased saddle-horses, and on the 8th started for the front, passing through Bridgeport and over Raccoon or Sandy Mountain by a rocky, difficult mountain-road, reaching General Rosecrans's head-quarters at Trenton, Georgia, on the afternoon of the 9th. Here we heard of the evacuation of Chattanooga, and on the morning of the 10th reached that place in company with a part of the General's staff. On our route we struck the river road from Bridgeport to Chattanooga, the latter part of which passes along the side of Lookout Mountain, over a rough, broken, rocky bed, cut into the mountain-side, over which loaded wagons pass with great difficulty.

"At Chattanooga we learned that the enemy were steadily falling back, — the rumors of the probabilities of an engagement constantly changing and contradictory. Should one occur, it was evident there would be great destitution; and, having ascertained by inspection of the routes by which supplies must be brought in, that practically Chattanooga was farther from Bridgeport than the latter place is from Louisville, we made immediate and persistent efforts to procure transportation, so as to forward as many stores as we could get at the earliest moment, and finally succeeded in getting through, with the first supply train that reached the place, seven wagon-loads of milk, beef, rags, bandages, dried fruits, hospital clothing, &c. Mr. Crary, our storekeeper at Stevenson, came through with the train, and immediately returned to superintend the forwarding of further supplies.

"We obtained an order for four more wagons, which was telegraphed to Stevenson, and the wagons were loaded and forwarded before Mr. Crary got through on his return. During the battle he sent forward additional supplies, which were turned back by an order stopping all trains, and did not reach Chattanooga before we left the place, but crossed the river and were taken in charge by the hospital steward of the 93d Ohio Vols., a faithful man, who undertook to get them through by the route on this side.

"Good rooms were secured at Chattanooga, our stores assorted and arranged for rapid delivery, before the battle commenced. Skirmishing occurred along the line for several days, and a few wounded men were brought to the hospitals in the town. These were supplied with such articles as they required from our rooms, and we also sent forward, by every safe means, a limited supply to the temporary hospitals in the front.

"On Saturday, the 19th, the general engagement commenced, and continued, suspended at intervals while changing positions or falling back, throughout Saturday, Sunday, Monday, and Tuesday. During this time there was no opportunity of making even the briefest memoranda, and the events, of which I am giving you this hurriedly written narrative, may not all be detailed in the order of their occurrence. My brother was severely sick, and had been so for several days. In fact, he was totally unfitted for work, but persisted in doing what he could, and continued the general superintendence of the work. Not a great many wounded were sent back on Saturday; but on Sunday they came in numbers far beyond the ability of all the medical officers to provide even tolerably for their comfort. At the request of the medical director, Dr. Barnum took possession of two large blocks, cleared out the rooms, fitted them up temporarily for the wounded, supplying them with clothing, bandages, and edibles from our rooms, procured and put up stores, dressed the wounds of those most requiring immediate assistance, and superintended the providing and cooking of rations for the men. All of the rooms were soon filled; and by his untiring efforts from 1500 to 2000 were rendered tolerably comfortable. On Sunday, I visited all the hospitals and temporary resting-places of the wounded, notifying the officers in charge of the location of our rooms and the nature of our supplies, asking them to send for everything we had so far as it was needed.

"Returning late in the evening, I found a large church on Main Street, where services had been held during the day, and saw that the steps were crowded with wounded men. Entering the church, it was found filled with a congregation from the battle-field, crippled with every variety of wounds, with no medical or other officer in charge, without food of any kind, without water, and without even a candle to shed a glimmering light over their destitution, — silent worshippers in the darkness, — patient, unmurmuring martyrs in a noble cause, apparently deserted by all except Him in whose sanctuary they had taken refuge. I immediately carried concentrated beef to the residence of Dr. Simms, near the church, — a resident physician of rebel sympathies, but a generous and warm-hearted man, in whose office we had some days before found quarters, and where my brother superintended the preparation of soup while I brought candles and a box of hard bread, had them carried to the church, and, procuring water, distributed it to the thirsty.

"Two thirds of the occupants of the church — some with shattered arms, and some with other ghastly wounds — were sleeping quietly upon the seats and the floor, unconscious of their many wounds. Never before had I so high an appreciation of 'Nature's sweet restorer, balmy sleep.'

"The soup was brought and distributed to the wakeful, and my brother and Dr. Simms commenced dressing their wounds, and continued their labor till sheer exhaustion compelled them to desist; — the waking men provided for, the sleeping were allowed to sleep in peace. I reported the condition of these men to the medical director, and medical officers were put in charge of them, and in the morning a chaplain took charge of vegetables and other eatables which I sent from the rooms, and superintended the preparation of food for the men. At this time, Monday, the streets were completely blockaded their whole length with army wagons, as an order had been issued on Sunday for the whole train to be sent across the river. This was done apparently to avoid confusion, and to save our train if our forces should be compelled to evacuate the place. The only means of crossing was one narrow pontoon bridge, and for two days the trains filled the streets. Our stores were needed everywhere, but nobody could get to our quarters. After applying to several head-quarters, I procured an order for three army wagons to report at our rooms for the distribution of stores. And, hastily riding to the different hospitals, I obtained approximately the capacity of each, the number of its inmates, and the nature of the articles most needed. The usual answer to the question, 'What do you need most?' was, 'Everything,' — a comprehensive, but almost literally a truthful answer. Returning to the rooms, I gave general directions to Messrs. Redding and Larrabee, who superintended the loading of the wagons, and piloted each one, when loaded, through the dense mass of teams to its destination.

"At first sight, it seemed an apparently hopeless undertaking; but the words, 'This wagon is loaded with stores for your wounded comrades; can you make room for it to pass?' operated like magic everywhere; and in no single instance did I find a driver who did not promptly and cheerfully open a way for the supplies, and that, too, through streets where there were three, four, and five parallel trains, the drivers all eager to reach the pontoon bridge first and secure precedence in crossing. In this way, we succeeded in getting a good supply: a full wagon-load each to the seminary building, and old rebel hospitals on the hill; to the old rebel hospital near the Critchfield Hotel (now called No. 2); to the Critchfield Hotel, where there were about 1500 wounded; to two churches next to the Critchfield House; to the Presbyterian Church, and to three blocks of buildings on Main Street; and to the officers' hospital, in a large brick building east of Main Street.

"The stores most in demand at Chattanooga were of edibles, beef, milk, stimulants, and dried fruit. The beef, on account of its intrinsic value, portability, and the readiness with which it can be prepared, is the most valuable of all, and at such a time as this there is no danger of an over-supply. Of clothing and dressings, bandages and rags were first in demand; then shirts, drawers, comforts, and blankets. Of the last we had but a few, and there was a great demand for them. Most of the wounded had lost their blankets. The nights were cold, and they suffered greatly on that account. I have mentioned only these few articles of prime necessity, but everything usually furnished for the sick and wounded was then, and is now, in great demand. We are able to provide for those who get through to the railroad what is needed in addition to the Government supplies, but it is essential that large quantities of all the usual articles be shipped through to Chattanooga as fast as possible. There the destitution and suffering have been, and must, for some time, be very great. Yet, you must not construe what I write here, or have written above, as an implied censure of the medical officers of the Army. I know how persistently the Medical Director of the Army labored to procure transportation for his supplies, and how ready he was to aid us in procuring transportation. I know, also, that war is and must be cruel; and, situated as our Army was before Chattanooga, even mercy to the wounded required that the Army, yes, even that the horses, should be fed, although the wounded suffered until the battle was over. Over roads, the difficulties of which no one will appreciate until he has tried them, supplies had to be carried for men and horses whose strength and endurance alone could save all of the wounded from thc hardships and destitution which the wounded prisoners would encounter at the hands of the rebels.

"If Chattanooga is to be permanently held, easier communication must be established by the river and by rail. The shorter carriage-route over Lookout Mountain, which has been blown up to prevent a flank movement, will be reopened, and we shall then be able to send forward additional supplies as fast as you can get them here. Thus far no time has been lost, for we have had all that we could get transportation for; and by the time a new shipment can reach us, we hope to secure transportation for all you can send us.

"If, when this reaches you, the telegrams from the front advise you that we still hold Chattanooga, my advice would be to send of all supplies as large a quantity as possible; for I believe that, already, this battle is one of the bloodiest of the war. Our loss must already be greater than it was at Stone's River; and I do not believe the rebels will fall back before our reinforced army without another desperate struggle."

With this record ends this imperfect sketch, and our thoughts are left to go with the Commission upon that bloody field, where so much of the youth and manhood of our country, of its nerve and genius, are lying dead.

Whilst victory and defeat have alike given us work on the Cumberland and on the Mississippi, the armies in Western Virginia and General Burnside's forces in the Department of the Ohio have been inspected and their wants supplied. From General Burnside, as might be expected, every assistance has been received by the Commission, and he has issued especial orders in its favor, similar to those of General Grant and General Rosecrans.

## ARMIES OF THE GULF AND THE ATLANTIC COAST.

During all this time work was going on upon many another field.

*Army of the Gulf.* — The control of the Federal Government over the coasts of the enemy was extended in December, 1861, by the success of a small naval expedition which took possession of Ship Island, and of the half-finished fort upon it. On New Year's day, 1862, the expedition under Major-General Butler sailed from Boston with reinforcements to this point, and with it went an Inspector of the Sanitary Commission, Dr. Geo. A. Blake, with large supplies from the Boston Branch. The expedition sailed in the transport "Constitution," with two thousand five hundred troops on board; and it was owing to the forethought of the Inspector, who took with him some vaccine virus, (none else proved to be on board,) that the ship was saved from the scourge of small-pox, — one case having appeared which they were able to leave at Fortress Monroe. The wretched condition of Ship Island, a barren, desolate sand-spit, left free for the most part to alligators and such reptiles as abound in the swamps and lagoons of that region; the painful and variable climate; the sufferings of the men from diarrhœa, influenza, and rheumatism; the badness of the food, which was of salt meat (no fresh meat being issued); the badness of the water, and the wretched system of cooking, made the presence of the Sanitary Commission not undesirable. A hospital was established on the Island and liberally furnished from the Commission stores, which had been replenished at Fortress Monroe. Whilst the Inspector's head-quarters were at Ship Island he found time and opportunity to visit Key West, and to examine and relieve the wants of the troops stationed there.

The condition of the sick on the Island being, after a time, so far improved that the depot could be left in charge of a relief agent, Dr. Blake believed that more real good might be done by his accepting a proposal of General Butler, to become temporarily the surgeon of the 26th Regt. Mass. Vols., and he joined the expedition against New Orleans, with the prospect of an advance up the Mississippi. As the expedition lay at anchor below Fort Jackson, during the bombardment, he found an opportunity to benefit the sister-service. The naval officers were anxious to establish a hospital at Pilot-town, in the Southwest Passage. The destitution of the gunboats in all medical and surgical appliances was found to be complete; nor was it possible to procure such appliances from any source whatever. A happy accident brought the Commission in their way, and they were liberally supplied with sponges, chloroform, oiled silk, adhesive plaster, bandages, lint, sheets, &c., &c.

Nothing can describe the suffering of the troops upon the crowded transports which are used for these expeditions; but it is wonderful how much misery our soldiers will cheerfully endure. Surely the wells of patriotism in their hearts are too deep to be drained by the prospect of any suffering, however great, or the experience of any hardships, however severe, incurred in the defence of our National Government. One of the ships employed to carry troops for this expedition had been chartered to carry British troops to the Crimea, and was then limited to the number of three hundred and sixty: our quartermaster thought her capable of carrying one thousand. The Commission was able at least to mitigate the sufferings of these men. A clean shirt was a boon to many a poor fellow, who recited to the Inspector the habits of cleanliness in which he had been trained, and told of the joys and comforts of that New England fireside, which he had left from a pure patriotism; and then whispered, with shame, that he was now ragged and covered with vermin.

On arriving at New Orleans the remaining stores were given to the St. James Hotel, then appropriated as a hospital, and the surgeons in attendance expressed their great indebtedness to the Commission, saying, that these stores enabled them to double the comfort of their men. At the same time a fresh supply of beef-stock, condensed milk, whisky, and brandy arrived from the depots of the Commission, and were distributed, as needed, to the different hospitals about the city. A free use of these stores was marked, after a short time, by the rapid change and recovery of convalescents.

At many of the posts it was impossible to obtain food suitable for the sick. In New Orleans everything commanded an enormous price, and, moreover, could only be obtained through the hospital fund, which did not then exist in a single instance. These stores of the Commission were therefore doubled in a cash estimate from the original value, and were in fact invaluable to the surgeons who could draw on them freely for their sick and convalescents. Many lives were saved and many thanks were rendered from grateful hearts for this bountiful expression of the sympathy which lives in loyal bosoms; and rebels were staggered by the sight.

The relations of the Commission and its Inspector to the officers of the Army were constantly of the most favorable kind. General Butler repeatedly gave assurances of his high appreciation of the efforts of the Commission, and there was scarcely an officer of the command but was ready and willing to listen to the many suggestions which were made for the removal of existing wrongs and imprudences. The medical essays of the Commission were freely distributed, and gladly received by the surgeons, who, with the regimental officers, were awakened to a sense of the necessity of sanitary measures; and it is believed that the improved condition of the troops in this department is largely owing in this way to the Commission.

In the summer of 1862, the field of inspection and relief in the Gulf Department included the forces stationed at Fort Pickens, Fort Barrancas, Ship Island; Forts Pike, Macomb, Jackson, and St. Philip; Carrollton, Bonnet Carré, Donaldsonville, Thibodeaux, Brashear City, and the forces in New Orleans.

The general and regimental hospitals in those places were visited systematically, and their wants relieved; but, as a general thing, they were well conducted and well supplied. In every instance a hospital fund had been created, and those hospitals near to the city were able to buy in the markets both for themselves and the other hospitals beyond them. The winter passed away in the current issue of supplies, and in a most careful inspection of regiments, from which valuable information is now being derived.

*Expedition into the Têche Country.*—On the arrival of General Banks's expedition early in 1863, the Commission forces were increased by Dr. Crane and others, bringing with them more than $17,000 worth of fresh supplies. When the expedition moved into the Têche country in March, 1863, Dr. Crane, and Mr. Mitchell, relief agent, left New Orleans for

Baton Rouge, with General Banks and Staff. On the General's arrival, the Army moved forward at once, leaving its sick, an aggregate of 2400, to be cared for in Baton Rouge. Contradictory orders, vacillations, and final hurry, caused much confusion in the work. Three fourths of the sick were left on the bare floor of barracks; some were in deserted camps, and the majority left in charge of a few nurses, their surgeons being of course with the regiments. The depot of the Commission being established at Baton Rouge, every assistance was rendered to these unfortunate men, while at the same time supplies were sent forward with the Army.

Had an engagement occurred, as all expected, and had Baton Rouge been filled with wounded men, the services of the Commission, ready as it was for the emergency, would have been signal. It is, however, none the less a satisfaction to know that, what work there was, it did well, and that hundreds of sick were benefited and made comfortable by its presence at this point.

The attack on Port Hudson proved a feint; and the Army returned within a week to its quarters at Baton Rouge, where it found the benefits of the depot of the Commission. During this brief period, three thousand articles of clothing and six hundred pounds of beef-stock, condensed milk, &c., were issued from it.

The advance towards Port Hudson was but the first step to a series of brilliant movements on the part of the Army, each one of which was followed by the Commission. Agents and supplies were pushed forward to Brashear City, following the advance of the Army to the Red River. When an engagement occurred, and the wounded were sent to the rear beyond Franklin, they were taken in charge by the Sanitary Commission, and conveyed for the most part in steamers to New Orleans. Indeed all, but fifty-seven severe cases left at Brashear City, were thus removed by the agents of the Commission, who gathered up on their way the sick upon the Têche, at Pattersonville, and at other places. As the Army rested at Opelousas and Washington, *en route* to Alexandria, its wants were studied and relieved by the Commission. Five hundred pounds of ice, with condensed milk, appear among the items issued at the request of the medical director. Each wing of the Army investing Port Hudson was accompanied by an Inspector and Relief Agent, with a depot of stores useful in the daily supply routine, and ready for any emergency. During all the military operations against Port Hudson, on the battle-fields of May 27th and June 4th, and at Springfield Landing, the agents of the Commission attended to the removal of the wounded, and to the care of them at Baton Rouge, to which place they were conveyed. The Inspector's head-quarters were with General Weitzel on the right. An estimation of the services he and the other agents rendered during this campaign can be formed from the fact that some officers who had looked on the Commission as a "meddlesome concern," now voluntarily went to the Inspector, and, surrendering their old ideas, thanked him for what had been done by the agents of the Sanitary Commission.*

At the present moment, the thoughts of those stationed in New Orleans under the charge of Dr. Blake turn to the expedition preparing under General Banks.

A "Woman's Union Aid Society"—or rather, in this instance, let us say a "Union Women's Aid Society"—is at work in New Orleans. "I bade them God speed," says the Inspector; "their work is useful as an example of loyal principle, besides its value in actual results." And here at the North we echo his benediction.

*Army in North Carolina.*— The next great point of attack and lodgment on the Southern Atlantic coast was first reached by the expedition under General Burnside, which left the harbor of New York, and rendezvoused at Fortress Monroe, sailing thence at midnight, January 11th, 1862.

* See Appendix K.

With this expedition sailed an agent of the Sanitary Commission. At its dreary resting-place on Hatteras, the stores of the Commission became at once important. General Burnside issued immediate orders to put the regiments into marching condition. The sick were to be sent into one of the barracks. But how were they to be provided for? A hundred of them arrived before dark, and before dark the Commission had arrived also. A hundred beds were ready, with blankets and pillows for the weary heads, and food and stimulants for the exhausted and fevered bodies. The relief which this timely aid gave to the surgeons, the satisfaction which it brought alike to officers and men, and especially to the medical staff, can only be realized by one in actual contact with the utter desolation of the forsaken sand-spit on which this military post was established, — where the elements were in constant strife, seeming to be presided over by evil genii possessed with the spirit of eternal unrest.

Reaching Roanoke Island, the Commission found that, although the hospitals were suffering from a dearth of supplies, medicines, sick-food, and furniture, yet the sick, especially the wounded, were doing well, owing, beyond a doubt, to well constructed, or rather well ventilated barracks, and to the conscientious care of their surgeons.

The energy with which General Burnside

pushed on his preparations for a forward movement left but few of the troops *in situ* long enough for purposes of inspection; and the attention of the Inspectors was more particularly given to the hospitals, on which the supplies held by the Commission were freely bestowed: — supplies which were available at a time when they were most grateful both to the surgeons and patients. The generous reception of the Commission by many of the general and other officers, and their cordial promise to facilitate the work in every way, did much to encourage and cheer those who had it in hand; one of whom remarks, — "In fact it was within the lines of the Army that I first began to appreciate the high estimation in which the Sanitary Commission is held by the service."

When the advance on Newbern commenced, the Commission was called upon to replenish the already exhausted stock of stimulants, anæsthetics, and narcotics, besides supplying other necessary and useful articles. For instance: the colonel of a Massachusetts regiment told the Inspector that one or two hundred of his men were about to start on the expedition, with the prospect of forced marches and hard fighting, but with no stockings on their feet. The Inspector gave an order on a depot of the Commission which the regiment was to pass on its way forth. A few days later he received grateful acknowledgments on behalf of the regiment, which bore a gallant and honorable part in the victory which ensued.

General Burnside, with his wise forethought for the good of his men, permitted and aided the Commission to follow him to Newbern; detailing men to its service, giving its vessel a position in the fleet, and promising that it should be taken seasonably to a point at which the stores of the Commission could be most readily available on the scene of action. Large supplies were left for the hospitals at Roanoke Island, and then the Commission went forward with the Army.

After the battle, it found ample occasion to bless the kindness which had placed it where it could be most useful. Its stores were landed on the battle-field, where, in many instances, so great was the emergency, so pressing the demand, that an exhausted Commissariat *could not* meet it. The stores of the Medical Purveyor, for which there was no transportation, were still at Roanoke Island, whither all requisitions had to be sent. The Commission then became, as it were, a necessary department of the service, and the right arm of the Medical Director, who more than once acknowledged heartily the timely relief.

In the establishment of hospitals at Newbern, the Commission gave much assistance; also, in the shipment of wounded for the North. After this, it fell back into its steady routine,—that routine which quietly goes on, in every part of the land, wherever the United States troops are to be found, and which is only broken in upon by special emergencies.

One little proof may be given here of the results of inspection and respectful advice. The Inspector found that, from the peculiarity of the soil, the water was impure, and filled with poisonous vegetable decay and mould. He submitted to General Burnside a paper suggesting a simple means, based on natural laws, by which to remedy this alarming evil. The paper was read at a council in the General's tent, and the plan adopted. The General gave orders that the necessary material should be supplied the next morning, and requested the Inspector to superintend the construction of as many wells as the various camps required. Wherever the design was faithfully carried out, its object was realized. It is refreshing to find recorded, in a report of the Inspector some months later, that the hospitals at Newbern were "liberally supplied by the Medical Purveyor. They are," he says, "models of neatness and systematic arrangement in their wards, sinks, out-houses, and grounds." And such they have continued to the present time.

*Army in South Carolina.* — When the expedition to South Carolina sailed under Captain Dupont, Oct. 29, 1861, (that glorious expedition whose naval fame shall last forever,) an Inspector and relief agent of the Sanitary Commission went with it. The supply of medicines, surgical instruments, and hospital stores furnished to the expedition had been inadequate, and the greater part of what there really was had been thrown overboard, to lighten the ship in the great gale which the fleet encountered. These deficiencies were most severely felt. The abundant supply brought by Dr. Andrews, Inspector of the Commission, was more than sufficient to meet all immediate wants. On his first arrival at Port Royal, he found that an order had been issued for the vaccination of the troops, which could not be carried out from the impossibility of procuring the necessary virus. Dr. Andrews had with him a sufficient quantity to complete the revaccination of the troops, and to make a good beginning towards protecting the negroes. Unfortunately, no attempt was made to perpetuate the virus, and the government supply did not arrive. The small-pox accordingly broke out amongst those negroes who had not been vaccinated, giving a frightful glimpse into what might have happened without that forethought of the Commission.

In February, 1863, in view of the impending struggle in South Carolina and Georgia, a corps of Sanitary Commission Inspectors and relief agents, composed of excellent and tried men, possessed of experience in similar fields, was ordered to proceed at once to Port Royal, and establish a station at the nearest possible point to the national forces. On their arrival they received the approval of Major-General Hunter. The necessary orders were issued from Headquarters to the quartermaster's and other departments, and to the post-commander at Beaufort, S. C., where immediate steps were taken to establish the depot of the Commission.

At that period, speedy and extensive military movements were impending; and the agents of the Commission, ambitious that relief should be as prompt within their province as it had been on many memorable battle-fields, pressed forward their preparations with vigor and zeal. The various hospitals in Beaufort and Hilton Head were visited, their resources and appliances inquired into, their wants ascertained, and the surgeons in charge invited (as usual) to draw upon the stores of the Commission for those supplies which they could not otherwise obtain for the comfort of their men.

For some time this regular "Commission routine" went on. "The Cosmopolitan," a large hospital transport, able to carry 400 men, and held by the Government to follow the movements of the Army, was furnished liberally from its stores.

In no respect was the Army at this time in South Carolina as well supplied as the other armies in the field; nor had the troops the endurance, energy, and enthusiasm that have distinguished the Armies of the Potomac and the Cumberland, in their alternate triumphs and defeats. Under these circumstances, no one could contemplate the approaching military operations without the most mournful forebodings.

The sufferings of the sick, when discharged from the service and sent home, pressed earnestly on the attention of the agents of the Commission. They were, habitually, placed in the steerage of the various boats bound North, without attendants, and unprovided, in many instances, with even straw to lie upon. Poor fellows just recovered from severe illness, or broken down by it, — some with bed-sores from long confinement, — suffered greatly. The Commission at once began to supply these men with necessaries; and having called the attention of General Hunter to the abuse, it was reformed. A medical officer was sometimes sent with the men; but from that time an orderly was invariably detailed to wait upon them during the voyage.

A faithful band of Commission agents is at work at Beaufort and Hilton Head at the present moment, when all eyes are turned to that spot. The work is in charge of Dr. Marsh, who, with his wife, is watching before Charleston for those opportunities to give relief, which are a painful joy to such as are engaged in the service. During the summer, vegetables and ice have been liberally issued from their depot, together with an immense amount of supplies, sent chiefly from the branch depot in New York. The Commission has a good-sized brig, employed as a store-ship, stationed with the fleet in the harbor of Charleston. Mrs. Marsh writes: "The brig sailed from here on the 8th with stores which would gladden the hearts of those who have friends exposed. The effect of these home offerings brings tears to the eyes and encouragement to the hearts of men ready to die. . . . . . On Sunday some 200 men were brought to Hilton Head. I hear that the Commission is operating very successfully with men and appliances stationed at intervals from the front to the hospital-ships stationed seven miles in the rear."

On the day of the first attack on Fort Wagner, the men were in fine spirits; and the Commission, in the anxious hope to strengthen them for their work, passed through the ranks giving to each man hot soup and crackers. Previous to the engagement each little squad of the Commission people had its duties assigned, and discharged them in such a manner as to win the public approbation of the U. S. Medical Director. He was heard, during and subsequent to the removal of the wounded to the ship, to exclaim, "God bless the Sanitary Commission!" General Strong, Colonel Chatfield, and other officers requested, when carried from the field, to be taken to the quarters of the Commission.

The *Port Royal Free Press* (an army newspaper) says: "The officers of the United States Sanitary Commission have won for themselves a splendid reputation in this department. They have by their discretion and zeal saved many valuable lives. Under the guns of Wagner, in the hottest of the fire, their trained corps picked up and carried off the wounded almost as fast as they fell. As many of our men were struck while ascending the parapet, and then rolled into the moat, which at high tide contains six feet of water, they must inevitably have perished had they been suffered to remain. But the men who were detailed for service with Dr. Marsh, went about their work with an intrepidity and coolness worthy of all praise. The skill and experience of the members of the Commission have, since the battle, been unremittingly employed to render comfortable the sick and wounded."

In a recent letter from Mrs. Marsh, she says: "A soldier from the 115th New York came into the office and inquired, 'If they ever paid money here?' To my reply, that everything was gratuitous, he answered, 'Oh, yes! I know that. I have never needed anything myself, but I have seen others made so comfortable through your aid that I want to give a little something to be expended for somebody;' and laying down one dollar he insisted that it should be thus appropriated. Not only are the material wants of the soldier met by the liberal gifts of the country, but they encourage him in the belief that he is not forgotten in his toil. . . . . Many an eye moistens at the thought of this link which binds the battle-field to the home."

We close this sketch with an extract from a letter already published in a Boston newspaper, which has the merit of impartiality, and with a General Order which speaks for itself.

"It is but just that I should notice, in connection with accounts of military affairs in this department, the operations of the Sanitary Commission here, under direction of its able and efficient manager, Dr. M. M. Marsh. I regret that some correspondents have either entirely ignored its presence, or declined awarding to it the high meed of praise to which the unremitting and indefatigable exertions of its agents, both in camp and upon the field of battle, have so eminently entitled it. I cannot, however, do better than give you facts which speak for it in abler and more potent language than I can command. The exertions of its agents for the preservation of the health of our troops during their almost superhuman labors in the trenches upon Morris and Folly Islands, as well as their timely and efficient aid in promoting the comfort of our sick and wounded during and after the engagements, form a theme of praise to which I confess the incompetency of my pen to do justice; but if the securing of an abundance of necessary supplies, and a liberal distribution of them at each and every point where they were absolutely indispensable, constitute an element of success in the working of a relief association, these gentlemen have certainly demonstrated, not only the wisdom of the plans of the Sanitary Commission, but the preëminent success of their practical working upon the fields and in the camps throughout this entire campaign. . . . .

"No faithful record of the services of these gentlemen upon the ever-memorable night of the 18th of July ever has or ever can be written. They seemed ubiquitous upon the field, removing the wounded, burying the dead, or staying the life-current where the bright red stain from a severed artery upon the white sands of the beach betokened its speedy ebb; and at the post hospital aiding in the operations, and up the dock receiving and disposing of the poor fellows as they were hurried on board, they seemed everywhere present.

"All were loud in their praise, and by none were their services more highly appreciated than by the medical faculty, with whom they worked hand in hand, and who, from skilled experience upon such occasions, were best competent to estimate the value of their services."

"DEPARTMENT OF THE SOUTH,
*Head-quarters in the Field,*
*Morris Island, S. C., September* 9.

"General Orders, No. 73.

"The Brigadier-General commanding desires to make this public acknowledgment of the benefits for which his command has been indebted to the United States Sanitary Commission, and to express his thanks to the gentlemen whose humane efforts, in procuring and distributing much-needed articles of comfort, have so materially alleviated the sufferings of the soldiers.

"Especial gratitude is due to Dr. M. M. Marsh, Medical Inspector of the Commission, through whose efficiency, energy, and zeal the wants of the troops have been promptly ascertained, and the resources of the Commission made available for every portion of the Army.

"By order of Brig. Gen. Q. A. GILLMORE,
"ED. W. SMITH, *Asst. Adj. Gen.*

"Official:
"J. S. SEALY,
"*Capt. U. S. A., Act. Asst. Adj. Gen.*"

# PART III.

## DEPARTMENT OF SPECIAL RELIEF.

This Department is organized for the relief and care of discharged soldiers, though other work is connected with it. It is under the direction of Mr. F. N. Knapp, "Special Relief Agent" of the Commission. The Commission, in assisting invalid soldiers, has thus far limited itself to the care of them whilst they are in that intermediate condition between the military and civil states, — no longer under the charge of regimental officers, or of hospitals, nor yet protected by their homes. In this state the Commission, by its various agencies, (providing lodging-houses and food, rescuing them from the hands of sharpers, collecting pensions and pay, correcting their defective papers, giving them medical treatment and nursing when required,) seeks to be the guardian of the soldiers whilst they are thus *in transitu;* endeavors to protect them in their rights, and to see that all immediate needs growing out of their disabled condition are met by corresponding provision for temporary supply and relief. But the Commission, thus far, in making this provision, has endeavored to limit itself to the care of the soldier whilst he is in this intermediate state. It takes care of him after leaving the hospital; transacts his business; puts him through by railroad to his home: and here usually its responsibility ends. Now, however, the question is forced upon it, *Does its work rightly end here?* We turn from this subject a while, to tell the story of special relief up to this point, — which must open with the remark, that the arrangements for this Relief are becoming daily more generally known, applied for, and appreciated throughout the Army; and that the coöperation of the Medical Department, and of the Quartermaster's, Commissary's, and Paymaster's Departments has been, if possible, still more ready and cordial than before.

The first point to which we turn is the "Home" in Washington, (on North Capitol Street.) Its leading objects are briefly these: — To give food and lodging, care and assistance, to men who are honorably discharged from service, and who are afterwards delayed in obtaining their papers and pay; to communicate with distant regiments on behalf of discharged men whose papers prove defective, who, without such succor, would fall into the hands of claim-agents, and even suffer want; to act as an unpaid agent for those too feeble to present their own claims for pay or pension at the paymaster's; to send them by railroad, in care of a railway agent who will protect them from sharpers, and put them through to their destination; to see that discharged men leave at once for their homes, not falling a prey to temptation and evil company; to make them reasonably neat and clean, and to furnish them with the necessary means of reaching home, if, on investigation, their destitution and need is proved; and to be prepared to meet at once, with food and other aid, such necessities as arise when sick men, discharged from service, arrive in Washington in large numbers, from hospitals or distant fields of service. The only condition imposed on this relief is, that each man shall present his certificate of discharge.

In addition to this service there is another,— an occasional one. Whenever men have been brought to Washington or Alexandria, in large numbers, from battle-fields and hospitals, this agency has ministered at once to their relief. Not long since notice was sent in: "500 sick and wounded are on their way to Washington by the canal-boats; can you do something for them?" By the time the boats arrived, the special relief agents were ready with a wagon-load of supplies,—bitterly needed, as it chanced; for the men had come through a country full of guerrillas, no supplies had reached them, and they were destitute of everything.

At the present moment the "Home" is larger than it has ever been. A new building has been added, and it now makes up 320 beds, including the hospital, where such as are reduced by disease are kept until they are able to travel. Frequently they are too far gone to make even the care bestowed upon them available to save life. The record, for a period of nine months, sadly shows that 935 *very* sick men were received during that time, of which number sixty-one died.

A visit to this "Home" will indeed repay the visitor. Its condition does credit to the Superintendent, — a frank, cheerful man, with a look of kindly but keen intelligence. The beds are all clean, and ready for their night's occupants; there is a cheerful reading-room; several bath-rooms; a convenient wash-room; a baggage-room, where the knapsacks are ticketed and put away, with a care which many fine general hospitals would do well to imitate; and, lastly, on the ground-floor, is a large and lofty room, — the hospital, where the men seem resting, not only from bodily anguish, but, for the brief moment of their sojourn there, resting in the sense that a care is over them which puts aside their own anxieties. No one can look at the sweet, grave face of the matron (one who did her part in the Peninsular campaign) and see her work, without comprehending the sentiments of these men, expressed oftentimes with the pathos which this war has taught us to hear as an every-day sound. The diary of the present physician of the "Home," Dr. Smith, tells many little stories such as this: — "One of the men said to me, whilst sitting in the hospital and looking upon the completion of arrangements for his departure, 'Doctor, I have been so kindly treated here, and been helped so much more than at any time since my sickness, that I'm *afraid* to go beyond that door.'"

There is one sad thought connected with this "Home" to those who know its history. It is the death of Dr. Grymes, its first physician. He, too, served on the Peninsula, as surgeon of "The Daniel Webster" transport; and the constant thought of those who looked at the energy of that frail body, and saw the inward fire that consumed it, was, that he knew he was a dying man, and would alleviate death and suffering in others so long as life was in him. And the feeling was just. After the campaign, he returned to his old service at the "Home." His house was but a few paces off, and he continued to come to his work until it took him more than half an hour to get over those few paces. Then he died.

From December, 1862, to October 1st, 1863, 7187 persons have been received into this "Home." Since it opened, 86,986 nights' lodgings have been furnished, and 331,315 meals provided. "Homes" of the same description are maintained by the Commission, and conducted in an admirable manner, at Boston,

Nashville, Cairo, Memphis, Louisville, Cleveland, and Cincinnati. Since they were established, (Cincinnati, one of the largest and most efficient, excepted,) the whole number of nights' lodgings furnished by these "Homes" of the Commission amounts to 198,963; the number of meals furnished, to 659,160.

In Washington, lesser Homes, or "Lodges," have been maintained in the vicinity of railroads. Lodge No. 2 was discontinued, as no longer needed, after it had furnished 1500 beds and 2130 meals. Lodge No. 3 was likewise closed after furnishing 3760 beds and 17,960 meals. Lodge No. 4 has been lately established, and is immediately connected with the Paymaster's Department. Up to October 1st, 1863, it had furnished 9832 beds and 50,096 meals. This Lodge is one of the most interesting. Its cheerful white-washed buildings cluster around a planked court, brightened at the corners with little squares of turf, and leading at one end to the large waiting-room of the United States Pay Department. Making the circuit of the court, and looking into its various little houses, we come first upon the "Pension Office," and then upon the "Ticket Office," and so into the store-room, with its hanging rows of hams and bacon; lockers of tea, sugar, and all that's nice; next into the kitchen, clean and savory; then into the dining-room with a capital meal upon the table, — and lo! a table-cloth and china cups, first waft of home:—and so round into the Special Relief Office, with its ledgers and letter-books,—the grave explanation of the rest. To this office *are now sent* from the Pay Department (hitherto the Commission has had to hunt them up) all those soldiers, who, by reason of defective papers, &c., &c., cannot draw their pay. The case is noted, the man cheered and fed, lodged if necessary, and perhaps righted at once. If his difficulties are great, involving a long correspondence, (sometimes ten letters are written to clear up one case,) he is sent to his home, leaving his care upon the Commission. And as he leaves the Relief Office, some one takes him across the planked court to the ticket office, where he is checked through to his home at half price; and so good-bye to him. The last mention of his name will be found a week or two later on the letter-book, in some such record as this:—

"PETER JONES: Sir,—Please find your discharge and draft for $177, being the amount of your pay. Please acknowledge and oblige

"J. B. ABBOTT,

"*Assistant Special Relief Agent.*"

Connected with this Lodge is the Pension Agency, which has been in operation for eight months past, with branches in Philadelphia, Boston, Chicago, Louisville, and Cincinnati. The Examining-Surgeon and Director were both appointed by the United States Commissioner of Pensions. The services rendered to the soldier are entirely gratuitous in Washington and Philadelphia, but in Boston there is a small charge, the organization there not having originated in the Commission. This agency has proved most beneficent in many ways; it has saved to the soldiers already an aggregate expense of $7000, and has rescued them from imposition and from a vast amount of trouble and anxiety.

Another service rendered to the soldier is the collection of his "back-pay." It was found that many men in hospital, with families sorely in need of as much as they could give them, were unable to obtain what was due to them; or, at least, that it was so tied up as to be beyond their power to collect it. An agent of the Commission authorized by the Paymaster's Department, has entered on the work of investigation and the removal of difficulties. In the Stanton Hospital alone, the back-pay of fifty-six men, thus procured, in one week amounted to $3008.96, almost every dollar of which was sent to their families. "Cast your bread upon the waters and ye shall find it after many days," might be the thought of some of those wives and mothers who had given their mite to the Commission.

Lodge No. 5, near 6th Street Wharf, is a little place memorable for great things: giving food to the sick and wounded arriving by boat from Acquia Creek, and furnishing supplies to such boats, returning for fresh loads of wounded, as had no suitable provision for feeding the men on board. An ambulance is kept at this Lodge to take the men to the "Home." The Superintendent visits each boat as it arrives, and renders immediate assistance to the sick and wounded. No true account can of course be kept of issues like these; but on the 15th and 16th of June, 1863, it is recorded, in the Superintendent's reports, that the number of men met at the landing, and refreshed with a meal, was over five thousand; and amongst them several hundred seriously wounded.

The next Lodge is at the junction of the Washington and Alexandria and Orange Railroads. Colonel Devereux, Superintendent of the road, telegraphs to Washington when trains are starting with wounded, so that the Lodge may be ready to receive them as they arrive. Before this arrangement was made, the effect of moving badly wounded men, after such a journey, without fortifying them with food or stimulants, was so disastrous that many fainted from exhaustion; and of ninety men who were thus taken on one occasion to the Stanton Hospital, four died in a few hours, and one dropped dead as he tried to reach his bed.

Another lodge, called the "Soldier's Rest," is in Alexandria, "the gateway of the Army of the Potomac,"* — at the terminus of the same railroad, — established to succor and shelter the sick and wounded, who are frequently detained at that point before they can be transported to Washington. Since its establishment, in August, 1863, to October 1st, the number of lodgings furnished was 604; of meals, 5980.

There is also a relief station of the Commission, of great importance, at the Convalescent Camp in Alexandria; it is managed efficiently and successfully by Miss Bradley, once in charge of the "Home." She has the coöperation and confidence of all the officers of the post. Her ambulances come daily into Washington, bringing discharged men, whom she accompanies to the Pay and Pension Offices, or to the railroads. Within four months she has thus brought in men whose pay amounted to more than $100,000.

As the old Convalescent Camp (Camp Misery, it was called) has brought such dishonor upon the name, it will not be superfluous to speak of the condition of the present one. In December, 1862, orders were issued to break up the old camp and prepare the ground for another. The present matron applied at once to be sent there as Sanitary Commission Agent. When

* This was the favorite expression of the faithful superintendent of this lodge, James Richardson, who died Nov. 12th, 1863, from the hard, unceasing labor which he gave to his duties.

she arrived, there were one thousand men on the ground, and no tents pitched. Her first act was the distribution of clothing; her next, to get two large hospital tents pitched, into which the sickest men were taken. This hospital she kept up till April, when the barracks were completed. One hundred and twenty-three sick men were admitted during that time, nursed and made comfortable; the Commission supplying clothes, chickens, butter, farina, brandy, everything in fact but the ordinary ration. In the beginning of January, a new commander of the post, Colonel McKelvey, and a new surgeon in charge, arrived; and, from that time, rapid improvements have been made, until those who now visit the ground are made to forget the horrible reproach attaching to the name of "Convalescent Camp." Still, no one can go there, even now, without perceiving the curse which is upon all convalescent men in hospital, — the curse of having nothing to do.

The last branch of Special Relief which we shall name here (there are others) is the "Nurses' Home"; of which there is one in Washington and one in Annapolis, where women-nurses sick and weary for the time can rest. These houses have become lodges for the wives and mothers of men in hospital, who frequently come to Washington or Annapolis without thought of cost, and considering nothing but the dear face to be seen at the end of their journey. Utterly destitute, helpless, sometimes broken-hearted, they are found by the Commission, which receives and shelters them in the "Nurses' Home." This has proved, in its working, one of the *kindest* charities of the Commission.

Over all this work of Special Relief, spreading through the West and going off in other directions not mentioned here, presides a man whose soul is in it, — whose soul is of it, — whose spirit is shed upon those under him, until, next to their desire to do their duty to the cause, comes, with love and reverence, the wish to be like him.

And now let us ask, *Does the work of the Commission to discharged men end here?* The subject is one on which the Commission, as we have said, has thought long and anxiously. A large collection of data upon the point of what becomes of the soldier from the time when the Government and the Commission leave him, shows that the time is at hand when some wise provision for the employment and support of discharged and disabled soldiers must be had, or a large class of mendicants will have established their necessity and their right to live upon the charity of the people. At the present moment the Government has relieved the immediate pressure of the question by forming an Invalid Corps for service in hospitals and garrisons; but the time is perhaps near when the Sanitary Commission, once more called upon by the voice of the people, must charge itself with a duty left to it by the recoil of war. This is its work in the distant future; but thought and action upon it must not be delayed too long, or the evils to be averted will be upon us. It is of the utmost consequence to begin now to create a public opinion, which shall compel the adoption of the wisest policy in municipal and State governments, with respect to disabled soldiers, so as to discourage all favor to mendicity, all allowance of exceptional license to men who have been soldiers, all disposition of invalids to throw themselves, any further than is inevitable, on the support and protection of society.

This subject is one on which we would fain pause to dwell at length; but our limits will not allow it. A few, however, of the leading thoughts connected with it may be briefly given.

First: The first obvious law of public opinion should be to deal with the question according to the nature and principles of the American people; to encourage and save the spirit of independence; to preserve the self-respect and the homely graces and virtues of the people, on which all the real dignity and strength of the nation rest.

Secondly: To make the subject a National and not a State question. A war against State pretensions should not end without strengthening in every way the Federal influence. This war is a struggle for *national* existence; we have found a *national* heart and life and body. Now let us cherish it.

Thirdly: To avoid the danger of interfering with natural laws — a thing not to be tolerated in our young and healthy country — by any scheme of herding the invalids of war in public institutions. Such schemes would strike a blow at domestic order and the sacredness of home affections, whilst they would take from the soldier that spirit of independence which is his birthright and his safety. We do not want a vast network of Soldiers' Poor-houses scattered through the land, in which these brave fellows will languish away dull, idle, and wretched lives. But we want — and this is the last general idea which shall be stated here: we want —

Fourthly: An endeavor to promote the healthy absorption of the invalid class into their own homes, and into the ordinary industry of the country; there to live and labor according to their remaining strength,— sustained, honored, and blessed by their own kindred and community.

The Sanitary Commission, deeply impressed with the importance of this subject, is spending thought and study upon it. For the purposes of instruction, it has induced Mr. Stephen H. Perkins, of Boston, to prepare, during a recent visit abroad, a report on the pension systems and invalid hospitals on the continent of Europe. This report has been a most painstaking work, and is of great and lasting value. Associate members of the Commission are also engaged in studying the question in its American relations and bearings.

In November, 1862, the Hospital Directory, already alluded to, (page 95,) was complete for the hospitals in the District of Columbia, and the total number of names registered was 19,084. Encouraged by the good attained, the business was enlarged, until in June, 1863, the Directory embraced the sick and wounded soldiers in every general hospital throughout the land, — in all 233 hospitals. The number of names on record, after the system was fully established, was 215,221.

The total number of inquiries received in a period of six months for the Washington Office, four months for the Western Office, and ten weeks for the New York and Philadelphia Branches, was 9494. Of these inquiries no record is kept, but that of the simple fact, "One question, — one answer"; and what a history of loss and misery and wild joy is hidden beneath that business record!

A letter comes inquiring for two nephews; and closes with the assertion, "These are two out of fourteen nephews that I have no account of since the battle of Fredericksburg." Of the two thus inquired for, one was found in hospital; of the other no tidings were received.

A mother expresses "unceasing gratitude" for the information that her son is "doing well." A father, who enters the office with hopeful, trembling inquiry, sinks with audible gasp into a chair on receiving the announcement, from which there is no escape, that his son is lost to him and to the country; while another evinces almost equal emotion on being told that his boy is in the Craven Hospital.

A young wife is sent to the Office to obtain a recommendation for a pass to visit her husband within the lines of the Army. She is impatient at the "senseless delay" of consulting the records for his name; she "*knows* he is in Nashville;—please write the pass at once." "Are you sure he is there?" "Yes," impatiently. "You would have no objection to meet him *here?*" "You are playing with me, sir; give me the pass." "You do not want it. Here are directions by which you will find your husband in the next street." If an accident had not brought her to the office, she would have taken a painful and expensive journey, and would, probably, have missed him, after all.

Sometimes it needs a strong faith in the positive good done by this agency to endure the sight of what it reveals. Only a few weeks since, a soldier in hospital at Nashville wrote to his wife that he was very sick, and she must come to him. Two days later he was transferred to Louisville, but his letter advising her of the change was lost. It did not reach her. So she leaves home; passes one night in Louisville, and goes to Nashville; there she learns that he has left. She returns only to find that he died at midnight, on the very night which she had passed in that city. Had she gone to the Directory *there*, she might have once held him, still living, in her arms.

An old, old man enters the office. He has travelled from Northern Ohio to meet his son in Louisville. He has been told to inquire at the Sanitary Commission Rooms for direction to the hospital which contains him. While the clerk turns to the book, he chats of his son, of home, and of the different articles in his carpet-bag, put in, he tells them, by the mother and sisters at home. He is all animation and happy confidence. He seems at the very door of the realization of his hope. The record is brought, —"Died" that very morning. One question,— one answer!

The cost of keeping up this Directory is about $1500 a month, and the Sanitary Commission has lately discussed the propriety of discontinuing it on the ground of expense. But for the present it cannot bring itself to stop a work which is helping tens of thousands to find their lost ones, and spares them cost, suffering, and the bitterness of suspense.

## CONCLUSION.

The first question that we ask as our story closes, and the deeds of the Commission lie mapped before us, is one about its supplies, — What have really been its means for its work?

Some of us, perhaps, have said, in words or in thought, The Commission is making constant appeals: what can it do with all it gets? But now that we have had a glimpse of its work, are we not inclined to change the question, and ask, — Has it really had supplies *enough* to carry on these gigantic operations? How has it done *so much?*

It can be said in reply that the gratitude of the Sanitary Commission towards the People — which has called it into existence, given it the breath of life, and never ceased to pour into it both strength and power — is not to be expressed in words. But it cannot be said that the Sanitary Commission has never been pinched nor hindered in its work by the want of means. It cannot be said that the Sanitary Commission has done all it might have done. Do we wonder, therefore, that, as it stood on many a battle-field, and saw anguish that it could not reach, death that it could not stay, it has turned in anxious and burning appeals towards the country? For the most part, those appeals have been answered. Yet it would not be the truth which this book aims to tell, if the fact were withheld that the Sanitary Commission is in want of means. Our purpose, however, is with the past, and we turn back to tell, with gratitude, all that which *has been done.*

In a recent letter to the Branches from the Assistant Secretary, Mr. Bloor, the following particulars are given, which will very properly open what can here be said upon the subject:—

"In reviewing our labors in the past, and anticipating our prospects for the future, it cannot fail to afford matter of remark and congratulation, to realize the extraordinary support and confidence which has been extended to the Commission, and through it to the national cause, by the loyal women of the country. For, while money has been freely provided for its treasury by the rich men of the country, from the Pacific to the Atlantic coast, the articles of clothing, and the delicacies in the way of food, provided by the women,—rich and poor alike,—have tenfold exceeded, in cash value, the donations of the former. And it will perhaps encourage your correspondents to know, what I can assure them is the truth, that, of some twenty thousand cases of invoiced goods, some of them containing articles valued at several hundreds of dollars, which have been forwarded to *this* depot of the Commission, (Washington,) not more than one or two have failed to reach us; and it may also be satisfactory to know, that the proportion of money expenditure made by the Commission for the various purposes of the remuneration of its *employés*, rents, freight, postage, &c., and all other incidental outlays, does not amount to more than three per cent. on the cash value of the distributions made, through its agency, to the soldiers of the country. The losses by accident or casualties of war have been so trifling as scarcely to be named. With regard to the losses by dishonesty of agents, surgeons, stewards, nurses, and soldiers, I can only say that every charge of this kind made to this office has been followed up, and has, in every instance, fallen through at one step or another of the investigation."

To arrive at an exact estimate of the value of the goods which have been contributed to the Commission since its organization, would require more material than is available or necessary for a sketch like this. But an approximate estimate has been made, in a late report of the Assistant Secretary, from which it can be stated that the gifts of the women of the country, made through the Sanitary Commission, exceed in value the sum of $7,000,000. Every woman who reads this book, thinking, perhaps, how little she has done for the Commission, sees here the vast result she has aided to obtain.

There is another source of generous assistance which must not pass unrecorded; namely, the material aid given to the Commission by many of the business firms and companies with which, in various ways, it comes in contact. Many of the express companies, both East and West, carry its goods either free of charge or at reduced rates, and the telegraph is free to its use all over the land. Its name is a password to constant generosity of this kind. And even this book owes much to the liberality of its publishers, — especially to that of Mr. Augustus Flagg, a member of the firm; to whom is owing the fact that its entire profits go to the treasury of the Sanitary Commission.

The whole amount, in money, received by the Treasurer of the Sanitary Commission, from its organization to the 1st of October, 1863, amounts to $857,715.33; of this sum $501,101 was received from California. For the six months ending October 1st, 1863, the receipts were $115,752.42. The disbursements for the same period were $281,099.15.

It is clear, therefore, that fresh moneyed strength must be given to the Commission, or its work *must be cut down.* This question is, perhaps, the heaviest weight upon the minds of the Commission; for, although the supplies have, of late, diminished sensibly, it is felt that *they* are always comparatively secure: but without the money to place them where they are needed, even *they* will prove comparatively inefficient, and become reduced in actual value.

16

From this subject we turn to one which stands, perhaps, in juxtaposition to it, in the minds of many; namely, to complaints against the Sanitary Commission, its administration, its agents, and its use of the public gifts, which are heard from time to time. This is a subject which the Sanitary Commission declines to enter upon controversially. In some few cases, a brief reply has been made; but, as a rule, it has contented itself with asking that all complaints be brought to it for temperate examination, and, if need be, for correction. Many of them have proved to be unfounded; many more could never be induced to come into the daylight of investigation. There is one class of complaint, however, which is incapable either of proof or of refutation; but as the writer claims to have the ability of giving it its true answer, it will be mentioned here.

A painful and anxious note was lately received at the central office, in Washington, from a lady deeply engaged in one of its branches, enclosing a letter from the secretary of an auxiliary society. The letter was as follows: —

"Much commotion is caused here by the return of soldiers who are feeble, who have got a furlough for ill health. They report great neglect in the hospitals. One gentleman in particular, — one of our townsmen, a man whose good word goes a great way — *is believed*, in short. He says the sick and wounded *do not get* the luxuries and delicacies sent to them, and designed by the donors expressly for them. He was sick in a hospital in Washington, and would have died had he stayed there. He has perfect confidence in the surgeon in charge, but distrusts the steward. He says, sick as they were, they never saw a delicacy. A sick man, getting well, needs something besides a piece of salt pork and dry bread for his dinner. . . . . . All the luxuries he saw, were, as he passed through the steward's room, and found his table loaded with luxuries, jellies, dried fruits, &c. Knowing his wife, at home, engaged in the preparation of these things for the sick and wounded, he thought he might have chanced to get something from her hands (comforting thought to the sick soldier!) . . . . .

" Now, I ask, *where were* all the delicacies designed for the sick? Where did that steward get so much for his own table? There are some places, near here, which have done nobly, and are now doing nothing, because of these things. . . . . . We have some that won't do anything, for the reason above; some that are willing to do, even if the poor soldier gets only half; others who mean to send what they have to give elsewhere. I have battled these reports so long that it is folly to do so any more." . . . . .

It is certainly a coincidence that a few days before the lady of the branch enclosed this letter to the central office, her mother was at a hospital where the writer was in charge of a department. This lady requested the writer to obtain for her some of the "Mess-Hall diet," that she might herself judge if it was good. An orderly was despatched over the way to the Mess Hall, where the men were at dinner. When the diet was brought, she ate it with enjoyment and praise, and, in fact, dined upon it. Whilst she was eating it, the writer was called out to speak to a patient: "If you please, ma'am," said he, "*do* give me an order for something out of the diet-kitchens; I can't eat such stuff as we had in the Mess Hall to-day." That patient was a perfectly conscientious, reliable man, who will leave the hospital under the idea that the food was execrable.

In the same hospital, on a regularly recurring day, a certain stew was prepared for dinner. It was thoroughly good, and better than anything that appeared on the table of any of the officers of the post. When the day for it came round, the detail of men appointed to draw the extra and special diet would say to the woman in charge of the kitchen: "What is it to-day? Wednesday — S-t-e-w," — (and we all know how the intonation can be made to rhyme with "eugh!" and "pugh!") "then give us the tea and the pudding, for our men won't eat *that*." And, true enough, they would actually go without it.

In this lies the real answer to the letter which

we have quoted. So long as our men are brought up on a diet of pies and "saace," and pork and beans, so long will they hate stews and soups; and, alas! so long as they are convalescents in hospital, so long will they be looking about them for causes of discontent, of which the diet is the most obvious and the most fertile.*

Hospital stewards have always had a bad name, partly because they have done something to deserve it; but the devil is not so black as he is painted. Their position lays them open to many charges which are utterly unjust. They give to the Sanitary Commission an unconscious testimony that, in the main, they are honest, by the simple fact that the requisitions for the Commission stores vary with the condition and number of patients. With two exceptions, during a period of some months, the demand for hospital delicacies in the hospitals in the District of Columbia corresponded well with the number of very sick. Were the stewards in the habit, so often asserted, of using the good things of the Commission for their own benefit, it is reasonable to suppose that their greed for them would have been as strong at one time as at another.

* The writer is not to be understood as denying the *existence* of neglect of men in hospital. This statement is made to show that complaints of such neglect must be taken with great caution; for they are frequently made unjustly by men who are in other respects worthy of belief.

In general hospitals, the hospital fund *ought* to leave but little for the Commission to do; and this has been the case, for the last six months, in the hospitals in Washington. A current supply of certain things is, however, *always* needed even here, and experience and judgment alone can know the measure of the economy which can be practised. As a general thing, the stores of the Commission are issued through the channel of the women-nurses; but sometimes they go for issue into the hands of the surgeons in charge, most of whom, let who will say to the contrary, take a true and conscientious interest in the welfare of those under their care.

And here a few words may be said on the work that might — we dare to say that *should* — belong to women in general hospitals. If women comprehended their true work, and had the patience to show that they do so comprehend it, the deep prejudice against them, in the minds of the army surgeons, would be removed. Indeed, it has been removed in many instances. But women have not, as a general thing, seen their place or their duty. It is hard, perhaps, to do so. It is hard to realize that even benevolence must be obedient. And it is for this reason that the Sisters of Mercy, so far, have been preferred as nurses by the surgeons of the Army. It could, however, be shown that the work of women belonging in the world would be more useful than even the work of the Sisters, if such women would learn their true place. And if they learned it, and if they kept to it, the result would be that in the end they would have all the power of benevolence that even they would ask. For here it may be said, in deep conviction of its truth, that the surgeons of the Army of all grades are, as a general thing, desirous of doing well by those under their charge; — they are conscientious and faithful men. It is believed, and is, perhaps, capable of proof, that if a lady, (by which is meant a gentlewoman holding a certain social position,) and one fitted for the work, could be placed in charge of what may be called the Woman's Department in a hospital, — namely, the nursing of the very sick men, the special diet and the linen department, with a body of nurses under her charge, — a benefit to the hospital would follow, and the surgeons, far from complaining of it, would in the end welcome it with sincerity. If a system like this could obtain in Washington, — these ladies being in the service of the Government, yet allied to the Sanitary Commission, — a result would be reached which would remove all ground of complaint so far as the sick men and the stores are concerned. As for the convalescents, we fear they must always be expected to grumble.

And so, after all is said, there will be many who will continue to judge of the Sanitary Commission by what returning soldiers say of it; not reflecting that the well men of the Army have hitherto known comparatively little of it. The receipt of a box of stale pound-cake or mouldy gingerbread, admirably adapted to fill the hospitals with sick men, occasions much livelier sentiments of grateful regard than whole car-loads of hospital stores. To be sure, all this is changing. Now, when you visit a regiment to get discharge-papers rectified, or call a circle round you to teach them how to benefit by the Commission as they go home furloughed or discharged, or to learn from them, for friends at home, the fate of some missing comrade, the question comes into their mind, " Who is it that cares enough for us to do this? " But, as a general thing, the well men have known but little of the Commission, and even the sick man cannot always know from whose hand comes the pillow that bears his weary head, and the wine or food that revives him.*

* Not long since, Mr. Knapp, then Special Relief Agent, met a man who was saying, " For his part, he had never received anything, and he had never *seen* anything from the Sanitary Commission." Mr. Knapp eyed him a moment, and then said, " Now, my man, come with me, and let me examine the clothes you have on." As article after article came off, down to the socks, each was found to bear the printed stamp, " U. S. Sanitary Commission." The man did not mean to be untruthful, but — he could not read.

The reader must not suppose, however, from what is here said (and said to one point only) that the men who have been succored are ungrateful. Far, very far from it. See Appendix L.

It seems scarcely necessary to attempt to show in words that the Sanitary Commission has produced results which, in their several degrees, great and small, have served the soldier, the war, the country, and mankind. If the facts cannot show it, what words can do so? There is, however, one of its results, and that the most important, to which the story has made not the smallest allusion.

When the war began, the requirements of law provided that the senior surgeon of the Army should be the Surgeon-General: an arrangement that was liable to result in placing at that post an officer whose chief qualification for its varied duties of large responsibility was a good constitution, carefully preserved. There was no bureau of medical inspection established by law, nor any legal requirement in this corps for its maintenance. There was little incentive, aside from natural taste, considerations of pride, or conscientious impulse, to professional improvement, or especially zealous devotion to duty. Promotion, being by seniority of service, could not follow as a result of high qualification, nor, after the junior officer had passed his examination for a surgeoncy at the end of five years' service, was it retarded by incompetence or sloth. The tendencies of the system repressed the promptings of professional ambition, and favored contentment in the dry path of old routine.

It was no merit of the *system* that so many

medical officers rose above its debilitating influences, and made for themselves and for their corps a reputation going far to justify, by scientific attainments as well as by manly and honorable bearing, the designation once applied to them by an officer of another staff, — "the *corps d'élite* of the Army." The Commission felt that such a system was inadequate to the demands of the country, — that the highest talent and the most interested devotion should be given to the discharge of the multiform duties of the Medical Bureau. It urged its views upon the President, the Secretary of War, and upon Congress; and brought to bear on legislators the organized sentiment of thoughtful men throughout the country. It met the objections of Prescription and Routine, and pointed out a more excellent way than ever their feet had trodden. By the influence of public opinion, — moulded and organized and directed by the Sanitary Commission, it is not too much to say, — Congress, in April, 1862, passed a bill, which, approved by the President, became law on the 16th of that month, and which introduced new features of the greatest value into the organization of the Medical Bureau.

Besides increasing the number of officers in the lower grades, it added an Assistant Surgeon-General and a Medical Inspector-General, with the rank of colonel respectively; eight medical inspectors, ranking as lieutenant-colonels; and provided that these officers — as well as the Surgeon-General, who ranks as a Brigadier-General — should be hereafter *selected* for merit and eminent qualification from the whole number of medical officers in service, whether of the regular or volunteer army.

A striking illustration of what was to be expected from the new law was given nine days later, when the President commissioned Assistant-Surgeon William A. Hammond to be Surgeon-General of the Army. It is well known that the Sanitary Commission urged this appointment, but not on personal grounds; for only one of its members had ever seen him when their decision was reached that this would be the best appointment possible. But they presented his claims to the President and Cabinet, from his well-known devotion to science, his energy and executive ability, his comprehensive view of the great questions sure to arise in the administration of his office, and his evident readiness to meet boldly great responsibilities. His administration has justified the selection. He has introduced liberality and promptness into the purveying department of his bureau. He has greatly enlarged the supply table; for old hotels and seminaries, he has substituted airy and ample hospital buildings, conformable to improved architectural models; he has raised, by providing more rigid examinations, the scientific standard for admission into the army medical service; he has sought legislation to enlarge the hospital fund, to improve the system of nursing, to provide for more extended inspection of camps, barracks, hospitals, transports, and stores; to establish a legalized and humane system of ambulance, and to render, by other enactments, the corps more efficient and the system more complete.

By these efforts, by the just exercise of discipline, by his encouragement to scientific investigation, his fostering of army medical societies, his establishment of a museum of pathology, and his detail of accomplished members of the medical staff to write the medical and surgical history of the war, he has kindled afresh in the medical service a zeal and an *ésprit de corps* which can hardly fail to insure an enthusiasm noble in its aims, and a scientific progress fertile in its results. It is barely eighteen months since the Medical Bureau was fully reorganized by the President, and since its corps of Medical Inspectors — the aids of its Chief in securing an exact knowledge of the field before him — was confirmed by the Senate. But the experience of these months indicates the increasing gain likely to accrue to science from this measure of reform. For, under such guidance, reform is not likely to go backward.

It is obvious, however, that the working of this law has borne painfully upon the feelings of individuals, and we trust that we may be suffered to say, with great respect for the manly virtues of such men, that perhaps no greater tribute of patriotism has been given to the country than that of the spirit with which these officers have seen younger men called into their places by the exigencies of active war.

The Sanitary Commission is a great teacher: teaching many the true use of their faculties; teaching others that they have faculties to use, and giving to all the education of opportunity. Truly it is "a liberal education" — guiding the national instincts; showing the value of order, and the dignity of work; opening the hearts of men and women in unselfish trust towards each other; teaching the true principles of the true equality of human nature. But this book has ill-conveyed an essential truth if it has not shown that the life of the Commission sprang from the nation, and that it becomes a teacher because the instincts of the nation have risen up and demanded to be taught and moulded.

The true strength and glory of a free people lies not in its politicians, orators, poets, and historians, but in the faithful instinct, courage, and intelligence of the unnamed and unnamable millions; — showing a gradual lifting up, not of man as an individual, but of human nature in its likeness to God. From its hidden life this instinct has been roused by the war into a visible existence. Perhaps its purest voice is uttered through the Sanitary Commission, where Mercy and Patriotism speak and act together, and Self *is not*. The sound of this voice comes back like an echo to the nation, bearing the lessons taught by the performance of good deeds. *Thus* the Commission becomes a teacher; *thus* it reaches, as perhaps nothing else can reach, into the hearts of the men and women of our country. Nor does its work end here. It has within it the means for a national education of ideas as well as of instincts. This, however, is for time and not for prophecy to show.

And here this sketch must close. Its main object has been to show certain facts, and not to appeal directly to the reader; but it is simply impossible to lay down the pen and not say, from the depths of a tried conviction — "Friends! let us give to this Commission all that we have to give of talent and strength and money; for life will never give us such an opportunity again!"

This book may have shown — as it professed to do — that the Sanitary Commission has justified the confidence of the people, but there are some things which it cannot show nor say. They are said elsewhere; and with those words, deeply felt and valued by the Sanitary Commission, this little book shall end: —

"If pure benevolence was ever organized and utilized into beneficence, the name of the institution is the Sanitary Commission. It is a standing answer to Samson's riddle: 'Out of the strong came forth sweetness.' Out of the very depths of the agony of this cruel and bloody war springs this beautiful system, built of the noblest and divinest attributes of the human soul. Amidst all the heroism of daring and enduring which this war has developed, — amidst all the magnanimity of which it has shown the race capable, the daring, the endurance, the greatness of soul which have been discovered among the men and women who have given their lives to this work, shine as brightly as any on the battle-field — in some respects even more brightly. They have not the bray of trumpets nor the clash of swords to rouse enthusiasm, nor will the land ever resound with their victories. Theirs is the dark and painful side, — the menial and hidden side; but it is made light and lovely by the spirit that shines in and through it all. Glimpses of this agency are familiar to our people; but not till the history of its inception, progress, and results is calmly and adequately written out and spread before the public, will any idea be formed of the magnitude and importance of the work which it has done. Nor even then. Never, till every soldier whose last moments it has soothed, till every soldier whose flickering life it has gently steadied into continuance, whose waning reason it has softly lulled into quiet, whose chilled blood it has warmed into healthful play, whose failing frame it has nourished into strength, whose fainting heart it has comforted with sympathy, — never, until every full soul has poured out its story of gratitude and thanksgiving, will the record be complete; but long before that time, ever since the moment that its helping hand was first held forth, comes the Blessed Voice, 'Inasmuch as ye have done it unto one of the least of these my brethren, ye have done it unto me.'

"An institution asking of Government only permission to live and opportunity to work, planting itself firmly and squarely on the generosity of the people, subsisting solely by their free-will offerings, it is a noble monument of the intelligence, the munificence, and the efficiency of a free people, and of the alacrity with which it responds when the right chord is rightly touched.

. . . . . . . . .

"The blessings of thousands who were ready to perish, and of tens of thousands who love their country and their kind, rest upon those who originated, and those who sustain, this noble work. Let the people's heart never faint and its hand never weary; but let it, of its abundance, give to this Commission full measure, pressed down, shaken together, and running over, that, wherever the red trail of war is seen, its divine footsteps may follow; that, wherever the red hand of war is lifted to wound, its white hand may be lifted to heal; that its work may never cease until it is assumed by a great Christian government, or until peace once more reigns throughout the land. And even then, gratitude for its service, and joy in its glory, shall never die out of the hearts of the American people."

# APPENDIX.

## APPENDIX A.

At the last session of the United States Sanitary Commission, Oct. 9, 1863, the following action was taken on the resignation of Mr. Olmsted: —

The President communicated the previously announced resignation of Mr. Olmsted as General Secretary and as a member of the Commission, and offered resolutions expressive of the feeling of the Commission, viz: —

*Resolved,* That this Board accepts the resignation of Fred. Law Olmsted, as General Secretary, with profound regret.

*Resolved,* That, from the beginning of our enterprise, the organizing genius of Mr. Olmsted, trained by rich experience in other large and successful undertakings, has been a chief source of whatever merit has characterized the operations of the Sanitary Commission; and that we find our consolation in the loss of his personal services in the fact that his plans and ideas are so ineffaceably stamped on our work, that we shall continue to enjoy the benefit of his talents and the inspiration of his character as long as the Commission lasts.

*Resolved,* That these resolutions be transmitted to Mr. Olmsted, with a letter expressive of our warm personal attachment, and an earnest expression of our wish that he will withdraw his resignation as a member of the Board.

The resolutions were adopted, and the President was requested to prepare the letter referred to.

*(Copied from the Minutes of the fourteenth Session United States Sanitary Commission.)*

The officers of the United States Sanitary Commission are now as follows: —

| | |
|---|---|
| H. W. Bellows, D. D. | President. |
| A. D. Bache, LL. D. | Vice-President. |
| George T. Strong, Esq. | Treasurer. |

| | |
|---|---|
| J. Foster Jenkins, M. D. | General Secretary. |
| J. S. Newberry, M. D. | Associate Sec'y for Dep't of the West. |
| F. N. Knapp | " " " " East. |
| J. H. Douglas | Asso. Sec'y, and Chief of Inspection. |
| A. J. Bloor | Assistant Secretary. |
| R. T. Thorne | " " |
| E. B. Elliot | Actuary. |
| John Bowne | Accountant, and Superintendent Hospital Directory. |

## STAFF OF INSPECTION.

| | |
|---|---|
| Dr. H. G. Clark | Special Inspection of Hospitals. |
| Dr. L. H. Steiner | Inspector Army of the Potomac. |
| Dr. Gordon Winslow | " at Gettysburg. |
| Dr. George L. Andrew | " Louisville. |
| Dr. A. N. Reed | " Army of the Cumberland. |
| Dr. George A. Blake | " Department of the Gulf. |
| Dr. H. A. Warriner | " Army of the Tennessee. |
| Dr. E. A. Crane | " Department of the South. |
| Dr. J. W. Page | " Department of N. Carolina. |
| Dr. A. L. Castleman | " Army of the Cumberland. |
| Dr. —— Fithian | " Army of the Tennessee. |
| Dr. C. W. Brink | " at Washington. |
| Dr. T. B. Smith | " and Pension Examiner. |
| Dr. J. S. Nichols | " on detached duty. |

| | |
|---|---|
| Dr. Alex. McDonald....... | Inspector Army of the Potomac. |
| Dr. Wm. F. Swalm......... | " " " " |
| Dr. M. M. Marsh........... | " " in South Carolina. |

In addition to the above, the roster of the Commission shows that there are now —

| | | | |
|---|---|---|---|
| Clerks, in all Departments.... | 44 | Surgeons.................... | 2 |
| Relief Agents................ | 25 | Hospital Visitors and Canvassing Agents.......... | 6 |
| Storekeepers................. | 21 | Porters, Watchmen, &c...... | 12 |
| Superintendents of Homes.... | 10 | Cooks, Laundresses, Servants, &c................ | 27 |
| Matrons...................... | 6 | Wagon-drivers.............. | 7 |
| Nurses....................... | 5 | | |
| Messengers................... | 4 | | |

---

# APPENDIX B.

## CIRCULAR LETTER.

*To the Presidents and Officers of the various Life Insurance Companies of the United States.*

Gentlemen: — You are directly and largely interested in the lives of our brave soldiers, so many of whom are insured in your several offices. Their principal danger comes, as you are well aware, not from the force of the enemy, but from the ravages of those diseases always active in camps and fortresses, and especially so among inexperienced volunteer troops suddenly subjected to change of climate, to unusual heat, and to great exposure. The officers in charge of the principal portion of these lives are brave, intelligent men, ready to shed their blood for the liberties of the country; but they are without experience in the care of their soldiers, and, with the best intentions, must fail, if not supported by extraneous efforts and experience, in saving them from pestilence and destruction in a ratio too fearful to name. In view of the enormous responsibility thrown by extraordinary events upon the Medical Bureau, and at the urgent instance of medical men at large, a Sanitary Commission has been appointed by the Government of the United States, to advise the War Department and the Medical Bureau of the most efficient way of preventing disease among the troops, and warding off general pestilence and rapid decimation, and to coöperate with them in their efforts to this end. Reasonable fears exist, that, unless the most energetic efforts are made, one half our whole volunteer force may not survive the exposures of the next four months. This Commission is now in full organization, and ready to go to work. It wants money. It needs twenty thousand dollars in hand to proceed with vigor to its sublimely important work. It has declined asking or receiving money from the Government, for fear it might thus forfeit its independent position, and lose in moral strength what it gained by government patronage. If the Government supported it, its members would be appointed by the Government, and acquire a political character, or be chosen not for their competency to the work, but from local and partisan reasons. We choose, then, to depend as long and as far as we can on the support of the public. And we look to the Life Insurance Companies, whose intelligent acquaintance with vital statistics constitutes them the proper and the readiest judges of the necessity of such a Commission, to give the first indorsement to our enterprise by generous donations, — the best proof they can afford the public of the solid claim we have on the liberality of the rich, the patriotic, and the humane.

We beg to remind you, moreover, that even those Life Insurance Companies which have no war risks outstanding are directly and deeply interested in promoting the objects of this Commission. For no fact in medical history is better established than this, that diseases breaking out among soldiers in camp or garrison, for the want of prudent sanitary measures, and extending among them on any considerable scale, are soon shared by the community at large. The mere presence in any country of an army extensively infected, is a centre of poison to its whole people. If pestilence do not break out (as it commonly does), ordinary maladies assume a malignant and unmanageable type, and the general ratio of mortality is heightened in a fearful degree.

Our case is urgent, and every hour's delay is a serious blow to our success. We ask for prompt, nay, for immediate action. We wish to send skilled agents to every point of danger, — men armed with the influence and authority of the Sanitary Commission, — to put all general officers and all medical men, the captains and all other responsible persons, whether in camps or fortresses, upon their guard; to arouse an unusual attention to the subject of good cooking, regular meals, absolute cleanliness, proper ventilation, and the use of prophylactics. An examination of the papers accompanying this appeal will show you the ampleness of our powers, and the vigor and completeness of our machinery. We can do a vast work in a short time, if we have abundant means. Fifty thousand dollars would, we seriously think, enable us to save fifty thousand lives. Can there be any hesitation in furnishing such a sum for such a vast and holy purpose? And ought not, must not, your Life Insurance Companies lead boldly and generously in this imperative duty? We are willing to give our time, our thoughts, our energies, and whatever of skill, experience, and knowledge we may possess, to this work; but we look to you and to the wealth of our cities to supply us with the money required to effect the beneficent objects proposed by the Sanitary Commission.

Very respectfully and fraternally yours,

HENRY W. BELLOWS, *President.*
ALEX. D. BACHE.
WM. H. VAN BUREN, M. D.
WOLCOTT GIBBS, M. D.
C. R. AGNEW, M. D.
JOHN S. NEWBERRY, M. D. (Cleveland.)
FRED. LAW OLMSTED.
GEO. T. STRONG, *Treasurer.*
ELISHA HARRIS, M. D., *Cor. Sec'y.*

SANITARY COMMISSION,
(In Session in New York,)
*June* 21, 1861.

## CIRCULAR ASKING CONTRIBUTIONS.

SANITARY COMMISSION, WASHINGTON, D. C.,
TREASURY BUILDING, *June* 22, 1861.

SIR: — The Sanitary Commission just ordered by the United States Government has a field of labor open to it of vast importance and immense urgency. The lives of 250,000 troops, four times more endangered from disease than from the casualties of war, are now hanging in the scales; and whether fifty per cent. of them are carried off by dysentery, fever, and cholera, in the course of the next four months, or whether they are maintained at what, under the best condition, is the double risk of life, depends, under God, upon the most efficient application of sanitary science to their protection. In the sudden and enormous responsibility thrown upon the Government, the usual medical dependence is so strained that extraordinary means are necessary to meet the case. Under these circumstances, our Commission, with special power and duties, has been brought into existence. To avoid political jealousies, and secure a board of harmonious and high-toned advisers, it has been thought desirable to derive the support of the Commission from the public, rather than the Government. The Commissioners freely give their time, experience, and labor to the country. But they must keep active agents at numerous points constantly and vigilantly at work, in urging the preventive measures on which they depend for success; and this involves a large expenditure of money. It is supposed that fifty thousand dollars could be expended with the greatest advantage during the present year in the work of the Commission, and that every single dollar so spent would save one life. Every dollar less than this placed at the disposal of the Commission must be considered as the needless exposure and probable loss of a life! It is hoped that the character and standing of the Commissioners is the only warrant the public will require for their energetic and faithful performance of the duties assigned them. Under these circumstances, the undersigned, members of the Sanitary Commission now in session in New York, ask the immediate contributions of the men of wealth in as generous a measure as the greatness of the interest at stake and the urgency of the case may prompt their humane hearts and forelooking minds.

It is hardly necessary to suggest that every soldier who survives the exposure of the next four months will be worth, for military purposes, two fresh recruits; that every man lost by neglect makes a complaining family, and forms a ground of unpopularity for the war; that every sick man deprives the ranks of one or two well men detailed to take care of him; that pestilence will demoralize and frighten those whom armed enemies cannot scare; that the men now in the field are the flower of the nation; that their places cannot be filled, either at home or in the ranks; and that the economical, the humane, the patriotic, the successful conduct of this war, and its speedy termination, is now more dependent on the *health* of the troops than any and all other conditions combined.

Help us, then, dear sir, to do this work, for which our machinery is now complete! Help us generously; help us at once!

In the name of God, humanity, and our country!

Yours, fraternally,

HENRY W. BELLOWS, D. D.
A. D. BACHE, LL. D.
ELISHA HARRIS, M. D.

---

## APPENDIX C.

A SERIES OF SURGICAL AND MEDICAL MONOGRAPHS, PREPARED AND PRINTED BY THE UNITED STATES SANITARY COMMISSION.

Introductory Essay. Valentine Mott, D. D.

Advice as to Camping. Issued by the British Government Sanitary Commission.

A. Report on Military Hygiene and Therapeutics.
B. Directions to Army Surgeons on the Battle-field. By G. J. Guthrie, Surgeon-General to the British Forces during the Crimean War (reprinted by United States Sanitary Commission).
C. Rules for preserving the Health of the Soldier.
D. Quinine as a Prophylactic against Malarious Diseases.
E. Report on the Value of Vaccination in Armies.
F. Report on Amputations.
G. Report on Amputations through the Foot and at the Ankle-joint.
H. Report on Venereal Diseases.
J. Report on Pneumonia.
K. Report on Continued Fevers.
L. Report on Excision of Joints for traumatic Cause.
M. Report on Dysentery.
N. Report on Scurvy.
O. Report on the Treatment of Fractures in Military Surgery.
P. Report on the Nature and Treatment of Miasmatic Fevers.
Q. Report on the Nature and Treatment of Yellow Fever.

# APPENDIX D.

## UNITED STATES SANITARY COMMISSION.

*List of the Special Inspectors of the General Hospitals of the Army, Sept. 1, 1862, to May 1, 1863.*

Henry G. Clark, M. D., Surgeon Massachusetts General Hospital, &c., Inspector-in-chief.

Abbott, S. L., M. D., Mass. Gen. Hospital ....... Boston.
Armor, S. G., M. D., Prof. University, Mich...... Ann Arbor.
Ayer, James, M. D. ........................... Boston.
Bell, John, M. D. ............................ Philadelphia.
Bell, Theod. S., M. D., Prof. Theor. and Pract. Univ. ........................... Louisville.
Bemis, Charles V., M. D. ...................... Medford, Mass.
Borland, J. N., M. D. ......................... Boston.
Bowditch, H. I., M. D., Phys. Mass. Gen. Hosp... Boston.
Brinsmade, T. C., M. D. ....................... Troy, N. Y.
Buck, Gurdon, M. D., Surgeon N. Y. Hosp...... New York.
Buckingham, C. E., M. D., Consulting Physician City of Boston ....................... Boston.
Cabot, S., Jr., M. D., Surg. Mass. Gen. Hosp..... Boston.
Coale, W. E., M. D. ........................... Boston.
Cogswell, M. F., M. D. ........................ Albany.
Comegys, C. G., M. D. ........................ Cincinnati.
Draper, John W., M. D., Prof. Chem. Univ. N. Y. . New York.
Ellis, Calvin, M. D., Pathol., &c., Mass. Gen. Hospital ........................... Boston.
Flint, Joshua B., M. D., Prof. Clinical Surgery, Univ. ........................... Louisville.
Foster, S. Conant, M. D. ...................... New York.
Fowler, Edmond, M. D. ........................ Montgomery, Ala.
Gay, George H., M. D., Surg. Mass. Gen. Hosp... Boston.
Gould, A. A., M. D., Phys. Mass. Gen. Hosp. .... Boston.
Gunn, Moses, M. D., Prof. Surgery, Univ., Mich.. Detroit.
Hodges, R. M., M. D., Surg. Mass. Gen. Hosp..... Boston.
Homans, John, M. D., Ex-Pres. Mass. Med. Soc. . Boston.
Hun, Thomas, M. D. ........................... Albany.
Hunt, William, M. D. ......................... Philadelphia.
Jackson, J. B. S., M. D., Prof. Morb. Anat. Mass. Med. Coll., &c. ........................ Boston.

Jacobi, A., M. D., Prof. Infant. Path., &c., Med. Coll.......................................New York.
Jarvis, Edward, M. D., Member of American Statistical Society...............................Boston.
Johnson, H. A., M. D., Prof. Physiol. and Histol. Univ. Lind...............................Chicago.
Judkins, David, M. D.........................Cincinnati.
Krackowizer, E., M. D.........................New York.
Lee, Charles A., M. D., Prof. Mat. Med. Med. Sch. of Maine...............................Peekskill.
Leonard, F. B., M. D...........................Lansingberg.
Lewis, Winslow, M. D., Consult. Surg. Mass. Gen. Hospital...................................Boston.
March, Alden, M. D., Prof. Surgery Med. Coll....Albany.
Mendenhall, G., M. D.........................Cincinnati.
Minot, Francis, M. D., Phys. Mass. Gen. Hosp. ..Boston.
Mitchell, S. Weir, M. D.......................Philadelphia.
Morehouse, G. R., M. D.......................Philadelphia.
Morland, William W., M. D..................Boston.
Pitcher, Z., M. D., Emer. Prof. Univ. Mich.......Detroit.
Pollak, S., M. D., Surg. Eye and Ear Infirmary..St. Louis.
Post, Alfred C., M. D., Prof. Surg. Univ. N. Y., &c., &c...............................New York.
Reid, David B.,* M. D.........................St. Paul's.
Rochester, T. F., M. D., Prof. Clin. Med. Univ. of..Buffalo.
Sager, Abram, M. D., Prof. Obst. Univ. Mich....Ann Arbor.
Shaw, Benjamin S., M. D., Supt. Mass. Gen. Hosp.......................................Boston.
Shattuck, G. C., M. D., Prof. Theor. and Pract. Med. Coll., &c...........................Boston.
Slade, Daniel D., M. D.........................Boston.
Smith, Stephen, M. D., Prof. Surg. and Surg. Bellevue Hosp.............................New York.
Snow, Edwin M., M. D., Health Officer, &c. .....Providence, R. I.

* David Boswell Reid, M. D., Fellow Royal Society of Edinburgh; Fellow of the Royal College of Physicians, London; Member Medico-Chirurgical Society of St. Petersburg; formerly Director of Ventilation at the Houses of Parliament of Great Britain; late Professor of Physiology and Hygiene at the University of Wisconsin. He died in the service of the United States Sanitary Commission, being at the time of his death Special Inspector of Ventilation in Hospitals.

Terry, Charles A., M. D. ........................ Cleveland
Vanderpool, S. O., M. D., late Surg. Gen. N. Y. .. Albany.
Walker, Clement A., M. D., Supt. Lunatic Hosp. . Boston.
Ware, Charles E., M. D., Phys. Mass. Gen. Hosp. . Boston.
White, James P., M. D., Prof. Obst. Univ. of .... Buffalo.
Williams, H. W., M. D. ........................ Boston.
Wyman, Morrill, M. D., Ex-Prof. Mass. Medical Coll. .................................... Cambridge.

These gentlemen, distinguished in their profession, with the care of large practices, or other responsibilities upon them, accepted the duties of Special Inspectors of the Sanitary Commission, solely from motives of patriotism and humanity. Their remuneration was very slight. It merely paid the travelling expenses of many of them. Others, who travelled lesser distances, gave what was due to them to the special relief agency of the Commission.

The reports of these gentlemen are contained in over four thousand folio pages of writing. They have been tabulated under the supervision of Dr. Clark himself. They contain answers to a series of questions, in addition to the professional and scientific observations of the Inspectors themselves. Thus it may be said that they give the most thorough and pertinent knowledge which can be had about the general hospitals of the United States. Those who are disposed to doubt the condition of these hospitals would do well to examine these reports, and assure themselves that, in a great degree, their doubts and fears are unfounded.

We must here mention, what should have been stated elsewhere, that the first plan for a barrack hospital in this country (the most important improvement which has taken place in general hospitals) was made and given to the Government by the Sanitary Commission. The Judiciary Square Hospital, in Washington, was built upon that plan; and every general hospital since erected has been of barrack structure.

---

## APPENDIX E.

### UNITED STATES SANITARY COMMISSION.

*Woman's Central Association of Relief, Third Avenue, 10 Cooper Union.*

NEW YORK, *Jan.* 13th, 1863.

MADAM, — A council was held in Washington, at the rooms of the United States Sanitary Commission, on the 22d and 24th of last November. It was composed of delegates from the different branches of the Commission, — Chicago, and Louisville, Ky., being represented, as well as Boston and New York.

The following conclusions were arrived at: —

1st. There are 130,000 sick and wounded soldiers now scattered among our hospitals and camps.

2d. Our Government is most liberal and humane in its care of these suffering soldiers, and the Surgeon-General of the Medical Department zealous and efficient in the performance of his duties.

3d. The historical experience of all nations in time of war (as well as our own) shows that, notwithstanding the utmost liberality of governmental provision, there is a large amount of suffering which must be alleviated, if at all, by the volunteer aid of the people.

4th. After an experience of eighteen months, it is acknowledged, by the officers of the Army of the United

States, that the best and safest channel (because the only one authorized by Government) through which the gifts from the people to the soldiers can pass is the United States Sanitary Commission. The Commission works in perfect harmony with the Government.

5th. The Commission collects supplies from all the loyal States, and distributes them to the soldiers of the United States, without distinction of State or regiment, giving first to those who *need it most*, and *wherever the need is the greatest.* This is the federal principle, upon which all the operations of the Commission are based.

6th. Out of 25,000 boxes sent to the Commission, but one has been lost. There are at least 25,000 boxes of hospital supplies, directed to individuals in regiments, now in the storehouses of express companies in Washington, who are unable to deliver them because the owners cannot be found.

7th. Supplies, even when *received* by regiments, cannot be used by the very sick or seriously wounded men of that regiment. These men are transferred to general hospitals, where they are no longer under the care of the regimental surgeon.

8th. Although our Army and Navy is now larger than ever, with a corresponding increase of sickness, the amount of supplies now received by the Commission is ten times less than the receipts of a year ago.

9th. In view of this fact, a more thorough organization of the whole country should be attempted, and soldiers' aid societies, tributary to the Commission, established in every city, town, and village throughout the loyal States. If possible, the contributions should be made regularly, that the Commission may know what supplies it may depend upon.

10th. There is at present no reserve stock of supplies in the storehouses of the Commission, either at Boston, New York, Philadelphia, or Washington, with the exception of lint, bandages, old linen, old cotton, and pillow-cases. The most imperative need is for flannel shirts, flannel drawers, socks, slippers, bedsacks, quilts, and blankets.

And, lastly, we acknowledge that the magnitude and importance of this work have only lately burst fully upon us, with the heavy responsibility attached to it. We hope that every loyal woman in the country will feel this responsibility with us, and look upon this work as a sacred duty. It requires sacrifice; it requires time and money, and earnest, steady, relentless work, which is to last as long as the war lasts. Let us think of it as a privilege as well as a duty, with a deep conviction of the high principles which govern it,—humanity, patriotism, Christianity.

We are desirous of making every explanation in regard to the above statements which may be desired.

As Secretary of the Soldiers' Aid Society of your town or village, an auxiliary of the Woman's Central Association of Relief, branch of the Sanitary Commission, will you be kind enough to answer the following questions, which I ask with the view of obtaining such information as will lead to the furtherance of our common object, — the care of our sick and wounded soldiers and sailors: —

1st. What is the state of feeling which exists in your community in regard to the Commission?

2d. Is the broad, federal principle upon which it is based thoroughly understood by the people, and do they agree that it is the right one?

3d. What reports, if any, prejudicial to the Commission are in circulation in your neighborhood? And what difficulties have you to contend with?

4th. When was your Society organized, and how often does it meet? Please send me the name of your society, and the names of its president and secretary. Is it the only one in your town or village?

5th. What circulars, issued by the Commission, have lately been received by you? Is this printed matter read aloud at the meetings, and is it received with any interest?

6th. Have all supplies sent from you to us been acknowledged? If not, please send a list, made out in detail, of the contents of each box missing, with the date of forwarding. We have received many unknown boxes, which we would gladly acknowledge.

7th. To which branch of the Commission is it most economical for you to send supplies, and what facilities have you in regard to transportation?

I shall be much indebted if you will send me a friendly letter, in answer to the above questions, within ten days after the receipt of this, if possible. Any suggestions from you, by which the work can be made more effective, will be most gladly received by me.

LOUISA LEE SCHUYLER,
10 *Cooper Union*,
*New York*.

Miss ELLEN COLLINS,
Mrs. T. D'OREMIEULX,
Miss GERTRUDE STEVENS,
Miss LOUISA LEE SCHUYLER,
Mr. S. W. BRIDGHAM,
W. H. DRAPER, M. D.,
*Committee on Correspondence and Supplies.*

I propose to answer the questions contained in this circular separately, each answer being based upon returns made in two hundred and thirty-five letters; these letters representing the feeling of the people throughout New York State, Connecticut, the western parts of Massachusetts and Vermont, and the northern part of New Jersey.

*Answer 1st.* The state of feeling which exists in regard to the Commission is *favorable;* more so at the present time than ever before. The degree of favor is in direct proportion to the efforts which have been made to enlighten and instruct those who are interested in the care of the soldier, as to the principles and workings of the Commission.

*Answer 2d.* The federal principle upon which the Commission is based is more thoroughly understood and appreciated throughout the State of New York, and in Massachusetts and Vermont, than in Connecticut and New Jersey.

*Answer 3d.* The Commission has *lived down* most of the prejudicial reports in circulation concerning it. It is still accused of dishonesty, and all other crimes, by those whose only motive is to undermine the confidence of the people in anything which tends to strengthen our national cause. There are always returned soldiers bringing with them stories of dishonest surgeons and nurses, some of which must necessarily be true in so large an army as ours. We never deny these reports, but the *proofs* (names and dates) are asked for, with a promise of investigation, and the punishment of all convicted delinquents. We have not, as yet, been able to trace back any of these reports to anything tangible. The man in Troy, who was so willing and anxious to swear that he had bought sanitary stores from one of our agents, disappeared the day before the oath was to be administered. In almost every village there is the story of a returned soldier who spent his last dollar for a pot of jelly, and then finds his mother's name on the wrapper. But where is the soldier, and what was his mother's name? A lady goes to Willard's and finds in her room sheets marked with her own name and the stamp of the Commission. But who is the lady? and where are the sheets? One more story, the scene of which is also laid in Washington. A sick and discharged soldier, too weak to go on his homeward journey without a few days of rest, while lying on a comfortable bed, was seen to shake his head, rub his eyes, and gaze intently at the handsome quilt spread over him. Suddenly he fell back, exclaiming, with deep emotion, "It is—yes, it is my wife's best spare-room quilt." We do not give his name; the *place* was the "Home for Sick Soldiers passing through Washington," established by the Sanitary Commission.

The chief difficulty our auxiliaries have to contend with is the want of funds. The households have been gleaned of all superfluous linen and cotton, and the price of new materials is double and treble the usual rates. By offering to pay the freight-charges at this end of the line, it would throw the moneyed burden upon this city, and thus enable the little towns and villages to put all their funds into materials. This would relieve them very much, and would increase our own receipts.

(Answer 4th is omitted as unimportant here.)

*Answer 5th.* In the country, the printed matter issued by the Commission is received with the greatest interest.

It is read aloud at the meetings, passed from house to house, and extracts from the circulars and reports are very generally read from the pulpit. Every day letters come to us asking for more.

(Answer 6th omitted as unimportant here.)

*Answer 7th.* The facilities in regard to transportation vary. Some speak of boats and railroads passing their doors, and so down to a letter from Delaware County, N. Y., which says: "It is most convenient to send to New York. We cart our supplies *fifty miles* to the Hudson River, and then forward by boat or railroad." In several instances, they are carted fifteen, twenty, and thirty miles. But comparatively little freight has been carried without charge, and these transportation bills are enormous. The Long Island, Jamaica, and Haerlem Railroads are the only ones which have consented to carry packages for the Commission free of charge, though all our railroad companies have been applied to. Similar applications have been granted by all the New-England railroads centring in Boston; and the Western railroads carry the supplies of the Commission entirely free, or at very reduced rates.

This whole correspondence is most interesting. Some of the letters are from fourteen to sixteen pages in length, — friendly, sympathetic, and encouraging letters, some of them even confidential, and all so full of interest in our work, and regrets that they are unable to do more for it. It is the farmers and villagers who are making the real sacrifices for the war. They work early and late for the soldiers, before and after the day's work is done; they walk and drive for miles, through snow and mud, to the weekly sewing-circle; they go from house to house, begging money and materials; they *deny themselves.* "I, and a few friends, have determined not to buy any more new material for our own clothes, now that the prices are so high, and the hospital supplies are so much needed," writes one of these women; "we cannot afford any longer to give both to ourselves and to the soldiers."

The work is no longer being carried on from motives of humanity, as it was at first; it has become a test of *patriotism.* Those who are the truest patriots, the real lovers of the Union, are the earnest, steadfast workers. It is the "grumblers," the "Peace Democrats," the "Secessionists," and the "Copperheads," they tell us, who will not understand it, who discourage it in every way.

*Plan of Organization.* — The original plan of organization of the Commission for the seaboard States was the establishment of three branches, or distributing depots, at Boston, New York, and Philadelphia. Each of these branches was to collect supplies from that part of the country which would naturally seek it as its nearest or most convenient depot. The large cities and towns in these fields were to be "centres of collection," gathering supplies from their vicinities, and forwarding them to the distributing depots. The branches were to organize and canvass their respective fields as they thought best.

At the council held in Washington, last November, the plan of organization of the Boston Branch was thought superior to all others, and we have consequently adopted it. This is the division of the country into sections, these sections being determined, not by county lines (although these are often most convenient), but by lines of transportation, rivers, and railroads. One or more associate managers are appointed to each section.

The duties of an associate manager are, —

1st. To ascertain whether soldiers' aid societies exist in every town and village of her section; and, if so, for what they are working.

2d. When they are not working for the Commission, to use all her influence to induce them to do so, meeting all objections by bringing forward, in a kindly spirit, the convincing proofs furnished by the published documents of the Commission, and the testimony of the officers of the Army of the United States.

3d. When such societies, tributary to the Commission, do not exist, we wish to have them organized by our associate; or, if preferred, she may send us the name of the right person, in the particular town or village, to whom we should address ourselves.

4th. To visit all the auxiliary societies in her section, from time to time, for the purpose of giving information, answering questions, dispelling doubts, and encouraging workers, — this personal intercourse being thought very desirable. This, however, would be at the option of our associate, who can judge better than we can how best to produce the desired result in her own section.

5th. To keep the broad federal principle, upon which the Commission is based, ever before the people. Our whole experience shows that our people are truly liberal in spirit, and only ask for information as to *the best way* of working for the sick and wounded. Where, during the past year, whole communities have worked for special regiments, it was only necessary to explain the national principle upon which the Sanitary Commission rests, and it was immediately adopted.

6th. To bring every influence to bear which may stimulate this work, the responsibility of which we feel so deeply, and which may tend to make it more thorough and efficient. It should always be presented on the high grounds of duty, patriotism, and Christianity.

7th. To keep herself thoroughly informed of the working of the Commission, by frequent correspondence with this office. When questions are asked us which we cannot answer, we write to the General Secretary at Washington for information, or refer our Associate directly to him.

8th. To send us a friendly letter once a month, with a report of the condition of things in her section, pointing out any errors on our part, and making any suggestions which may help us to make our work more effective, and which will be gladly received.

In addition to this, several gentlemen have been lecturing for us in behalf of the Commission, at intervals during the last three months. Mr. Furness has been speaking in the towns and villages upon the Hudson River, and has lately returned from a most successful tour along the line of the New York Central Railroad and the centre of this State. The Rev. Mr. Hadley has been canvassing the line of the Haerlem Railroad, and is now in Saratoga and Washington counties. The Rev. Herbert Lancey is now in the western part of this State, and Chaplain Phillips has been speaking in the Presbyterian churches of this city. The Rev. Mr. Tiffany is doing most excellent service in Connecticut. He, and Mr. Hadley, and Mr. Lancey, are the only lecturers at present assigned to this branch by the central office in Washington. The result of these efforts, so far as we can judge, has been most beneficial.

I will give but one interesting incident from the reports of these gentlemen. Mr. Furness had just been addressing an audience in Rochester, N. Y., and writes: "While I was talking, a man came in and took his seat, listening very attentively. After I had finished, he rose and proceeded to tell how the lives of sixteen Rochester boys were saved by the Sanitary Commission; and so earnest did he become, that at last his voice trembled, his eyes filled, and he fairly sobbed out, — 'And I pray God every day to bless every man connected with that noble institution.' Coming, as this did, without any possible collusion, and from the man who, as well as I could learn, had been deputed by the city of Rochester to look after the soldiers, it went home with thrilling effect."

In another month we shall have closed the second year of our work; and we may feel gratified at the proofs which are now daily received of the way in which the Sanitary Commission has grown into the confidence of our people and our Army. We are still, however, too dependent upon the sympathy of our friends not to appreciate and feel grateful for a compliment lately received from one of our correspondents, who was "so glad to find we were *not a soulless corporation!*"

Respectfully submitted,

LOUISA LEE SCHUYLER,

*Mem. Executive Com.*

## APPENDIX F.

The Branch of the United States Sanitary Commission at Chicago, Ill., represents the Northwest, namely, the States of Illinois, Wisconsin, Michigan, Iowa, Indiana, and Minnesota. Fed by the patriotism and liberality of these States, it has done, and is doing a magnificent work with the armies of the West. The earnestness and devotion of its agents, both men and women, has not been and cannot be surpassed. They have lately been employed on a great enterprise called "The Northwestern Fair for the Armies." A letter received at this last moment from the Associate Secretary for the East, dated at Chicago during the progress of the Fair, speaks of it as "a splendid success"; and adds, "I cannot express too warmly the energy and devotion of these admirable women." *

The Chicago Branch of the Commission receives important assistance from a large society in Milwaukee, Wis. We cannot dwell at length upon what this society has accomplished; but Mrs. Colt, the lady to whom is owing, in a chief degree, its great success, has written a few words addressed to the women of her State, which contain so vital a truth and so wise a prayer that they must be given here, in the hope that they may, in these pages, carry their influence to the women of the whole country. She says:—

"A great difficulty which our surgeons have to contend with in their patients is homesickness. Medicines are then useless. If the men are not all heroes, let the women try to be all heroines. And let me beg every

* We learn that the sum of money given to the Commission, as the proceeds of the Fair, exceeds $50,000.

woman to write to her soldier cheerfully, encouragingly, and heroically, or not at all. If they knew the effect of their letters of condolence and complaint, they would be more careful. A soldier came to me in Nashville, choking with emotion, his wife very sick, and he unable to go to her. I promised to write and have her cared for; and it was only by reiterated promises that the letter should be written and sent at once that he could be soothed and comforted. As soon as my letter reached Wisconsin, she was perfectly well, and no doubt sorry she had written while feeling ill and lonely. I was surprised that letters from home sometimes pain instead of cure.

"Women of Wisconsin! Our country, bleeding at every pore, needs her soldiers, and needs them to be brave and cheerful; and we look to you to keep them so. It is better than any other labor of love which you can do. If you must grieve, keep it from your sons and husbands. It is unwomanly to put your burden upon them. It is unworthy of our country's daughters! And let me assure you, that, inevitable as are the horrors of war, everything is done by our Government for the wants of her soldiers; and when she from her ponderous machinery works slowly, the United States Sanitary Commission with its quick messengers of mercy is always ready." . . . .

Oh, that all women would lay these words at heart! We say *all*, for we know that there are many wives and mothers and sisters who give to their soldiers the cheerful courage which *none but they can give*. But there are others who do not do so. To such women it must be told that, not very long since, a poor, weak, suffering man, harassed by the fretful letters of his mother, said to the writer, "She worries me more than my wound."

# APPENDIX G.

*Supplies furnished by the Sanitary Commission to the Army of the Potomac, July 1st to 31st August.*

| Hospital Furniture. | | Personal Clothing. | | Hospital Delicacies. | |
|---|---|---|---|---|---|
| Quilts | 30,197 | Shirts | 87,994 | Condensed milk, cans | 2,624 |
| Blankets | 13,500 | Drawers | 48,303 | Jelly, jars | 6,959 |
| Sheets | 42,945 | Socks | 80,322 | Tea, lbs. | 541 |
| Pillows | 35,877 | Slippers | 14,984 | Spirits, bottles | 1,026 |
| Pillow-cases | 49,096 | Handkerchiefs | 43,606 | Wine, dom. gals. | 570 |
| Pillow-ticks | 2,269 | Towels | 65,164 | Wines, foreign, gals. | 450 |
| Bed-ticks | 11,716 | Wrappers | 10,235 | Vinegar, bottles | 692 |
| | | Flannel bands | 3,684 | Syrups, " | 1,435 |
| | | | | Beef-stock, liquid, lbs. | 634 |
| | | | | Beef-stock, solid, lbs. | 1,052 |
| | | | | Farinaceous food, lbs. | 12,268 |

Besides these things, a vast amount of miscellaneous articles, from rubber cloth of every kind, crutches, oiled silk, flannel, to eggnog, porter, and ale, was furnished.

The work of collecting and forwarding these supplies was one of the heaviest of the unobtrusive works of the Commission. The hospital transports arrived at the various ports of Washington, Philadelphia, New York, and Boston, especially at the port of New York. Each vessel had to be met on her arrival with arrangements ready to unload her freight of sick and wounded men. She had to be overhauled, cleaned, and entirely refitted for the needs of another voyage. Besides this, the requisitions sent up from White House or Harrison's Landing, to meet the needs *at those points*, had to be carefully and liberally filled, and the vessel loaded and despatched. Sometimes three of these vessels arrived in New York during one week. Nor did the work end here. Surgeons, dressers, nurses, agents, &c., &c., had to be obtained, their qualifications examined, besides many other laborious and worrying details which cannot be given here.

To Dr. Agnew, in New York, special thanks are due, also to Dr. Jenkins, in Washington, (during part of the time,) for their share in this work, which was extremely laborious and most successful. No mention has been made in the text of the "St. Mark" and the "Euterpe," two magnificent clipper ships fitted up by the Sanitary Commission in New York as hospital transports. Owing to their want of steam-power, and their great draught of water, they were unable to go up the rivers, and were therefore used chiefly as receiving hospital ships in the waters of Hampton Roads.

On Mr. Olmsted's return from Harrison's Landing he collected and sent down, at the most pressing need of the Army, (the shadow of scurvy was then hanging over it,) a vessel freighted with vegetables. A cargo of ice had already gone down. These vegetables proved of inestimable service, and were distributed to all the regiments at Harrison's Landing.

---

## APPENDIX H.

Constant and finally successful efforts were made by the Sanitary Commission for the release of these gentlemen. No doubt their release was given the more readily because of an earnest appeal in their behalf addressed to General Lee by twelve surgeons of the Confederate army who were within our lines after the battle of Gettysburg. On the return of these agents to Washington, they stated that Dr. Wilkins, surgeon in charge of the C. S. Military Prison No. 1, (the Libby Prison,) had informed them, that, if supplies of clothing, bedding, and reading-matter should be sent to his care from the Sanitary Commission, he would guarantee their distribution among the Union prisoners. They also stated that Capt. G. W. Alexander, A. A. G. and A. P. M., Castle Thunder, made a similar promise with regard to reading-matter within his precincts.

These gentlemen added that the above supplies were greatly needed by our men, and that a distribution of such things would be of inestimable benefit to them.

Of course it was questionable whether, if such supplies once passed the line, they would be permitted to reach their destination; but the Commission gladly acted on the merest chance of their doing so, and felt justified in taking any trouble or expense in forwarding supplies over our lines, provided such a course involved no violation of military rules and exigencies on our side.

Accordingly, and in behalf of our brave and unfortunate officers and men now pining amid want, squalor, and mental inoccupation in the noisome prisons of the enemy, the Sanitary Commission brought the subject to the notice of the Secretary of War, who replied as follows:—

"War Department,
"*October 3d,* 1863.

"Mr. Alfred J. Bloor, *Asst. Sec. U. S. Sanitary Commission.*

"Sir,—In reply to your letter of the 2d instant, transmitting correspondence with General Meredith, in reference to forwarding Sanitary Commission supplies to the prisoners at Richmond, the Secretary of War desires me to convey to you his consent for the transmission of the articles named, through the lines as requested.

"Very respectfully,
"Your obedient servant,
"JAS. A. HARDIE,
"*Assistant Adjutant-General.*"

Supplies of those articles which were mentioned by the Confederate officers were at once forwarded by the Sanitary Commission, which has continued to forward from time to time supplies of the same nature; also articles of sick-food, which are now permitted to be sent by the Confederate officers.

Our Government has now, however, undertaken the supply of clothing and bedding.

---

## APPENDIX I.

### *Hospital Cars.*

THE importance of some improvement in the railway transportation of wounded men was deeply impressed on Dr. Elisha Harris, and other members of the Commission who witnessed the painful journeys of such men over the memorable route from Fair Oaks and Savage's Station to White House. To Dr. Harris the great alleviation given by the invention of the hospital cars is chiefly due. These cars may properly be termed ambulances, for they are not only fitted up exclusively for the transportation of military patients, but they are furnished with beds, (swung on elastic springs to prevent the jar of motion,) couches, pillows, and reclining chairs, a medicine closet, a complete *cuisine* and all the appliances and attendance of a hospital. They are ventilated, warmed, and lighted with special reference to the wants of sick and wounded men, and most of them are grooved to run upon railways of different gauges, so as to avoid needless transfers of patients. Fourteen such cars have been prepared after the plans and specifications of the Commission, and were wholly or in part furnished and managed by it. Ten of them are now running regularly on long routes, — four of them on the route connecting Louisville and Nashville with the nearest railway point to General Grant's Army. The dedication on the part of railway officials of the use of these cars has been generous and patriotic. The superintendent of a railroad company which constructed one such car, turned it over to the Sanitary Commission with these words: "I have no preferences as to where you run the car that has been fitted up in accordance with the plans and specifications furnished by yourselves. I therefore turn the car over to you, to dispose of as you deem proper, believing that you only desire to alleviate the sufferings of the sick and wounded."

---

## APPENDIX K.

In this connection a little story must be told, — not that it is a very rare one, but because it happened only a few days ago, and has a freshness and charm from the manly character of the officer about whom it is told.

One of the associate secretaries had occasion to visit

a post in the vicinity of Washington. The commanding officer, at the close of the conversation, said: "Now I must tell you something. I was colonel of a regiment when the war broke out, and one of your Inspectors came about my camp, and put me through the closest set of questions I ever had to answer. I do believe there were hundreds of them. Well, I did not like it, and I believe I told him I hoped I might never see him in my camp again. But since then I've been sick and wounded, and I fell into the hands of the Sanitary Commission, and so have many of my poor fellows; and, do you know, the other day that same Inspector came out here. I knew him. I don't know whether he knew me; but there was only one thing I could do; so I went to him and offered him my hand, and I said, 'May God give me the opportunity of helping the Sanitary Commission.'"

And in this same connection we will give a letter published some time ago in a Wisconsin paper. The writer was an army surgeon. His mission to White House after the battle of Hanover Court House is distinctly recollected by some of the hospital company stationed at that point.

"I was reminded so much by —— of what I have myself seen, that I feel like telling my own experiences with the National Sanitary Commission.

"When I went into the field in 1861, I found a large proportion of the surgeons, for some cause which I have not learned, opposed to that Commission. It of course took me but a little while to become strongly prejudiced and bitterly opposed. Every agent sent to inspect us was made the subject of not very flattering remark. Every pamphlet which it issued was criticized. One evening a number of surgeons met in my tent. The Commission soon became our subject; something must be written against it, and I must write it. I was full of the subject, and I threw into my article all the force I could command. I had nearly finished it when the sound of artillery came booming over the country, — heavier and heavier grew the roar, — a battle was being fought at Drainesville. The surgeons dispersed to collect appliances for the wounded. The sufferers in the battle began to arrive. We had scarcely anything they needed. The noise of the battle had reached Washington, and by the time the wounded were examined, in came those sanitary agents with the very articles of comfort which Government had failed to supply. My article, which had been hastily thrown aside, I now put away to finish at a 'more convenient season.'

"Time passed on and we found ourselves on the Peninsula. In the haste of moving, most of the appliances of comfort had been left behind. . . . After the battle of Lee's Mill, I was almost without medicine, or any articles of diet for the sick, though I had been for weeks striving to procure them. What should I do? Just then were discovered a number of 'those sanitary chaps who are always poking their noses into everybody's business.' Somehow or other they had the very things we needed. That night, after having finished my labors with the wounded, I went to my trunk, took out that article 'on the Sanitary,' and read a few lines. It did not read as well as I thought it would, so I raised a garment and put it under, where it would not stare me in the face every time I looked in.

"The battle of Williamsburg followed; and before the smoke of the battle had blown away, right alongside of our Army lay one of those ever-present sanitary steamers, freighted not only with necessaries, but with luxuries for the sick and wounded. They had only to be asked for and they were distributed to us without limit. Another shirt was thrown over that article!

"I was in charge of Liberty Hall Hospital at the time of the battle of Hanover Court House. Here both the sick and wounded were crowded on me. Five hundred were piled in at one time. I had not a bed, not a dozen blankets, not a cooking utensil, and nothing to cook. In vain did I appeal to the medical director,— in vain did he appeal to higher authority. The necessaries of life were scarcely to be had. I begged, I plead,— no use. A few days after the battle, on the breaking up of other hospitals, the wounded who could not be moved to a greater distance were sent to me,— some of them in a most loathsome condition, their wounds gangrenous and alive with worms. Again I appealed for assistance, and with such importunity that I was threatened with dismissal from the service. I procured a pass to White House. There I found the United States Sanitary Commission. I told them the story of the soldiers' suffering. Hundreds of clean sheets, blankets, bedsacks, and pillows were packed in less time than it needs to read the story. Boxes of condensed milk, farina, army soup, tea, coffee, sugar, oranges, and lemons were sent off with astonishing celerity. When I departed there was not a State represented in my hospital but found some article bearing the marks of home: New York, Pennsylvania, Connecticut, Vermont, Massachusetts, Rhode Island, and Wisconsin, all were there, —both in their soldiers and in their gifts. As I led one poor fellow from Pennsylvania to his bed, and he saw upon the clean white sheet the name of his family and his home, his convulsive sobs shook the building. . . . . The whole hospital wept; and as I took my paper and thrust it at the bottom of my trunk, it may be that a few watery drops had fallen amongst its leaves. . . . .

"The Army arrived at Harrison's Landing. The sick had been sent ahead of us. In this connection I shall state but a single case in illustration. A young man from Milwaukee, in whom I felt a great interest, was found, after a long hunt, in an ambulance. He had all the symptoms of an approaching attack of typhus fever. Government transports were at the wharf taking on the wounded. I had the ambulance driven to the river, and asked a place for this young man. It was denied; the transports were only to take the wounded. 'But he is in more danger than hundreds of wounded.' 'Our orders are peremptory. We take only wounded.' Thirty hours there would be certain death to him. What could I do? I succeeded in reaching a transport which the Sanitary Commission had. I appealed to them. 'We have only two hundred and forty on board; — we will take him.' He was sent to his home. And does the mother of that young man ever enter the Sanitary Commission rooms without gratitude to that Commission, — and without feeling that the means for furnishing the conveyance which saved his life were perhaps drawn from other States? I pass over other scenes of suffering relieved which I witnessed at Centreville, South Mountain, Crampton's Gap, Antietam, and Fredericksburg.

"At Antietam I took the paper from the bottom of my trunk, and, lest I might see it again, burned it. And now I declare upon my honor that I never wrote it, and that I never will do so again."

# APPENDIX L.

When this book was already in type, it occurred to the writer that it contained no sufficient record of the gratitude of the soldiers themselves for the relief and succor of which the book has given a history. It was then too late to do more than make a selection from a few instances of their affectionate sense of what has been done for them, which happened to be at hand at that last moment.

This omission must be excused on the ground that the gratefulness of the men, especially on or near the field itself, is so unceasing that it comes to be a matter of course, — forgotten at the moment, though remembered afterwards. It is indeed a chief source of strength and courage for the work of relief; and it seems as if it must always be understood as underlying the history of it.

The following letters, &c., are, as we have said, hastily selected from a very small number of others happening to be at hand.

"TARRYTOWN, *May 22d*, 1863.

"MR. J. B. ABBOTT, *Assist. Special Relief Agent.*

"DEAR SIR, — Yours of the 20th came to hand, together with the draft for ninety-two $\frac{15}{100}$ dollars, being the amount due from the Government to Thaddeus Seymour Davis, my son, (who is now dead,) for services rendered in 32d New York State Volunteers. I thank you for your kindness in this matter, and I know that many poor fellows bless you who have been the recipients of your kindness, and God will bless those whose mission it is to bind up the wounds and minister to the needy in this holy cause.

"Believe me truly yours,
(Signed) "G. T. DAVIS."

"WILLIAMSBURG, LONG ISLAND, *Feb.* 9th, 1863.

"TO THE SAME.

"SIR, — With grateful feeling I acknowledge the receipt of yours of February 6th, enclosing the draft for the amount due my dear brother. You have conferred a great favor on us. Accept the sincere thanks of my widowed mother — mine also —for your kindness. May I ask you, if not too great an intrusion on your time, to tell me what means my mother should take to secure the bounty to which my brother was entitled. If your time does not admit, then do not give it a thought. Present my compliments to the gentleman who accompanied you to the hospital, (I did not ascertain his name.) I am much indebted for his kindness, and yours too.

"Yours with much respect,
(Signed) "MARGARET E. CURRAN."

"ST. PAUL, MINNESOTA, *August* 13th, 1863.

"MR. FOWLER, *Chief Clerk U. S. Sanitary Commission, Washington.*

"DEAR SIR,—Yours of the 4th and 6th were received yesterday. I sincerely thank you for the kind spirit which you have manifested, and the trouble which you have taken to assist me. May heaven reward you, for earth is too poor. I am very sorry to hear of Rev. Mr. K.'s illness; please give him my best respects. 'T is no wonder he broke down; his labors were severe. I hope he may soon recover. I shall follow your kind advice relative to my pension. May God bless you and your noble associates, is the fervent prayer of

"Yours truly,

"JOHN T. HALSTED."

*To the Ladies who direct the Affairs or contribute to the Funds of the Cleveland Branch of the United States Sanitary Commission.*

"I want to thank you. I was wounded at Stone's River on the last day of December, 1862. Since then I have run the gauntlet of the hospitals from Murfreesboro to Cleveland. At every stage of my painful progress I was the grateful recipient of your priceless gifts. I owe the preservation of my life to a bottle of blackberry cordial, which was labelled 'Cleveland,' and sent to me by Mr. Atwater, Agent of the United States Sanitary Commission, at Murfreesboro. It came to me at a time when I had scarcely any vitality left. It restored my appetite, which I had lost entirely. That wine *could not* have been bought with money, — it was made and given by some great-hearted countrywoman. God bless her!

"When I left Nashville the hospitals were well supplied, and the rooms of the Sanitary Commission were filled and overflowing. May they never be empty until the war shall close.

"Yours, respectfully,

"S. W. SHANKLAND."

*From a report of Mr. Knapp, Special Relief Agent.*

"There is one other point which, although not strictly connected with sanitary affairs, seems to me worthy of mention. Among these thousand and more of sick men whom we have had in charge, I have met scarcely one whose anxiety for renewed health did not seem actually to centre chiefly upon this idea, namely, to have strength enough to fight for his country. Hundreds of those men go home with a feeling of bitter disappointment, to think that they can never strike that blow in their country's cause for which their arm and heart both were once so strong, while now the arm is palsied. I am more and more impressed, not merely with the patience of these men, but with their deep-seated spirit of patriotism. I am convinced that many persons in the community attribute to a mere love of excitement and to the attractiveness of a military life what ought to be credited to a genuine, earnest purpose. I have had peculiar opportunity here to get at the real feelings of a great many of these men, and I see more and more how strong and real a current of life flows down southward from our northern hills. Again and again have I wished that all doubting or lukewarm patriots could witness some of these scenes, which, to my eye, have so much real pathos in them, — men returning to their friends and their homes simply to die, yet without a complaint or regret, except that they were too weak to bear arms. Even those men who were prisoners at Richmond, but who have now been allowed to return, (as they are maimed for life, nearly every one having lost a limb,) even these men utter no complaints. There have been ten of them with us the past two weeks, getting their papers of discharge and of pension, yet I have not heard a murmur from one. It has seemed to me right, in my report, to give this measure of testimony.

"I will append to this report one letter of many, which, although addressed to me personally, belongs to the Commission and to the public, whose charities I am allowed to bestow. The letter is printed just as it was received: —

"*Sept. the* 29 —61.

"DEAR SIR, on account of a feeling of gratitud towards you I sit down to write a few lines to you — to let you know that my son arrived home on the 24th in very feeble health, about the same as when he left your House — & stil remains as week with verry bad Cough — when I herd him tel of the kind treatment he receaved from you an entire Stranger and the kindness you Showd him, and the things you gave him — I could not refrain from Sheding tears of Gratitude I feel as though he found a friend in need which is a friend in deed.

"I feel as though Heaven would Reward you for your kindness — it would be a pleasure to me to See Such a good Soul — as it is not money you was after I beg you to accept our cincere thanks and may God bless you — if we never meet on Earth may God prepair me to meet you in Heaven

"Yours truly this from your obedient Servant"

"—— ——.

"P S my son will write you Soon if able Excuse my poor ignorant letter"

"Did circumstances call for it, I could add many similar assurances of gratitude, which come from humble homes, indeed, but from wives and parents who appreciate kindness bestowed upon husbands and sons.*

"Respectfully,

"FRED'K N. KNAPP,

"*Special Relief Agent of Sanitary Commission.*"

*From a sister who carried home living a brother who had lain for some time at the point of death.* After giving an account of the journey, she says: —

"James says, though he wanted to get away, and he is at home now with all the family, he almost wishes he was back where he had so much that was kind done for him. He says, 'Tell them, if I ever do any good in my life it belongs to them, for they saved my life and showed me what it was to be good.'

"And I'll never forget your kindness for giving me board and lodging, and so enable me to stay near my dear brother." . . . .

*A man writing from the Army, says:* "We soldiers know best what the Commission is. You all see it, but we *feel* it. I bless the Sanitary Commission every time I see its name posted up — or think of it."

*From a private soldier (name unknown) in a ward of a General Hospital.*

"DEAR LADY, — Please pardon me, but I *must* say God bless you. I have watched you as you pass. I have witnessed with heartfelt gratitude your kindness and sympathy for the poor, sick, and dying soldiers. I am one of those who love humanity; — and may the

* See a little pamphlet published by the Sanitary Commission called "The Lord will provide."

heavenly influences of the departed loved ones ever be with you, is my prayer. God bless you.

"FROM A SOLDIER.

"*July 23d*, 1863."

The following poem was addressed to Mrs. ——, by a private of the 16th Regt. New York Vols. He had been in her care on board of a Commission boat at White House. After he returned to the regiment he sent her these lines. Surely no lady has ever received a more graceful acknowledgment of kindness:—

From old St. Paul till now,
Of honorable women not a few
Have left their golden ease in love to do
The saintly work which Christlike hearts pursue.

And such an one art thou,— God's fair apostle,
Bearing His love in war's horrific train;
Thy blessed feet follow its ghastly pain,
And misery, and death, without disdain.

To one borne from the sullen battle's roar,
Dearer the greeting of thy gentle eyes,
When he aweary, torn, and bleeding lies,
Than all the glory that the victors prize.

When peace shall come, and homes shall smile again,
A thousand soldier-hearts in northern climes
Shall tell their little children in their rhymes
Of the sweet saint who blessed the old war-times.

*On the Chickahominy,*
*June 12th*, 1862.

CPSIA information can be obtained
at www.ICGtesting.com
Printed in the USA
LVHW110811120522
718525LV00003B/66

9 783375 002930